Alessandro Perissinotto

Blood Sisters

D1150956

Translated from the Italian by Howard Curtis

 Hersilia Press

First published in Great Britain in 2011
by Hersilia Press, Oxfordshire
www.hersilia-press.co.uk

2 4 6 8 10 9 7 5 3

Originally published as *Una Piccola Storia Ignobile*
© 2006 RCS Libri S.p.A., Milan
English Translation © 2010 Hersilia Press

The right of Alessandro Perissinotto to be identified as the author of this work has been asserted.

This is a work of fiction. Any resemblance to actual persons, living or dead, is purely coincidental.

Printed in Great Britain by
the MPG Books Group, Bodmin and King's Lynn

To Barbara

What a squalid little story
is the one I have to tell you
just a stupid story like so many
not even worthy of
an item in the paper
or a slightly rhyming song
not even worthy of
the attention of people
with more important things to do

(Francesco Guccini, *Piccola storia ignobile*)

There comes a moment when you start to wonder how you got to this point. And you wish you could disappear, be somewhere else, you wish it had never started. Maybe this is happening to me because I'm a woman, because I'm not a detective, because the day I graduated in psychology I thought everything would be different.

Here I am, in the middle of the night, in the gloomy undergrowth of the South Milan Agricultural Park, and I'm scared. I'm digging with the little folding snow shovel Stefano gave me, which I've never before taken out of the car. I know that, soon, a hand will start to emerge from the ground, or maybe a foot, or a piece of material, and gradually, if I'm brave enough, I'll unearth a dead body, or what's left of it. It's the price I have to pay to be sure it's all true.

It's quieter than you'd expect just a few kilometres from Milan. Far away, on the main road, lorries pass, but from here all you can hear of them is a deep, muffled vibration. So the sound of my shovel hitting the earth echoes a lot more than I'd like. Fortunately, there are dogs barking loudly in the surrounding farmyards, and that partly covers my digging. Only the cars passing on the nearby unpaved road make much noise, but they're few and far between and the drivers stop beside the fires of tyres and crates lit by the prostitutes: prostitutes from a Europe that's adopted the laws of the market with unseemly haste, the laws that say 'everything's for sale, anything can be bought'.

But how did I get to this point? In my mind, I go over the whole story, to persuade myself that it's worth going on, seeing it through to the horror of a body buried and disinterred without pity in a small wood on the edge of a city. And when I go over the story in my mind, I see it in an orderly way, as if written in a kind of imaginary diary. And that bureaucratic clarity makes it seem all the more tragic.

I can't help it, if I search in my memory I always find the hook, the point of departure. And from then on, the events fall into line, complete with dates and hours. And that hook, that point of departure, is Valentine's Day.

Monday, 14 February, Valentine's Day

At seven, the unpleasant screeching of my old rotary dial telephone put paid to any hopes I might have had of making up in the morning for the hours of sleep my backache had stolen from me during the night. Even Morgana had spared me her hungry dawn miaowing, but the telephone was less merciful. I got up, and my body moved with the unnatural lightness it has after it's been given a copious dose of anti-inflammatories. As I took the first few steps from the bed to the desk, I hoped that the ringing would stop, that the person at the other end would get bored or the battery of their mobile phone would pack up suddenly. But it didn't happen. For a moment, still hovering between sleep and waking, I felt touched: Valentine's Day greetings! No, it wasn't possible, not any more. I lifted the receiver and a hoarse 'Hello?' emerged from my mouth.

Ignoring all the disappointment concentrated in that one word, the female voice at the other end began, in the tone of someone who isn't used to waiting or being contradicted, 'Signora Anna Pavesi, I presume?'

'Yes, that's me.'

I expected a 'Sorry to disturb you at this hour', or something similar, instead of which the voice continued, 'I was given your number by Signor Crocetti, of the firm of Crocetti and Borghi in Turin. My name is Benedetta Vitali. I need to talk to you urgently and in person. I'm in Milan right now. If you can see me this morning, I'll leave immediately.'

'This morning would be fine,' I replied, still groggy with sleep.

'Could you give me your address, please?'

'10 Vicolo Aquila Nera, Bergamo.'

'Is that in the Upper City?'

'Yes, just after the Piazza Vecchia, coming from the funicular station.'

'Is there somewhere to park?'

'Nowhere at all. In fact, there's no thoroughfare, except for residents…'

'That's all right. I'll be there in an hour.'

'Could you give me some idea what – '

But she had already hung up.

I collapsed onto the sofa, trying to put my thoughts in some kind of order and figure out what this woman – who, from her tone, sounded like some princess from an old noble Roman family – wanted of me. The one clue was the name of Signor Crocetti, whose missing son I had tracked down a year earlier.

To be honest, the whole idea that his son had been missing was the father's version of events.

'Signorina,' he had said in his best declamatory manner, handing me a cheque for a decidedly generous amount, 'you found my missing son and reunited us. I'll never forget that.'

But his son hadn't gone missing at all, he'd actually run away from home, or rather, given that he was twenty-two years old, had simply moved house. He hadn't been hard to find, I'd gone around the squats in Turin and in two days I'd tracked him down. The hard part had been persuading him to return home. Fortunately, I knew some of the other squatters, kids who'd occasionally spent time in the hostels where I worked in those days. They were the ones who'd helped me, telling him that his political commitment could be just as effective at home, because he'd be fighting the system from within. They'd done it out of friendship for me, but above all, I think, to get that daddy's boy out of their hair. So he'd let me take him home and his father, after the cheque and the ritual celebrations, had asked me to give the young man a little 'psychological help'. We'd had four or five sessions, but then Signor Crocetti had come to the conclusion that his child's recovery was too slow, so, to speed up the process of welcoming him back fully into the bosom of his family, he'd bought him a Porsche and I'd refused to continue with my assignment. That was the story of Signor Crocetti: perhaps Signora Benedetta also had a son who was squatting and could be won back with the aid of psychotherapy and luxury cars?

I got dressed, without taking too much care over it, then closed the bedroom door and, occasionally taking a sip from a cup of scalding hot tea, tidied the other room, which served as kitchen, living room and consulting room combined.

I'd just done the absolute minimum necessary in order not to feel too ashamed of the state of my apartment, when, leaning out of the window to open the shutters, I saw a woman get out of a taxi and walk towards the front door of my building. After a moment the entryphone rang and I opened. I calculated the time that had passed between the phone call and the woman's arrival. There was no way she could have come by train. She must have taken a taxi all the way from Milan: one more indication that I was going to have to deal with another poor little rich kid.

But as soon as Benedetta appeared at the top of the last flight of stairs, it immediately struck me that she didn't have children, that she was a woman who would never have children. Like me, but for other reasons. The heels of her shoes, high but not excessively so, sounded discreetly on the stone steps. The small slit at the side of her skirt opened and closed rhythmically as she climbed: I could see it because she was wearing a short overcoat, a coat I was sure I'd seen in a shop window in Via Montenapoleone.

When she reached the landing, she held out her hand and shook mine firmly, but without any warmth, and without smiling.

'Please come in.'

'Thank you.'

I motioned her to the sofa. She sat down and looked around with a puzzled look on her face. 'Perhaps you'd have preferred to see me in your office?'

It surprised me that a woman like her would call a psychologist's consulting room an office.

'I don't have a proper consulting room, I do consultations where I need to, on the spot.'

Again she made a puzzled face. 'Signor Crocetti,' she went on, 'with whom I frequently deal in my work, has told me a lot of good things about you, how capable you are, and, above all, how honest. Again for reasons of work, there have been a couple of occasions when I've had to deal with people in your profession, and I have to confess I didn't find them pleasant company, in fact I found them rather vulgar and insensitive...'

I thought about some of my colleagues and was forced to agree with her.

'...whereas you seem a straightforward kind of person.

Perhaps because you're a woman. May I tell you the reason I've contacted you?'

'Please.'

'As I said, my name is Benedetta Vitali, but I almost always use my mother's surname.'

She handed me a business card on which the name Benedetta was followed by one of those double-barrelled surnames typical of the upper classes of Milan, the kind you read in the pages of glossy magazines reporting on opening night at La Scala. Beneath the name, next to the words *Marketing Director*, was the logo of a well-known designer.

'The Vitali name was a kind of accident, if you like. My father was a very handsome man and my mother was too young. It was a kind of Cinderella story, but in reverse: the dances took place at her house, and the only glass slipper he provided was his smile, which is also the only thing I remember about him.'

Entranced by the fairy-tale metaphor, I was stupid enough to ask, 'So they met at a dance?'

'No, at university. It was 1969. I'm sure you know what I mean. Protests, sit-ins, Mao's *Little Red Book* in one pocket of the anorak, Marcuse's *One Dimensional Man* in the other. That's the background against which they met, abandoned their studies and got married.'

'Against your family's wishes?'

'No. My family has a long democratic tradition. They tried to warn my mother of the risks of such a... such an unbalanced marriage, but in the end they respected her decision. Unfortunately, though, my grandparents were right. Within a year, by which time I'd come into the world, the Cinderella story was over. They tried to keep it going for another three years, then they gave my father a sizable cheque and asked him never to show his face again. With another cheque they obtained a discreet separation and a discreet divorce, and that was the end of it. I never saw my father again, and he never asked to see me. From time to time, he would write to my mother to let her know how he was and to ask for photographs of me, but that was all. My mother says the letters always came from different places, though all of them in the area around Grenoble.'

'Did you keep those letters?'

'No, they were always thrown away.'

Psychologically speaking, the situation was becoming clearer, or at least so I thought: *she* was the poor little rich kid. I didn't interrupt her with questions so as not to jeopardise the climate of trust that was being established.

'My father moved to France. First to Paris, to enjoy the bohemian life with the money from what you might call his severance pay. It was after that that he moved to Grenoble, and found work as a mechanic, like his father. He remarried. His second wife was a Frenchwoman of North African origin named Zoulika. In 1982, he had a child with her, Patrizia Vitali, my half-sister. It's because of her that I'm here.'

The Cinderella references were increasing, but becoming more confused. Anxious to get to the nitty-gritty, I interrupted her monologue. 'Did you ever meet your half-sister?'

'Only once, five years ago, at my father's funeral. He died with his wife in a car accident. It was Patrizia who informed us, so we went up there, to Domène, where they'd been living, and met her.'

'What is she like?'

'What *was* she like: she died too. A girl so plain she looked almost dowdy. An eighteen-year-old girl who looked no more than fifteen but acted as if she was forty: quiet, composed. She'd taken care of everything, the funeral, the obituary notice, the little reception for the friends and relations. And I mean little, because there were only two or three friends, neighbours of theirs, and my mother and I were the only relatives: there was no one from Zoulika's side. And there was Patrizia, offering canapés to those people and talking to us in almost perfect Italian, without any tears. I can still see her showing my mother the last photographs of my father, convinced she was pleasing her, that seeing that fifty-year-old face would revive the affection she had felt thirty years earlier for a young man in an anorak.'

'And you never saw her again after that?'

'No. Nor did I ever hear from her. To be honest, I made no attempt to keep in touch. Then, suddenly, last week, the Carabinieri in Corbetta, which is between Milan and Magenta, phoned my mother's house and asked for me. The reason they wanted to speak to me was because Patrizia had died in December in Magenta, also in an accident. She'd been knocked over by a hit and run driver. They told my mother they hadn't found any relatives, either in Italy or in France, and that it had taken them more than two months to finally locate me.'

'Do you have any idea what your half-sister was doing near Milan?'

'They told me she was working as a clerk in a small firm in Vittuone, four or five kilometres from Magenta, but why she was in Italy in the first place I really don't know. I can only assume she had nobody left in France and felt like spending time in her father's home country.'

Once again, I was disoriented by the measured, detached tone of her reply: what did someone who could stay so calm at the thought of her sister's tragic death want from a psychologist like me? I was about to interrupt again when she herself started getting to the point.

'And now I come to the matter that's brought me here today. The Carabinieri suggested I collect the few things Patrizia had left, then asked me an embarrassing question. They asked me if I wanted to transfer the body to our family vault. I told them I'd think about it.'

'Embarrassing': she had used the word 'embarrassing'. It was time I started digging into her subconscious.

'Why did you find that question embarrassing?'

'Because it put me in an obviously embarrassing position. On the one hand, I was even less interested in Patrizia's body than I was in her when she was alive. On the other hand I couldn't openly show them how little I cared. It would have been bad taste.'

'So what did you decide?'

'I talked to my mother and she didn't think twice. According to her, it was unacceptable for our family not to take care of my sister's body, even though she was only my half-sister. It was a matter of honour and tact. Patrizia had to rest in our family vault, even though she was a Vitali, because when you came down to it I was a Vitali, too. So I resigned myself to the idea of having her transferred to our family vault in the cemetery at Meina on Lake Maggiore.'

She was still skating around the subject, but that was normal. The first session with a therapist is always a kind of taster session, where you sound each other out. That's why many of us don't charge for it.

'Last Thursday was the day the transfer was supposed to take place. I went to the cemetery in Magenta, where they'd buried Patrizia. There was just a temporary stone, without a photograph. I stood there looking at the grave for a few moments, trying to see if I felt any grief, but I don't think I did. The gravediggers came up to me and asked me if they could start. I told them to go ahead and they started moving the earth with a small excavator. The man who was working the excavator must have been having a bad day. The others told him to be more careful, but he became even more heavy-handed, as if he was in a hurry. After a while, we heard a sharp noise and we all realised what had happened: the machine had broken the lid of the coffin. Two of the gravediggers leaned over the edge of the grave to try and see how bad the damage was, and as soon as one of the two looked down he said, "Oh my God, that's terrible." At that point I leaned over and almost fainted: the coffin was empty, completely empty.'

I confess I was surprised, too, but then I told myself the moment had come to really get down to my work.

'I think your sister's empty coffin is a good point to start our dialogue.'

Benedetta gave me a puzzled look, and I asked her the question I should have asked her from the start. 'Signorina Vitali, what kind of help do you expect from me?'

'I want you to find my half-sister's body and get it back to her family. Its disappearance is a scandal we have to avoid. The gravediggers buried the coffin again and were appropriately rewarded for their silence, but now I want you to find the body.'

It was a classic comedy of errors. We'd been talking for half an hour about two different things we'd thought were one and the same. I went straight to the source of the principal misunderstanding.

'I assume Signor Crocetti told you I found his missing son and brought him home.'

'Didn't you?'

'Not exactly.'

'But you are a detective?'

I didn't know what to think of Crocetti. He was the one who really needed "psychological help", not his son. He refused to accept the idea that his son had left home, or that he needed support: to admit that meant admitting defeat. So much better to insist on the theory of the mysterious disappearance and the detective investigating and solving the mystery.

'No, Signora Vitali. Whatever Signor Crocetti told you, I'm not a detective, I'm a psychologist. All I did for Crocetti was talk to his son and persuade him to return home. Nothing more. No chases, no stakeouts, no gun battles, nothing like that.'

She leaned back in the chair and brushed her fringe away from her forehead, as if her hair was stopping her thinking. 'So you really can't do anything for me?'

'My job is to talk to people and try to understand them, which isn't easy to do with someone who's dead. I work with the living. I tracked down Crocetti's son to a squat because I tried to think the way he would, to get inside his head. That's not possible with a dead body.'

'What if you tried to think the way Patrizia thought when she was alive? What if you tried to understand what brought her here?'

'Would that help to find the body?'

'It might.'

How could it help? There were two possibilities: either Patrizia's death hadn't been entirely accidental and the removal of her body had something to do with the reasons for her death, or Benedetta had a guilt complex as high as a mountain where her half-sister was concerned and this quest was a belated attempt to show her love for her, hoping it would have some kind of retroactive effect.

I looked again at Benedetta and for the first time she seemed a bit lost, not so well protected by the shell of her social position. Yes, I said to myself, even if she doesn't realise it, what she's asking me to do *is* a job for a psychologist. I know now that I was wrong, but at the time I was acting in good faith – or perhaps I was just attracted by the idea of a generous cheque. Yes, perhaps that was it. It was only two days since the hostel for drug addicts I'd been working for had closed down, and more than anything else that encounter with Benedetta meant money, meant being able to cope.

'All right,' I said. 'But I'll only talk to people who knew Patrizia in Italy, and try to get some idea of her personality. As far as the other thing is concerned – finding her body – you'll have to bring someone else in, a professional. Dealing with things I haven't been trained for could get me into all kinds of trouble. And I'll add one last thing. In my opinion, the body's gone missing because of some stupid error. The coffin somehow got mixed up with another one, something like that.'

Benedetta immediately regained her resolute air. 'Then I think you should start today', she said.

I thought about my sleepless night, my backache, Morgana who hadn't yet eaten and was huddled in a corner, silent and scared. I thought of all these things and found enough self-respect to say, 'Not today, it's out of the question. I'll call you this evening and we can arrange when to meet tomorrow.'

'Do I have to be there, too?'

'I think you do, at least at first. As I said before, I'm not a detective. I haven't the faintest idea where to start, and I have no authority to ask people questions. Either you go with me, because as a relative you at least have a reason to ask about Patrizia, or we don't go at all.'

In preventing Benedetta from getting out of it, I was deluding myself that she and her guilt complex were the real objects of my assignment. I really was deluding myself. I could never have imagined the truth.

We exchanged mobile numbers and fixed a time for me to phone her that evening, then I called her a taxi, said goodbye, and watched from the window as she walked the thirty metres that separate my apartment from the Piazza Vecchia. Her heels landed without hesitation even on the irregular cobbles of the Vicolo Aquila Nera. Everything about her, from her walk to the way she looked at you, expressed an unostentatious self-confidence, the innate self-confidence of a superior race. This is one of the few things I've never been wrong about: there's no one better than an insecure person like me at assessing other people's self-confidence.

I looked up at the leaden sky. The thick clouds seemed to lie heavy over the roofs of the Upper Town. But I liked Bergamo even like that, even in the middle of winter. I thanked my mother's stubborn refusal to leave her little two-roomed apartment while she was still alive. Did she ever imagine that I'd be living in that same apartment one day?

Feeling the chill, I closed the window again. Morgana started rubbing herself against my legs. She was really hungry now, but still wasn't complaining. She seemed to understand that this was a difficult day, the first Valentine's Day for years that I'd be spending on my own, without Stefano. And then there was this new development, this strange job looming on the horizon. I stroked her, then opened one of the special tins for her.

While Morgana noisily devoured her salmon pâté, I sat down at the table, took an old diary that I used as a notebook, and tried to jot down a few notes on what I should do. I wrote two or three lines, then crossed them out. I wrote a few more lines, but they seemed just as pointless, and I angrily scratched them out with my biro. What kind of job was this? The mind of a dead woman: it was like the title of a low-budget horror movie. I ended up with just two words: *Carabinieri* and *Hospital*. That was where my journey would start the next day.

I spent the day at home, tidying, cleaning, doing the laundry: the whites on one side, waiting for the pile to become a little more substantial, the dark colours straight into the washing machine at forty degrees, rapid cycle. But what about my green sweatshirt? It's hard to know where to put green: put it with the light colours and it stains them, put it with the dark ones and it gets stained. The one solution would be to wash it by hand... I envied the women in the commercials, who had nothing to worry about except how to get everything as clean as possible and how best to wash delicates. I wasn't yet used to spending long afternoons at home, even though the amount of free time I had had increased to a worrying extent lately: I didn't really have a private clientele, and the co-operatives were closing one by one for lack of funds. The State cuts funding to local bodies, the local bodies cut funding to the co-operatives, the hostels close, the addicts go back to being addicts, and the psychologists stay at home doing the housework. I didn't yet know it would all soon be different, I didn't know that things were about to get worse.

If nothing else, the thought of that strange assignment had kept my mind occupied, but about a quarter to seven I felt I had to go out, I had to breathe. I closed the door, making as little noise as possible, and just as silently descended the stairs: Signora Ghislandi, who lived alone in the apartment below mine, was always on the alert, and at the merest hint of a human presence would rush out onto the landing in search of a chat. And I didn't want that, however sweet Signora Ghislandi was.

There was almost nobody in the street. By the light of the street lamps, you could see the dampness of the evening gathered in fine droplets that hung in the air. Despite the cold, a few students stood chatting in the portico outside the Angelo Mai library: I heard their occasional bursts of laughter, gradually fading as I continued along the Via Colleoni. The shops had emptied, and through the windows I saw the proprietors tidying the shelves and counters, anxious to close and get home. I waved at Signora Ada, who owned the dairy, then turned left, towards the slope. I didn't have any desire to return home, or any pressing reason. I carried on walking, stepping on the round cobbles of the Via Salvecchio, the ones that make tourists twist their ankles. When a true native of Bergamo walks next to someone who isn't local, they motion them to walk on the paved, level border at the side of the street. I'm used to these stones, they say, to me it's just like walking on the floor of my own home. It isn't true, of course, they only say it because they still have the rough but polite ways of mountain dwellers.

In the air you could smell, in gusts, wood burning in the fireplaces of the very rich who had recently taken over Upper Bergamo and in the stoves of the few remaining poor people who had always lived there.

I walked for a long time, as far as the walls, then all the way up to Colle Aperto, then back down along the Via Colleoni. Halfway down, I thought over my options: dinner in my kitchen, with Morgana sitting under the table and the TV on, or else dinner at the Circolino?

I opted for the Circolino. Bad mistake.

Once under the austere vaults of what used to be the city prison, I saw a host of couples doing the textbook things, looking into each other's eyes, holding hands under the table as they waited for the next course. Even the big tables usually reserved for groups had been broken up into smaller, more intimate tables. I was about to leave, but one of the waitresses, a girl I usually exchanged a few words with, pointed to a still empty table in a corner, next to another one occupied by three women about my age.

'They just called to cancel the reservation,' she said, as if apologising for the fact that there was a free seat in a restaurant on the evening of Valentine's Day. So, I thought, now that I was pushing forty I had to be content with the scraps from the lovers' tables, literally.

I ordered what, over time, had become for me a kind of fixed menu: casoncelli with butter and kebab. I allowed myself the luxury of a bottle of Valcalepio red, though I limited myself to drinking only a couple of glasses. The three women at the next table, on the other hand, were really going to town on the wine, and their voices got louder and louder until their chatter echoed through the room, as if they were deliberately trying to annoy the other customers, as if they wanted to take their revenge on anyone who was there to whisper sweet nothings.

I ate quickly, without much appetite, managing as usual to drip butter from the casoncelli onto my clothes. I left, and as soon as I got a signal on my mobile I called Benedetta.

I cut short the pleasantries. 'Let's meet at ten o'clock tomorrow morning,' I said, 'outside the Carabinieri barracks in Corbetta.'

'Do you know where it is?'

'No, but I'll find it.'

'I'll see you tomorrow, then.'

'See you tomorrow.'

Before putting my mobile back in my pocket, I set the alarm for seven the next day: from Bergamo to Milan and from there to Corbetta might take quite a while during the rush hour.

It really was time now to go home.

I walked some more. The street was deserted, and shiny with dampness. I entered the building, climbed the stairs, and by the time I reached the third floor I could already hear Morgana's miaowing: she had recognised my steps and was welcoming me.

I had just closed the door behind me when the old rotary dial telephone let out its unpleasant, old-fashioned screech.

I sat down on the sofa and lifted the receiver.

'Hi, it's me. How are you?'

'Fine, and you?'

'Fine.' Silence, then he continued, 'I called to wish you a

happy Valentine's Day.'

'Separated couples don't wish each other a happy Valentine's Day.'

'Okay, but it's not against the law.'

'Then happy Valentine's Day to you too.'

'Good night.'

'Good night.'

I put down the receiver, switched out the light. And cried.

The ground has been made hard by the frost, but once I get past the surface crust, in this spot where it was shifted some months ago, it yields more easily to the thrusts of my little folding shovel. I ought to have a real shovel, a big one, the kind you can press down on with your foot. I'm getting exhausted, but I keep going all the same. Even though it's not too late to turn back.

There's no fog. Damn it. In this area there are at least fifteen fatal accidents a year due to fog, but tonight the air is clear, and there are stars in the sky. At least there were before I entered this cluster of trees, which by day is a ridiculous little wood on the edge of the city but by night turns back into a dark, forbidding forest.

If there was only a little mist I'd feel more protected, protected from the eyes of anyone whose suspicions might be aroused by the noise, but there isn't any mist at all. The fires of the prostitutes on the dirt road glow clearly. You can see the profiles of the women as they approach the flames, holding out their hands paralysed by the cold. The cars, the few that there are, pass slowly – the drivers are window shopping. A few stop. Then the girl approaches the lowered window and starts haggling. I imagine that on a night like this, some of them, Alina for instance, would be prepared to get laid for a couple of euros, just to get out of the cold for a while. If it weren't for their pimps I think they'd do it, but they have to please the pimps, who are increasingly greedy and violent. Out of every two or three drivers who stop to haggle, one buys, and the girl gets in. A quarter of an hour later, back she comes and everything starts again.

I, too, stop from time to time, to catch my breath and wipe the cold sweat from my forehead, then start again. And when I stop I look at them, hoping they can't see me from the road, hoping I'm sufficiently hidden by these skeletal trees.

I keep digging, thinking about the prostitutes' hard lives in order not to think about my own. I dig and dig. But what will the body be like once I've dug it up? Better not to wonder about that, better to pick up the thread of my memories.

Tuesday, 15 February

I opened my eyes a second before the alarm on my mobile phone started ringing. It was another difficult, confused awakening. The bedroom looked unfamiliar, until I realised it was the kitchen. I had slept on the sofa, fully clothed, sunk in the leaden sleep that hits me suddenly after I've been crying.

I had a quick shower and got dressed. A pill for my headache, a few bites of cat food for Morgana in her bowl, and I was out in the street, without even having breakfast, in order not to waste time. Stopping only to grab a cappuccino at the Corsarola coffee bar, I hurried to the car park in the Piazza Mascheroni.

I looked for my Opel Agila and, despite the bright yellow bodywork, had some difficulty finding it, hidden as it was among the station wagons and people carriers of the upper classes.

I reached the autostrada. *Occasional tailbacks*, said the lighted signs. More than occasional, actually, but I was prepared, I'd even brought a novel with me just in case I had a few long waits: *The Pledge* by Dürrenmatt. I find having something to read quire reassuring, even though often, as happened that day, I don't even open the book: the main thing is not to read, but to know that I can.

I reached Corbetta as the church bells were striking ten. I drew up at the kerb and asked a passer-by where the Carabinieri station was.

'Via Montenero,' he said, in a marked Eastern European

accent. He added a few directions.

When I arrived, I saw Benedetta Vitali standing outside the door, looking like someone who hasn't been waiting more than five minutes but still thinks it's too long. I held out my hand, without apologising for the delay, and she shook it as curtly as the day before.

We went in, and the Maresciallo, who must have been informed of our arrival by a phone call from Benedetta, came towards us, smiling almost obsequiously: the surname – not Vitali, but the other one, the double-barrelled one – always did the trick.

'Maresciallo Pietri,' he said, giving a kind of military salute. He was a stocky man, not ugly, but a little overweight, rather different from those you see in police series on TV.

He immediately took us into his office.

'How can I help you?'

'My cousin,' Benedetta said, indicating me, 'is a psychologist. I've asked her to try and get some idea of the kind of person my sister, who I hardly knew, was when she was alive. I know nothing can bring her back, but finding out something about her would at least be a small consolation.'

Was this a piece of play-acting to arouse Pietri's pity, or did she have a dissociative personality? She had said she was my cousin, which was probably a good idea, but how to explain this belated interest in Patrizia? How to explain Patrizia's promotion from half-sister to sister?

I thought it best, though, to back her up. 'My cousin's right. Getting a better idea of what we've lost can help to fill the void. And in order to get an idea of Patrizia, I need to start with her last days and then go back all the way to her childhood.'

'I don't really know much about her last days,' the Maresciallo replied. 'I know she'd been working in the office of a small factory in Vittuone for five or six months, and that she'd found lodgings on a nearby farm.'

'A farm?'

'Yes, there are still a lot of them around here. This area is called the South Milan Agricultural Park. The factory where Signorina Vitali worked is just on the edge of the park, and the farm is just over a kilometre away. The owners often let rooms in the farmhouses to seasonal workers, and even though your cousin wasn't seasonal...'

He gave me a slightly embarrassed look. I think he was wondering how close a cousin I was: if I was Benedetta's cousin on her mother's side, and therefore nothing to do with Patrizia, or on her father's side, which would place me in the poor half of the family. I got the impression that he opted for the second hypothesis, because he continued, 'As I was saying, I don't know anything else about your cousin. I don't even know very much about the accident itself. All I can do is go with you to the scene. As long as it's not too painful for you.'

He had addressed these last words to Benedetta, and it was she who replied, contritely, 'Let's go. Can you take us there now?'

'Of course.'

He lifted the receiver of an ancient intercom, one of those blue ones with six buttons at the bottom. He pressed one of them.

'I'm taking the two Vitali ladies to Vittuone. I'll be back in an hour. If you need me, use the radio.'

He had clearly put me in the poor branch of the family, ignoring my muttered 'Anna Pavesi, pleased to meet you' when we had been introduced.

We went down to the courtyard.

'I'm taking one of our cars, but perhaps the two of you could follow me in yours.'

I don't know if he said this because the regulations forbade him to carry civilians, or if he was thinking that a Benedetta with a double-barrelled name might feel uncomfortable being seen in a Carabinieri vehicle. Whatever the reason, I followed him in my little car and Benedetta followed me in her Mercedes coupé.

Once he got onto the main road, the Maresciallo turned right and I kept just a few metres behind him, trying not to lose him in the mist, which was growing thicker. We joined the slow, serpentine line of cars and lorries that wound endlessly around Milan. After a few minutes, travelling at thirty kilometres an hour, we passed a bilingual sign announcing that we were entering the municipality of Vittuone, in Italian, or Vituon, in Lombard. Another hundred metres, and the Maresciallo's car turned right onto a side road that cut across the landscape of what a few triangular signs indicated as the South Milan Agricultural Park. I followed him, checking in the rear-view mirror that Benedetta was doing the same. Although we were in the Agricultural Park, or at least on the edges of it, the first thing we passed on the road was a factory composed of a few small, ill-assorted buildings inside a perimeter wall. I saw the Maresciallo gesturing towards the factory, and I was already about to pull over when he accelerated again and drove on.

By now, we were on an unpaved road lined with slender, leafless trees, beyond which were bare fields, wreathed in mist that was like smoke. Between the trees and the fields, on our left, ran a ditch. It was deep, and overrun with brambles, but there was no water in it, except in a few places where it widened, forming what looked like small ponds covered with a thin crust of ice. A grim place to die, an even grimmer place to live.

The Maresciallo pulled up beside one of these ponds, and Benedetta and I did the same, parking the three cars in a row at the side of the road.

'Here,' Pietri said, indicating the point where the ditch started to widen, 'is where we found Signorina Vitali. The impact threw her a few metres. She was lying face down, with one hand in the water.'

He seemed to be searching for the most exact, most precise words, clearly hoping to make an impression on Benedetta.

'We found the bicycle your sister used for getting to work,' he continued in the same tone. 'It was lying over there, bent out of shape. The car that knocked her down had driven over it and continued without stopping. It was a good thing the signorina was thrown off the bike, otherwise she would have been crushed by the tyres of the vehicle and would have died on the spot.'

As soon as he realised what nonsense he was talking, he fell silent. Is it better to lie dying for a week or to die immediately? I had my own answer to that, although it might not have been a widely shared opinion. Perhaps, in the case of a young woman of twenty-three, living another week had mattered. To me it wouldn't have mattered at all.

I decided to stick to more down-to-earth questions. 'What time did the accident occur?'

'We don't know exactly. My officer and I got here at

seven-fifty. The call had come in about seven-forty, but it's possible the accident happened earlier, maybe about seven.'

'Who reported it?'

'An anonymous caller, from the phone booth at the junction of this road and the main road. The officer who took the call said the voice was male and Italian.'

'Could it have been the hit and run driver himself?'

'I don't think so. He didn't say there'd been an accident, just that there was a woman's body lying in the ditch, as if he'd arrived after she'd been knocked down.'

While Pietri was briefing me, Benedetta was looking around her in silence, apparently distracted and even slightly vexed at having to be there when she probably had a thousand more important things to do.

'Excuse me, Maresciallo,' I said. 'Earlier, when we passed that factory, you made me a signal I didn't understand.'

'I just wanted to show you the company where Patrizia Vitali worked. I think it's called Vittuone Heat Treatments. All the details are in the documents we gave your cousin.'

'I brought them for you,' Benedetta cut in, as if waking up. 'I have them in the car, I'll give them to you before I go.'

'Do they include the address of the farmhouse where Patrizia lived?'

'Of course,' the Maresciallo said. 'Actually it's the one over there, the yellow one.'

Following the direction of his finger, I saw a large, two-storey, ochre-coloured building in the distance, standing out above the low sheds that formed the other three sides of the farmyard. Surrounding it were a few fir trees, green against the uniform grey of the sky and the dark brown of the ploughed earth.

'Was Patrizia conscious when you got here?'

'No, she was unconscious. I climbed down into the ditch and checked that she still had a pulse. She did, though it was weak.'

'Did you call the ambulance?'

'Of course, immediately. I didn't trust myself to move her. In a case like that, there's always a risk of making things worse. Within a quarter of an hour an ambulance arrived, with a doctor on board. When he saw the state the girl was in, he immediately said, "She won't make it".'

Benedetta gave a start, and Pietri realised he had been tactless for the second time in five minutes.

'They took her straight to the hospital in Magenta,' he continued, trying to conceal his embarrassment. 'The doctors will be able to tell you the rest. Unfortunately, there was nothing else we could do except trace the people who knew her in some way: her employer, her landlady, and of course, her family, although that was a bit more difficult.'

His third blunder. He really liked twisting the knife in the wound!

From the open door of his car came the croaky voice of the radio. The Maresciallo ran to answer it, and sat in the car for a while with the door closed so that we couldn't hear his conversation.

'You must excuse me,' he said, coming back towards us. 'I have to go. I don't suppose you'll have any problems finding your way back.'

'That's fine,' I assured him.

'If you need me for anything,' he added, looking into Benedetta's eyes, 'don't hesitate to contact me.'

'Thank you for everything, Maresciallo,' she said.

'Goodbye.'

He drove off, raising dust and gravel.

Benedetta walked to her car and came back with a small-ish padded yellow envelope. 'Here, take this. There are the documents the Maresciallo was talking about. All the papers Patrizia had with her. You can take your time looking at them, I have a copy.'

'Seeing that we're cousins, we could be more familiar with each other. It might be more convincing when we're playing our parts.'

'You're right, best not to make any mistakes.'

But it was obvious that neither the idea of being my cousin nor that of being on more familiar terms with me filled her with enthusiasm.

'Shall we go to the hospital?' I suggested.

'Yes, that's a good idea. Unfortunately, I don't have much time.'

'Shall I lead the way?'

'Yes, I've never been there.'

As it happened, I'd been to the hospital in Magenta a few times in September, to continue therapy with one of my addicts, who had suffered multiple fractures after crashing his father's car into a lamp post while on heroin.

I got back in the car, paying attention to where I was putting my feet. Looking down at the ground, I saw three condoms in the space of a square metre. I put the car into gear and, in order to do a three-point turn, described a quarter-circle with the wheels. I ended up with the front of the car on the opposite side of the road, nearly hitting a folding seat that had been propped against a tree. First the condoms, now the seat: it wasn't hard to figure out that this was an area where prostitutes hung out. This probably was-n't a time when they plied their trade, or perhaps the sight of the Carabinieri car had scared them off, but there was no doubt that it was an area for prostitutes.

We rejoined the main road, going back the way we had come, and then past our starting point and as far as Magenta. As we got further from Milan, the endless line of vehicles gathered a bit of speed. I passed villages that were nothing but collections of houses on either side of the road, connected by a long string of warehouses, motels, car and lorry showrooms and discount stores, followed by more warehouses, showrooms and discount stores. Once they had been isolated little villages, now it was only possible to tell where one ended and the other began thanks to the signs. Vittuone/Vituon, Corbetta, Magenta.

We came to a roundabout, passed under the railway line and, at the end of a straight street, found ourselves in the hospital car park. Benedetta got out of her Mercedes, look-ing lost. She was one of those people who feel quite at home in New York or Sydney, but then, finding them-selves deep in the provinces, even though not far from their own homes, need a guide dog. I took on that role.

Approaching the hospital, Benedetta stopped for a moment to look at the structure towering over the entrance, which looked like one of those futuristic arches they had built at La Défense in Paris.

'Is it a private clinic?' she asked me.

'No, it's a public hospital.'

She seemed surprised. To people like her, 'public' meant chaos, ugliness, waste.

Her astonishment increased inside, when she saw the

shiny floors, the ornamental plants, the wood finish, and reached its climax at the sight of a grand piano on a raised area in a corner of the entrance hall. What she was seeing was a world she could barely conceive of, a world where people could be treated without using their credit cards or having to fight cockroaches and falling plaster.

'Now where do we go?'

I went up to one of the notice boards where the layout of the various wards and departments was indicated with bands of different colours, looked at it, and said, 'Let's try trauma, fifth floor.'

We went up and, once we reached the department, we stopped a nurse who was coming out of a room carrying a tray with two phials and a used syringe.

It was Benedetta who stepped forward to speak. As I was now starting to realise, whenever she found herself in the presence of other people she regained all the self-confidence she lost in her solitary moments.

'My name is Benedetta Bellandi Serzoni. I'd like to speak to anyone who dealt with a patient named Patrizia Vitali, who died here on…' – she took a piece of paper from her pocket and read – '…6 December last year.'

No plucking at the heartstrings this time, no long-lost sister to be cherished in memory. Faced with a nurse – nurses, according to a widely-held view, being the kind of people who devoured glossy magazines and gossip columns – Benedetta had again played on her family name.

'I'll get Dr Callegari right away.'

Hard to say if the nurse would have been so eager to carry out her mission if it had been some ordinary Signora Rossi who'd asked her. Whatever the case, Dr Callegari appeared less than a minute later. One metre ninety tall, with a tan redolent of tropical beaches, the kind of mahogany-coloured tan you might see on a dentist or a lawyer, not a hospital doctor in mid-career.

Benedetta introduced herself, with her three surnames, one after the other. She mentioned her sister Patrizia. I was again her cousin, a poor one of course.

'Let's go in the lounge.'

Even a lounge, for conversations with patients' relatives!

We sat down and Benedetta took charge of the conversation.

'The thing is, doctor, as you will surely have realised, my sister and I didn't see much of each other, in fact, we barely knew each other. She was actually my half-sister, my father's daughter. I never saw anything of him either. He's dead now...'

Depending on who she was talking to, she pitched her own grief and her degree of kinship with Patrizia differently. Callegari listened carefully, without appearing to judge, simply waiting for her to come to the point of her visit – rather as I had the day before.

'...now, though, that Patrizia is dead, I feel as if something is missing...'

Yes, the body was missing, but she couldn't say that.

'...something of her, of her life. And so, together with my cousin, who is a psychologist, we're looking at the last days of her life as a way of finding out about her personality, and building up the memory of her that we don't have – in fact we don't even have a photograph of her to put on the family vault.'

Was this involuntary self-mockery on her part, or was she sending coded messages to the doctor?

'I understand,' he said, smiling. It wasn't exactly a forced smile, more a professional smile, I would have said, the smile of someone who, in his job, has to show an understanding he doesn't always possess. Then he turned to me, with a different smile.

'Unfortunately, as you know, we don't deal with personalities, with characters, we deal with bodies, bones, muscles. All I can tell you about Signorina Vitali is contained in her medical records. I'll go and get them.'

His white coat fluttered as he went out. Under it he was wearing a pair of light trousers and an orange Lacoste T-shirt: apparently, he didn't just spend his time on tropical beaches, he actually commuted every morning between Zanzibar and Magenta.

Left alone in the lounge, Benedetta and I didn't say a word, didn't even look at each other. Luckily, Callegari wasn't away for more than five minutes.

He sat down, opened the folder and started reading aloud, skipping parts of it, summarising and paraphrasing.

'Patrizia Vitali, born in Grenoble, France, 13/1/1982. Brought into the Emergency Department last 30 November at 8.15 a.m.'

He looked up from the sheet of paper and I saw him quickly remove a pair of reading glasses and slip them into the pocket of his white coat: I hadn't even noticed him put them on. Without reading any more, he started telling us the story we had come to hear.

'I remember when they brought her in. She had abrasions everywhere, partly due to the impact of the car, partly due to branches, brambles and other things. She was unconscious. But the most serious damage was to the spine. Here, look at the X-ray I asked for as soon as she arrived.'

He took the X-ray and showed it to me, as if he assumed

my training had been similar to his and I'd be able to interpret an X-ray. Tracing an imaginary circle with his finger, he indicated a particular spot where the more or less regular sequence of the vertebrae seemed to be broken. I thought I understood, not because I'd studied such things, but simply because, ever since I'd had that accident on the rocks at the age of twelve, I'd seen hundreds of X-rays, all showing the same part of the body: the back, my back. Just thinking about it gave me a spasm that made me grimace with pain, but nobody seemed to notice.

'Here, you see, there's a lesion. A serious one. In my opinion, if she had survived, her legs would have been permanently paralysed. Although you can never be sure.'

Another spasm, this time in my back, but coming from the brain, from the memory of those words my doctors had repeated ad nauseam: '*It's a miracle she wasn't paralysed.*'

'Did you treat her until she died?'

'No. I'd temporarily taken over my colleague Dr Maestri's patients. He was at a conference in the United States, but was due back that day. In fact he arrived at two o'clock – I think he'd come directly from Malpensa airport – so I handed over to him and Patrizia became his patient.'

'And she never regained consciousness?'

He reopened the folder and made an effort to find the answer without having to put his glasses on again.

'Here it is. I remember it well. The day she was admitted, Patrizia woke up, about one o'clock in the afternoon. I think she remained conscious until five, then fell back into a coma and never came out of it. Of course, for the details you really should ask Dr Maestri.'

'Is he here?'

'No, he was on call last night so he's off today. Later, if

you like, we can check his schedule.'

'What was the cause of death?' Benedetta asked.

'In a case like this, doctors tend to use the word "complications", but it can all be traced back to the initial trauma: she died because of the blow she sustained. I see here that my colleague also mentions a head injury which I must admit I never noticed, but…'

He broke off and searched in the papers and folders for something specific, but couldn't find it.

'There's a report on the X-ray that led Maestri to diagnose a head injury, but the X-ray itself is missing. It must have got stuck in the filing cabinet. But anyway it's all here: lesions to the spinal column, a haematoma in the cranium, respiratory problems, the kind of things people usually die of in road accidents.'

He leafed through the folder again and located the crucial paper.

'I was right. On 6 December, about six in the morning, Maestri notes the occurrence of serious respiratory problems. He himself takes her to intensive care, but by the time he gets there all he can do is note the time of death and fill in the certificate.'

He closed the medical record with a grimace that expressed, this time, a genuine compassion for Patrizia, an understanding that seemed to extend notionally to all the patients he hadn't been able to save.

'That's our profession, you see. A string of failures, with a few successes every now and again, though you tell yourself they might have recovered anyway. Like those stray dogs that get run over and somehow pull through. They may walk with a limp for the rest of their lives, but they pull though. The lucky ones, that is, the others die.'

His tone had suddenly turned bitter, and he didn't seem like a tourist now. He seemed more like a doctor, the kind you'd like to meet when you're ill.

'I'm sorry about your sister, I really am. When a young woman not yet twenty-three goes like that, we wonder what we're doing here. Believe me, it can be quite upsetting.'

It was as if he somehow knew that Benedetta's grief was fake and he wanted to contrast it with his own, genuine sorrow. Not necessarily at Patrizia's death, but death in general.

'As you see, that's all I can tell you. Perhaps Dr Maestri will be able to tell you more, but not much more, at least to judge from the medical records. Come, I'll see you out.'

He stood up, opened the door and let us pass, first Benedetta and then me.

'Wait a moment,' he said to us when we were halfway along the corridor.

He opened a door with the words *Doctors' room* on it. He came out again a moment later.

'Dr Maestri has today and tomorrow off. He'll be back on Thursday.'

He led us to the lifts and shook our hands. Firmly. His eyes were lively again, but I remember thinking it didn't necessarily mean that he was insincere, rather that he was someone who couldn't allow himself to look sad, at least not in front of the sick.

In the lift, Benedetta and I didn't exchange a single word, and I learnt by heart the sign showing the layout of the different departments. Then, as soon as we had left the hospital, she rushed ahead, and turned the corner towards the car park. By the time I caught up with her, she was standing by her car, finishing a conversation on her mobile.

'...in about forty minutes. There's not so much traffic at this hour. Did Caprioli complain about the cancelled appointment this morning?... All right, send him a scarf from the new collection, for his wife... No, not to his house, to his office, then if he doesn't want to give it to his wife he can give it to someone else.'

Benedetta reasoned like a man, perhaps that was the price you had to pay to stay at the top in her line of work – or perhaps someone like her would stay at the top anywhere.

She folded the mobile and condescended to talk to me.

'I really have to go now, I've been neglecting some really important things. I think you can continue on your own. You have the documents and you know as much about my father's daughter as I do. If you need anything just call me. I'm also leaving you my secretary's number, her name is Silvana. Naturally, you'll have to introduce yourself as my cousin and not mention Patrizia.'

'Naturally.'

The thought that Patrizia might be the thing she'd most neglected didn't even occur to her. I would have to do a lot of work on her, I thought: once you're going down the wrong road, it's hard to get off it.

She got in the car and started the engine, but almost immediately switched it off again. She opened the door and motioned me to come closer. Still sitting on the leather seat, one leg inside the car and the other resting on the ground, she took a cheque book from her handbag and wrote out a cheque.

'I believe it's normal to give an advance,' she said, as she handed it to me.

I ought to have said no, it was normal to pay one session at a time, or, at most, after a cycle of sessions. I should have put paid to the misunderstanding once and for all, but I thought of the last bank transfer I'd received from the co-operative: three hundred euros.

'The rest when funds arrive from the European Union,' they had said. In other words, never.

I looked at the figure. Three thousand: a real shot in the arm.

Benedetta's predictions were wrong, there was just as much traffic on the main road as before. I drove back to Corbetta, and then on as far as Vittuone. I drove slowly, switching on the windscreen wiper from time to time to remove, not rain, but a kind of dense vapour, a mixture of dust and smog.

Waiting at a traffic light, I heard the mobile ring, a single, prolonged, irritating sound: a message had arrived. I looked for the phone in my bag and viewed the text: *Tomorrow 10.30 meeting with regional education board to discuss results new cases. Waiting for you. Laura.*

I would have liked to reply that while they might be waiting for me, I was waiting for my money, so Laura and the whole of the Progetto co-operative could go to hell. But I didn't do it. The lights turned green and I set off again, slowly.

Where the warehouses, car showrooms and discount stores left room for a little of the surrounding world, the road was lined with leafless poplars and partly-tilled fields. The only patches of colour continued to be the advertising signs with their almost fluorescent hues: *Furniture ware-*

house: complete furnishings from 20 euros per month. Motel Rode: soundproof rooms, light and mirror effects, whirlpool bath. Gardenland, for your garden.

I looked for my Paolo Conte cassette to put in the car stereo. I found it, wound the tape forward to the right spot, and turned up the volume.

...in the Po Valley, between Broni and Stradella, it's like being in a glass of water and aniseed, oh yes....

It couldn't have been more appropriate.

The line of cars ahead of me slowed down even more, and stopped.

...and Broni, Casteggio, Voghera are grey too, there's only one red light up there...

Enough. Enough tailbacks. I decided to avoid Milan and turned north, towards Carnate, or Usmate or another of what Buzzati, or someone like him, called the 'villages ending in -ate', in search of an empty road I wouldn't find.

At home, Morgana was waiting for me as usual, impatient and affectionate. And as usual I was late for her lunch, and for mine, too. I poured a few bites into her bowl and cooked myself some pasta – plain with butter, the way Stefano used to like it. The TV news was saying the same things as usual: attacks in Iraq, no change in the inflation rate, Inter Milan in crisis; and was silent about the same things as usual: bombing of Iraqi villages, redundancies, etcetera, etcetera.

When they announced an item about fashion, I switched off the TV and quickly cleared the table. Morgana was sleeping next to the stove, curled up and snoring slightly. From Signora Ghislandi's apartment downstairs came the muffled signature tune of a game show. There was no other sound.

I picked up the envelope with Patrizia's papers and sat down on the sofa. I started with the identity card, which was in French.

nom: Vitali
prénom: Patrizia
née le: 13 janvier 1982
à: Grenoble (Isère)

Looking at the photograph, I had to admit, reluctantly, that the description Benedetta had given of her fitted her perfectly: a young girl with an old woman's eyes. If you wanted to be more indulgent, you could say they were eyes that contained a great deal of suffering, but the gist was the same: they were an old woman's eyes. She wasn't ugly, but there was nothing pretty, nothing attractive about her: she had shoulder-length brown hair, parted in the middle, a straight, fairly large nose, and a dark complexion, obviously inherited from her mother.

From the big envelope I took out a smaller, white one. It contained photographs, of different formats, and taken at different times. One was of a woman with Arab features. On the back was written the word you might have expected: *Maman.* The second was a black and white passport photo, showing a young man who looked remarkably like Antoine in the days when he sang *La tramontana.* I turned it over. This time, too, I knew what to expect: *Papa à 25 ans.*

There were rather more words on the back of the third photograph: *La plus drôle des maisons où j'ai habité, où j'ai été heureuse.* The image did indeed show a very strange house, made of stone and grey concrete like so many others, but with one side extending out over the waters of a stream and supported by tall concrete pillars that looked like giant stilts. An unusual place to live, but not as much as Patrizia thought: I remembered seeing a very similar building on TV, in a documentary or something like that. Anyway, she had been happy there, which seemed highly unlikely to me.

The last photograph showed a white puppy, a poodle with not especially curly hair: *Vanille*, according to what it said on the back.

The words were all in the same handwriting, and had all been written in purple biro. It was as if at a certain point in her life, probably just before leaving France, Patrizia had created a meagre archive of the things she had loved – which didn't amount to much.

I put the photographs to one side and looked at what was still in the envelope: five pay slips from the company where she had worked, printed with a dot matrix printer on standard forms.

Company: Vittuone Heat Treatments, proprietor Giovanni Imperiale, 2 Strada alle Cascine, Vittuone (MI).

Employee: Patrizia Vitali, c/o Caterina Bono, 33 Strada alle Cascine, Vittuone (MI).

I assumed that the Carabinieri had also recovered Patrizia's personal effects and handed them over to Benedetta. Clothes, underwear, a few books. These were the things I needed to see, not just the papers. I made a mental note to ask Benedetta for these other objects, the ones that could really tell me about her sister. In any case, the following day I would begin to reconstruct Patrizia's last days on the basis of those papers, starting with the company where she had worked and the farmhouse where she had rented a room.

I hadn't realised how much time looking through those documents had taken, because when I raised my eyes to look outside I saw that the colour of the sky had turned dark grey, verging on black. It was five-twenty.

I switched off the nightlamp I'd been reading by and went to the window to watch the orange light of the street lamps rapidly replacing the daylight. My internal clock registered that this was the hour of melancholy. When I lived in Turin with Stefano, it had been the hour of anxiety – the supermarket, the journey home, the tailback on the Corso Novara, dinner made with a maximum of love and a minimum of time – the hour of the good wife. Then came the hour of waiting, putting the pasta on the gas to boil, on a low light that would be turned up at the sound of his voice through the entryphone: 'It's me, I'm just putting the car in the garage and I'll be right up.' And I would look at the clock in the kitchen: eight-thirty, nine, nine-thirty, depending on how late he'd been kept at the office. In my hour of melancholy, all that remained of that anxiety, and that stifled anger at his lateness, was a vague memory, a bizarrely sweet aftertaste. Memory is often wrong, because it's much too indulgent.

I savoured that aftertaste for a while longer, watching as the lights came on in the buildings opposite and gradually revealed kitchens, laid tables, families settling down to see themselves reflected in the TV.

Finally I went to the cooker and made two hamburgers, one for me and the other for Morgana. When they were done, I put them on two plates and put the plates down on the table, then motioned to Morgana to jump up. She looked at me in surprise: how could I of all people be inviting her to break the most sacred of taboos? For a moment she hesitated, turning her nose alternately to me and the unseen source of that aroma that made her nostrils quiver, before finally leaping up and starting to eat her meat. At least I wouldn't be having dinner alone.

From time to time I shine the torch, masking it a little with my hand and pointing it at the ground. I don't seem to have made much progress in my digging, and that's not because the torch doesn't give enough light, it's because the ground is hard and heavy. The metal handle of the shovel is hurting my hands and the cold seems to paralyse me. Or perhaps it's fear that's freezing me, making me shake. How much earth will I still have to shift to find the body? And will I find it before someone finds me? What am I doing at night in the middle of the countryside, in the middle of this stench that won't let me rest?

Wednesday, 16 February

33 Strada alle Cascine. I parked my car in an unpaved open space filled with the rusty parts of agricultural machines that seemed to belong to a bygone age. As I got out, I was immediately struck by an acrid, all-pervading smell of chemical fertiliser. I walked along a short, tree-lined drive until I came to the farmyard. Around the yard were cowsheds and hay lofts full of round bales of hay. It was a strange feeling to hear cows mooing such a short distance from the housing estates on the edge of the city. Apart from that, everything was silent, motionless. The sun shone down through thin clouds, and the farmhouse looked like the set of one of those German TV series in faded colours, like *Derrick* or *The Black Forest Clinic.* Under a tractor, a man in blue mechanic's overalls was carrying out some kind of repairs, but all you could see of him was his legs, perfectly still, as if he was engaged in a piece of precision work or contemplating how to proceed. I decided not to disturb him and headed straight for the house.

I knocked at a glass door that opened directly onto the yard and a female voice told me to come in. The door led straight into a kitchen which didn't look as if it had changed since the Sixties, apart from the annual Frate Indovino calendar. The furniture was of metal, painted white, the surfaces all of red Formica. Against the wall was a shiny steel dresser. On its doors, just under the central handle, a child who was now an adult had stuck some transfers, the kind you'd find in boxes of processed cheese about forty years ago. Even the wall cupboards were of painted metal. There was lino on the floor, the part of it under the long wooden table still looking like imitation parquet, the rest of it, where it had been trodden over day after day, reduced to a sheet of thin yellow foil.

'Signora Bono?' I asked the white-haired woman standing next to the kitchen sink.

'That's me,' she replied, wiping her right hand on her apron and holding it out to me.

'How do you do? Anna Pavesi. I was a rather distant cousin of Patrizia Vitali.'

'Poor girl, I still can't believe what happened. I can still see her there, sitting at her place at the end of the table. Because we eat all together, the family, the seasonal workers, the other lodgers. I cook for everyone, and treat the youngsters like my own children. Patrizia, of course, who'd lost her mum and dad, was my pet. But I didn't know she had relatives here in Italy.'

'Actually she only had a half-sister, my cousin, but they hadn't seen each other for years. Now, though, we'd like to try and understand how Patrizia was as a person, so that we can remember her better.'

'Ah yes, people always shut the stable door after the horse has bolted! Of course. Taking flowers to the cemetery is easier than getting close to the living.'

'You're right. That's why my cousin feels guilty, so guilty that she doesn't dare come here in person. She keeps saying she should have helped her before...'

'But Patrizia didn't need any help. She had a job, somewhere to live, and I had the impression she even had a boyfriend towards the end.'

A mischievous but good-natured gleam had come into her eyes, but it immediately disappeared, probably at the thought that the hit and run driver who had knocked the girl down had also obliterated that love story.

Grabbing two chairs from the back, she moved them away from the table. I noticed they were also covered in red Formica.

'Please sit down.'

'Thank you.'

'Would you like some coffee?'

'Yes, that's very kind of you.'

I should have caught in time the semantic difference between wanting *a* coffee and wanting *some* coffee. Signora Bono took a huge coffee maker from the unlit cooker and poured the contents into a saucepan, which she put on to boil.

'It's actually barley malt, so it won't get you over-excit-ed.'

I was lucky: in a bar in the centre of Milan, that pigswill would have cost me three euros. I wondered if she knew that her barley malt was a fashionable drink.

'Patrizia,' she resumed, sitting down, 'was always a very calm girl. A bit quiet, but calm. I could see it in her eyes.'

'How long had she been living here?'

'Since June last year. Workers often come here before they find permanent accommodation. They're good people, Arabs most of them, but good people. Patrizia was the first girl. I was pleased to have her here. She even gave me a hand laying the table in the evenings. And we'd have our little chats, you know, the way women do, though like I said, she didn't talk much. But she did tell me a little bit about France, and about her parents who died in a car accident. That was all.'

'Did she have friends?'

'I couldn't really say. At work, maybe, but I never saw anyone here. She practically never went out during the week. She'd go to the office early and come back about seven in the evening, eat, watch a little television with us, and by ten she was already in bed. My husband says she was like a nun, but she was just a well brought-up girl.'

'But you told me she might have had a boyfriend.'

'Yes, a boyfriend, or a girlfriend, you know how it is, these days you never know what to think. But I think it was a boy, because Patrizia seemed normal, not one of those strange girls with all sorts of ideas in their heads.'

'But what makes you think she had someone?'

'Because lately, from about the end of August, she'd seemed more lively, more… in love, that's it. Yes, she really seemed like a girl in love. On Saturday evenings and Sunday afternoons, someone always came and picked her up, but I never saw him because he never came to the house, he always waited for her in a car at the end of the drive.'

'Every weekend?'

'Almost every weekend. On Saturday evening at nine and on Sunday afternoon at three. And she never came back after midnight.'

She wasn't a nun, she was Cinderella!

'All I ever saw of the person who came to pick her up,' Signora Bono continued, 'was the car, an old car, dark red.'

'And was Patrizia close to the other people who live here?'

'She was kind to everyone and everyone was kind to her, but I can't say she made friends.'

'Do you know if anyone went to see her when she was in hospital?'

'I don't think so. I went once, but they told me she was in a coma and wouldn't let me see her. They told me they would call me if she woke up, but when they called me it was to tell me she'd died and that I should take some clothes to bury her in, if I had any. Poor thing. I took a pair of jeans, a blouse and a sweater. The only other thing I could do was go to her funeral, and it was a good thing I did because there were only two of us there, me and the owner of the factory where she worked. How sad, not even a girl-friend, not even a colleague. She really was a reserved kind of girl, alone and reserved.'

I realised I wouldn't get anything else from Signora Bono but further commiserations.

'I think I've already taken up too much of your time,' I said, getting to my feet.

'Not at all, I enjoyed talking about poor Patrizia. Sometimes it's nice to remember things, even sad things.'

'Thanks again for the coffee and for the chat.'

'Goodbye.'

'Goodbye.'

Outside, nothing had changed. Only the mechanic had changed position: now he was standing, near the top part of the tractor. Hearing the kitchen door close, he turned in my direction. I saw that he was very young, and an Arab.

I walked to my car and while I was searching for the keys in my bag, I saw, next to the other metal carcasses, a bicycle with a twisted frame and badly bent wheels.

I did an about-turn and went back to Signora Bono. I didn't even bother to knock.

'Excuse me, is the bicycle outside the one that Patrizia used?'

'Yes. Did you see what the bastard driving that car did to it? If the bike is like that, you can imagine how she was. The man who did that should be caught and given the death penalty. Some people don't deserve to live in civilised society.'

'You're right,' I replied, surprised myself at my genuine approval of the old woman's reactionary views. I finally got in my car, put it into reverse, and headed towards the main road. Destination: Vittuone Heat Treatments, proprietor Giovanni Imperiale, 2 Strada alle Cascine, a couple of kilometres away.

I was starting to familiarise myself with the place: the skeletal trees, the misty fields, the low, grey sky and the ditch, with its pools of stagnant water, which were a disgusting chemical green colour. Then the narrow road, the wider stretch where Patrizia had been knocked down, and the traces left by prostitutes who were nowhere to be seen at that hour.

I passed the triangular sign that marked the boundary of the Agricultural Park and, after about a hundred metres, turned left towards the factory. I parked next to four or five cars so beat-up they made my yellow Opel Agila look custom-built, even though of course it couldn't bear comparison with the Porsche Cayenne resting in the shelter of a canopy a few metres further on. It wasn't that I was particularly interested in cars, but the Porsche Cayenne was constantly being mentioned on a radio programme I often listened to in the morning. The DJ who presented the programme would imitate a young businessman from Cantù unable to spend even a minute away from the tangible symbol of his success, his Porsche Cayenne. I'd once asked the petrol station attendant in the Via Suardi to describe the car to me, and his face had lit up. He had shown me a foolscap exercise book in which he had glued an incredible number of photographs of the Cayenne taken from every angle. 'One day I'll buy one,' he had said in a low voice, 'second-hand, third-hand, I don't mind, but I'll buy one.' I remembered I'd felt sorry for him, like the typically conceited intellectual I was.

I mentally closed the Cayenne chapter and followed the arrow pointing to the offices.

Actually, there was only one office, a kind of mezzanine, ten metres by five, converted from part of the workshop and closed off from it by an aluminium and glass partition. Next to the door was a desk with a metal base and an imitation leather top, with a not very recent-looking computer on it. The chair behind it was empty.

Turning to my left, I saw another, larger, though no more elegant desk, behind which a rather stout man was talking on the phone, or rather, listening on the phone, since he wasn't making a sound.

'Take a seat,' he said, covering the receiver with one hand. 'I'll be with you in a minute.'

From the few words he exchanged with the person at the other end, I gathered he was talking to his accountant. Then the call was over, and he immediately held out his hand and introduced himself. 'Giovanni Imperiale, how can I help you?'

I trotted out my little formula – the cousin of the half-sister in search of memories – and he didn't seem to find it at all suspicious.

'Poor Patrizia. She worked at that desk over there. An

exceptional young woman: punctual, regular. In the morning she always arrived before eight and if she had to stay late in the evening she never made a fuss. Even on Saturday, sometimes…'

In a few words, the man had expressed his whole philosophy of life, a philosophy shared by untold numbers of people on that foggy plain: work, work and more work. People judged each other on their productivity, and from that point of view Patrizia must have been a model worker.

'How did she come to be working here?'

Imperiale looked at me somewhat irritably. I had probably misjudged my tone, and my question had come across as: '*How the hell did she end up in a dump like this?*'

'Do you mean why did she come here from France or why did I hire her?'

'Both,' I replied, trying to make up for my blunder with a smile which I'm sure came out forced.

'Why she came here from France is a mystery to me, too. I asked her once and she told me she'd wanted to see her father's country, but it seemed strange all the same. Why I hired her is simpler. My wife was expecting a baby and couldn't handle the bookkeeping anymore, so I consulted a temp agency and they sent me Patrizia.'

'And did she come straight away?'

'I put in the request on the Friday and she started here on the Monday.'

'So it's possible she sent her CV to the agency before she left France.'

'I'm sure she did. The temp agencies have branches all over Europe. Let's say a Polish person needs work and says he's willing to work in Italy, they press a couple of keys on the computer and two or three days later he has a job in Agrate, or Treviglio, or Vittuone. That's how Europe works.'

'Do you have many foreign workers?'

'They're all foreign. But not European. I mean, not from the European Community or whatever they call it now. I have a few Belarusians, a few Moldavians, a few Albanians, but most are Moroccans. But mark this: Belarusians, Moldovans, Albanians, Moroccans, they all have residence permits and permission to work. Giovanni Imperiale doesn't have anyone working illegally. I suffered too much from that kind of thing myself when I was young, and I told myself that if I became a boss I wouldn't do to others what they'd done to me. Come, come and see.'

We stood up and went to the partition. He opened a window that looked out on the workshop. The continuous drone of machinery burst into the office like an explosion. He leaned out and motioned me to do the same. A dozen workers in grey overalls were bending and cutting and doing a thousand other things to sheets of metal whose function I didn't quite grasp.

'Do you see them? They all wear gloves and safety shoes with reinforced toes. Health and safety regulations are respected down to the last detail. They all get sick leave, paid holidays and a good Christmas bonus.'

He was saying these things as if they were exceptional, as if the fact of simply meeting the regulations should have drawn gasps of admiration from me. But perhaps that was the way it was. Perhaps, given the system that was becoming the norm even in that foggy plain that had once been the cradle of morality and strictness, Signor Imperiale, with his legal workers, was a real gem, or something like that.

Pointing to the machines he explained a little about the process.

'We used to do only heat treatments: chromium plating, nitriding, electrolytic baths. Then I added machine work, which is what you see here. We still do heat treatments in the older building on the other side of the yard.'

He closed the window and went back to his desk. Sitting down again opposite him, I took a good look at him. I guessed he was about forty-seven or forty-eight. He didn't look good for his age, he looked like someone who'd had a tough life, who hadn't studied much but had worked a hell of a lot. My first impression, that he was some kind of mindless slave driver, had given way to a more indulgent image. I considered his accent: it had undertones of various Italian dialects, both northern and southern, as if everywhere he had worked he had tried to become accepted by speaking the language of the place, finally adopting a Lombard he still hadn't quite made his own.

I persisted with my questions. 'Why did you choose Patrizia Vitali?'

'I didn't choose her, I took the only person they offered me. I should explain that I'd put in a very specific request. I wanted someone who knew a bit about bookkeeping, but especially someone who spoke Italian and Arabic well, because, sometimes, it isn't easy to communicate with the boys who come to work here. Patrizia spoke perfect Italian, which was her father's language, Arabic, which was her mother's language, and also French, so I told myself that if I wanted to hire someone from Senegal she could help me there, too.'

The telephone rang and Imperiale replied. I always feel

embarrassed when someone starts a phone conversation in my presence: I tell myself I ought to move away and let him talk in peace, or at least pretend not to listen. So I pretended to take an interest in the objects on his desk. Among them was a framed photograph of a baby in the arms of a woman who might be about my age. Not young, not beautiful, and yet, as they say of all wives and mothers, radiant, happy to have performed a miracle I probably never will.

Imperiale quickly got rid of the customer on the phone, assuring him profusely that the goods would be delivered as soon as possible.

'As far as you know, was Patrizia friendly with anyone else in the company?'

'I don't think so. Unfortunately for her, she worked in this office, and I'm the only one here. There are no other white collar workers, and she was the only woman in the whole firm. I sometimes asked her how she was, if everything was all right, but that was all. I didn't want to pry and I didn't want to embarrass her. Having always worked only with my wife, I don't really know how to behave with a female employee, and I didn't want certain things to be taken in the wrong way.'

I smiled at him. Bald, tubby and slightly seedy, he certainly didn't look like someone who felt comfortable around women, especially young women.

'Did you find out about the accident straight away?'

'Of course. I started to worry when she hadn't arrived by eight-thirty. She was always so punctual. Then I heard the sirens and went out to have a look. I remember I took the company van, because my car was being serviced. By the time I got there, they were putting her in the ambulance.'

'Did you follow it to the hospital?'

'No. I know it's a horrible thing to say, but in a place like this you can't drop your work for a minute. But in the next few days I kept in constant touch with the hospital to know how she was, if she had regained consciousness. The head nurse is a friend of my wife's and she kept me informed even though I wasn't a relative. She was the one who told me Patrizia was dead. Then, immediately afterwards, the Carabinieri arrived and asked me if she had relatives. I told them I didn't know but gave them the address in France, the one that was on her papers, which they also had at the agency, but they couldn't find anyone. So in the end I paid for the funeral. But I was happy to do it, believe me, and I don't want to ask anything of your cousin – Patrizia's sister, I mean.'

'Thank you, Signor Imperiale,' I said, standing. 'Thank you for what you did and for the information you've given me. I'm gradually building up a picture of the kind of person Patrizia must have been, though I doubt it'll really console my cousin. She neglected her for too long, and from what I hear she was a lovely girl.'

'I'm sorry you didn't know her well when she was alive, but if I can help you to find out something about her now, I'm pleased to be of use. In fact, if you leave me your address and phone number, I'll call you if I remember anything I haven't already told you.'

I left him my details and started towards the door. I had almost gone out when I remembered the main thing Benedetta Vitali was paying me for, the thing I had been relegating to the background in order to believe I was still a real psychologist. I turned back to Imperiale and asked, 'What was Patrizia's funeral like?'

'Sad, like all funerals, but even more than most. There was just me and the owner of the farmhouse where she was living.' There was a touch of reproach in his tone, a reproach I felt was partly meant for me: I was starting to get a little too deeply into my part.

Back in the open, I looked at the factory. It was small, but for a man like Imperiale it must have been a major achievement. His own factory. It must have seemed like a miracle to him. A dream. Like the third-hand Cayenne for the petrol station attendant in the Via Suardi. Except that Imperiale had been able to afford one brand new, at least to judge by the shiny black bodywork.

I looked at the factory again. Perhaps it wasn't as small as it seemed at first sight.

By now, it was one in the afternoon. In the centre of Vittuone, I went into a bar and had a sandwich and a still mineral water. Even the waiter looked at me sadly.

Then the ring road, the A4 autostrada, Seriate exit, shopping centre, hypermarket.

As usual, I filled my trolley with an excessive number of things. I hadn't yet adapted my acquisitive instincts to my new condition as a single woman. I was still buying pasta, cheese, detergent and toilet paper as if there were two people at home, cramming the little pantry in my small apartment to the brim and filling the fridge with things that would go off before they were even opened. Above all, I was still lingering in the men's clothing aisle, looking at the special offers, the sweaters and boxers in 3-for-2 packaging, wondering if Stefano would like them, if they were his size. But how did Stefano dress now? And who did he dress for?

How excessive my shopping was I didn't realise until I got to the checkout. When had I lost touch with the real economy? How long had prices been going in the opposite direction from my salary? But I could never ask Stefano for money. He wasn't exactly rolling in cash either. These were tough times for the middle classes! The day I'd graduated, I really had hoped for a better life.

I left the car in the Colle Aperto car park, the one reserved for residents. I had no desire at that moment to carry my shopping bags all the way home. It was cold outside, and the stuff certainly wouldn't suffer in the boot.

I decided to take a walk along the walls. The walls are perhaps the most beautiful part of Upper Bergamo. From them, you can look down over the Lower Town, you can see the historic sections and the spreading modern city, you can even see the countryside. Looking south-east, you have the impression you can see the Adriatic, but it's only an impression. When I got to the Porta San Giacomo, I sat down on the low wall. The day's mist had lifted as the hours had passed and now there was a gorgeous winter sunset. The stones of the walls and the fronts of the buildings were tinged with pink. Below, the last rays hit the windows of the Viale Papa Giovanni and bounced off them. Far away, the planes could be seen taking off from Orio and catching fire in the sun. The conditions were ideal for thinking.

I needed to think about what I was doing. It wasn't enough to go around asking questions. I needed to stop and think. Think about the fact that I was behaving more and more like a stupid amateur detective. Think about Benedetta's stubbornness in entrusting me, specifically me, with this mission. Think about my own stubbornness in looking for traces of Patrizia when she was alive without focussing on the main question: the missing body.

I wondered for the first time if Benedetta might be tricking me, using me for some scheme of her own that I couldn't figure out. Perhaps things weren't exactly as she said. For the first time, it occurred to me that Benedetta wasn't really interested in finding out what had happened to her sister just before and just after her death. What she really wanted to find out was what other people knew about her death, and perhaps shouldn't have known. A professional detective might have discovered something and blackmailed her, whereas I, whose one talent was to track down people who'd run away from home, was a less risky proposition.

Or perhaps someone was already blackmailing her. Someone who had stolen the body and was asking for a ransom, as had happened not long before with the body of that financier.

I decided to suppress my doubts and get my act together. If the missing body was the crux of the matter, then I might as well try to clarify what had happened in the period between Patrizia's death and the discovery that the coffin was empty – if it didn't offend my dignity as a psychologist.

As I walked back to my car to pick up the shopping bags, I made up my mind to pay another visit to the hospital in Magenta the next day and then try and talk to the firm of undertakers that had handled the funeral. Subsequently I was to wonder if Dr Marco Callegari and his dentist's tan had something to do with my decision to go back to the hospital, but I'm convinced it wasn't, I think it was only one last attempt to think rationally.

What's the source of my fear? The darkness around me? But darkness also means protection, peace. I've always liked the dark, I've always considered it restful. As a child I would spend hours in the dark, in my room, before going to sleep, looking at the blackness and telling myself stories in which I was the princess, the little mermaid, the girl who saved the prince from the dragon in the cave. Then later, as a teenager, I carried on daydreaming, but these dreams were of a more romantic nature now, personal adaptations of what I'd read in some book or newspaper before turning the light out. So no, I'm not afraid of the dark as such. I think again about my longing for darkness, the relief I felt when my mother, leaving my room after a hurried 'Goodnight', switched off the light and closed the door.

So if it's not the dark, what is it that's knotting my stomach with terror? The idea of a dead body? But I've seen plenty of dead bodies. There were times, when I was working with addicts, that you'd see some who looked deader than the dead. Yellow-eyed, hollow-cheeked, and so skeletal you could put your hand all the way round their arm. Some you managed to save, others you'd see again later in the morgue, really dead. Not that they looked all that different, except for the serene expression on their faces. Their parents too, coming to identify them now that the nightmare was over, also looked serene sometimes, though they tried to hide it.

But if it isn't an irrational fear that's paralysing me, what is it? It's justified dread, it's anxiety about the impending danger. Because inside me I know the danger is near, I know someone is threatening my life. The risk comes from the prostitutes. Not directly from them, of course, but from a man who uses their services regularly.

Thursday, 17 February

The slightly metallic voice of the lift announced: 'Fifth floor, trauma.' The doors opened and – I don't know if it was good or bad luck – the first person I saw was Dr Callegari, with his tan. He was standing by the coffee machine, chatting with a colleague in a very professional manner. With their white coats open, and plastic cups in their hands, the two men seemed to be taking a break after a long series of emergency procedures. The picture they formed could have been entitled *The Warrior's Rest.*

As soon as he saw me, Callegari took leave of his colleague and came towards me, holding out his hand.

'Good morning, Signora Pavesi, how can I help you?'

'I was actually looking for your colleague Dr Maestri, the one who treated Patrizia.'

'He was here a minute ago, but I think he went up to general medicine on the seventh floor for a consultation.'

'In the meantime, I need to find out something about the funeral. Obviously, my cousin would like to pay for any expenses incurred.'

'Then you ought to talk to the head nurse. Come on, I'll go with you.'

He led me along the corridor. The light coming in through the windows was curiously milky, I assumed because of the scaffolding that swaddled the outside of the building. Looking closer, though, I noticed that on that particular side there was no scaffolding. The thing that was filtering the rays of the sun, turning them white, was the fog, which had reappeared as if by magic.

At the end of the corridor, he opened a glass door and ushered me into a white-tiled room.

'Margherita,' he said, addressing a big woman of about fifty, 'Signora Pavesi is a relative of that patient of ours who passed away in December, Patrizia Vitali. She'd like to have some information about the funeral because the family would like to take care of the expenses, am I right?'

'Of course,' I replied, even though the expenses were only an excuse to talk about how it had all gone.

'I'll leave you, then. Dr Maestri should be here in a few minutes, Margherita can point him out to you.'

'Many thanks. Goodbye.'

'See you later.'

He went out, leaving the head nurse to inform me of what she knew.

'The funeral was paid for by the girl's employer, Signor Imperiale. But it was Dr Maestri who arranged it all. He was the one who took over her case. The care he showed her…'

She broke off, as if she'd let slip a personal impression that should have remained private.

I took advantage of the silence to insist, discreetly, 'Was she a special patient for Dr Maestri?'

'It's Dr Maestri who's special, in the way he treats his patients. Always attentive, always tactful. To him, they're not patients, they're people. I think seeing the girl like that, alone, no visitors, well, I think he really took her case to heart. That doesn't mean he shows any favouritism, I want to be quite clear about that.'

How could he have shown favouritism to a patient in a

vegetative state? All he could do was keep her going with drugs and machines. Unless the special treatment consisted of noting that she was dead, in which case I'd gladly have foregone the privilege. In any case, the way the nurse had spoken about him made him sound like the typical idol of the ward. From my experience of hospitals, every ward had its idol, usually a young doctor, the kind about whom people say that they'll never get anywhere in their careers because they're too honest, the kind that maternally-minded nurses fall in love with, even though it's usually the others they sleep with, those who are anything but honest.

'Unfortunately,' Margherita went on, 'there was nothing they could do for poor Patrizia. She had a serious lesion to the spine and a very serious head injury and that was what Dr Maestri said prevented her recovery.'

'Only Dr Maestri?'

'Well, Dr Falco, who ordered the CAT scan, said the haematoma wasn't extensive enough to cause brain damage, but Dr Maestri didn't agree and I think he was right.'

Beware of touching the idol, I thought.

At that moment the idol himself materialised in the nurses' room.

'Good morning, doctor. This lady is a relative of that patient of ours, Vitali, Patrizia Vitali…'

The doctor gave me a highly suspicious look. 'I didn't think she had any relatives.'

'I'm a cousin of Benedetta Vitali, Patrizia's half-sister.'

He looked puzzled, but said nothing.

He was young, between thirty and thirty-five, but I noticed that his eyes, just like Patrizia's, made him look older, much older. Or perhaps it was his gold-rimmed glasses, or the fact that he was almost completely bald, or his poor posture, drooping shoulders and thin chest. Only his voice, although not especially pleasant, fitted his age.

'The thing is, doctor, I wanted to find out something more about the time Patrizia spent here in hospital.'

'What do you want to know? I assume you and your cousin are aware of how the accident took place. As for the rest, all I can tell you is that she was in a coma for nearly a week, then died as a result of the head injury, on which we were unable to operate. Unless you want to know the details of the diagnosis, the treatment and the tests. Are you a doctor?'

'No, I'm a psychologist.'

'Then I doubt reading the medical records would mean much to you.'

I was finding it hard to believe that this ill-mannered man was the same person the head nurse had described as a model of tact.

Despite his clearly hostile attitude, I persevered. 'Dr Callegari told me Patrizia regained consciousness on the day she was admitted and stayed awake until about five in the afternoon.'

'That's right. I'd been here for an hour when she woke up. We asked her if she remembered anything, but she couldn't speak. Then she fell back into her coma and never came out of it. I signed the death certificate myself.'

That fact seemed to mean a lot to him.

'The head nurse was telling me you arranged the funeral, and I wanted to thank you for that on behalf of Benedetta.'

'Don't mention it. Perhaps Margherita also told you the funeral was paid for by – '

'Yes, she told me everything, but I really wanted to

express our gratitude for what you did.'

'I did what anyone would have done in my situation. Let's drop the subject.'

But I didn't want to drop the subject. I tried another tack. 'Now that Benedetta has become aware of her sister's tragic end, she'd like to have the body transferred to the family vault.'

Maestri gave a start, a gesture of annoyance which I interpreted as a sign that he was not at all pleased about this belated attention shown to a person who had deserved better when she was alive: idols don't find it easy to be understanding. 'I don't see what that has to do with me,' he said. 'I deal with the living.'

So do I, I would have liked to reply, *usually I also deal with the living.* But I held back from giving him a piece of my mind.

'The reason I'm telling you that is because I don't know any undertakers in this area, so I thought we could use the same one you contacted for the funeral. If you'd be so kind as to let me have the address…'

He turned to the nurse who, although pretending to be busy arranging some medicines in a cabinet, must have been listening attentively to our conversation.

'Margherita, do you remember who we called about the funeral?'

'I don't know, doctor, you did it all.'

'Yes, but the bills and the other papers ought to be here. Could you have a look, please, then we can give Signora…'

'Pavesi.'

'…we can give Signora Pavesi what she needs.'

'All right, doctor,' the woman replied, still adoringly.

'Now I really have to go. As I said, I devote my time to

the living, and there's never enough of it.'

He shook my hand as if it was a piece of wood, or a broom, then went out, closing the door behind him.

The nurse started searching in the drawers and filing cabinets, throwing files, forms and medical records on a desk. From time to time, she would linger over a sheet of paper, mutter something and then throw it among the others.

After about ten minutes during which she had not uttered a word apart from this vague muttering, she admitted defeat.

'Here,' she said, holding out a small yellow post-it with some words written on it, 'this is all I have left. It's got the name and telephone number of the undertakers. I don't have the invoices and the other papers, if you need them…'

'Don't worry, this is enough to be getting on with.'

'Thank God for that.'

'Thanks a lot. Goodbye.'

'Have a nice day' she said, disappearing again among the papers and records and starting to rearrange them.

In the corridor, I ran into Dr Callegari again, which made me wonder if he spent more time there than with his patients.

'Well?' he asked. 'Did you find what you were looking for?'

'I think so.' I went closer to him and lowered my voice. 'Although your colleague Dr Maestri wasn't exactly pleasant.'

'I have to admit that being pleasant isn't his forte, though he has a lot of good points. But perhaps I can help to improve the image of the hospital staff by inviting you to lunch.'

I don't know why I accepted. People like that usually annoy me. I can't stand their self-confidence, their ready banter, the speed with which they turn any situation to their advantage. I don't know why I accepted – perhaps I needed it.

He took me to a trattoria just outside Magenta. We went in his silver-grey 4x4, and as soon as I got in I couldn't help asking, 'Is it a Porsche Cayenne?'

He smiled in amusement: perhaps he listened to the same programme as I did, the one where they made fun of Cayenne owners. 'No, it's a BMW X5 and I'm not from Cantù, I live in the centre of Milan.'

He did listen to it.

The restaurant was really pretty. No flashy fake rustic furniture, no cartwheels used as chandeliers, no half casks filled with mediocre bottles of wine. Only wooden tables with tablecloths of rough paper, like the kind they used to use for wrapping breadsticks, and, against three of the four walls, dressers like the one in my kitchen which had belonged to my great-grandmother.

'Jungian or Freudian?'

At least he had an original way of breaking the ice.

'Freudian by training, though I don't do much psychotherapy, in fact almost none. I do most of my work with local educational co-operatives, working mainly with minors, so forget the couch, patients telling their dreams, and all the psychoanalytical jargon.'

'Do you work in Milan?'

'In Bergamo. That's where I live. But I don't yet have a permanent contract, I only moved there a few months ago.'

Actually, it was ten months, nearly a year, but I still thought of it as a short time, a temporary situation. It was as if, unconsciously, I refused to accept that Bergamo was my city now. Not because I didn't like the place. On the contrary. It was just that...

'Where did you live before?'

'Turin.'

'Nice city. Interesting, lively. Why on earth did you move?'

How many seconds had it taken to get to the crucial question? Forty, fifty at the most. Should I tell the truth or invent an excuse: that I wanted to be near my elderly mother, for instance? But why, in the twenty-first century, should a woman still feel it so hard to utter that word?

'Separation. I'm separated from my husband, and, as the apartment that used to be my grandmother's became available, I moved there. You know how expensive it is to rent a place these days...'

'Lower Bergamo or Upper Bergamo?' he asked.

'Upper,' I replied with a certain pride.

'You did the right thing.'

'Moving or separating?' I replied, thinking it was my turn to put him on the spot.

'Both,' he replied, not at all fazed. 'Seizing the opportunity to live in Upper Bergamo, because it's a wonderful place, and separating, because if you did it, that's a sign it needed to be done. Women never leave their husbands without a good reason.'

'What if it was my husband who dumped me?'

'Then he must have been an idiot.'

It was a gratuitous and not especially original compliment, but I needed that, too. And besides, it was true, I'd been the one to decide, I'd been the one to say: I've had enough.

The tagliatelle with mushrooms arrived and he poured me another glass of the oak-aged Barbera which he had ordered earlier without even looking at the wine list, like a real habitué. At the time, I didn't think about how many women must already have drunk that wine with him, how many women he must have taken to that trattoria. The conversation was too pleasant to think about all that.

We chatted a little about his work, lightly. He wasn't the kind of doctor who thinks he's always talking to his colleagues around the dissecting table. On a whim, I asked him where he'd got such a beautiful tan, and he replied that he had been in Mexico two weeks earlier, with his wife and son.

As the minutes passed, I became aware of what Stefano, during our bitterest arguments, had referred to as a 'pre-fuck atmosphere'. 'There are times,' he would say whenever I caught him out, 'when you find yourself in a situation that seems to lead inevitably to sex. You're away from home, maybe on business, and a bond is formed, a mutual attraction you can't resist, even though you know that the next day there'll be nothing left of it. In fact, you do it precisely because you're sure there won't be any consequences and that the woman you love is still the same woman and you love her just as much as ever. You know that when you're having sex, playing at sex I'd call it, you haven't taken anything away from her.'

But there were consequences, because he was a hopeless liar and there was always a well-intentioned person, a colleague of his, a mutual friend or someone like that, who would take it upon himself to arouse my suspicion. It wasn't that they'd been spying and knew the whole truth: there was no need, the suspicion was enough. When I questioned Stefano, he would collapse and tell me everything. The first time, he promised me it would never happen again. The second time, he tried to convince me of his theory that he had taken nothing away from me. The third time, I told him I'd had enough.

And now here I was, sharing a moment with a married man, starting to form a bond.

A caress from him, I thought, would make the moment perfect. A caress, nothing more, to complement the pleasure of the intimacy and the wine. But if that caress came, would it be possible to stop there? Or would we inevitably go further? If you're over fifteen and not yet eighty, is tenderness for its own sake even possible?

But the caress didn't come. In its place, the coffees arrived.

It was while I was eating the little chocolate that came with the coffee that Marco Callegari said, 'How about exchanging mobile numbers?'

'Sure.'

I wrote mine on a corner of the paper place mat and entered his in the address book of my mobile. It struck me that I should have asked him when was the best time to call him without disturbing him, but I didn't have the guts: I wasn't used to being with married men. Anyway, I assumed he'd be the one to call me.

Marco went back to work and I sat down on one of the benches in the tree-lined avenue at the side of the hospital. I took the post-it with the telephone number of the undertakers from my purse, and dialled it.

'Good afternoon, La Pace funeral directors.'

'Good afternoon, could I speak to the owner please?'

'This is Gandolfi, one of the two partners, what can I do for you?'

'I'd like to talk to you in person, if possible. Will you be in your office for a while?'

'Another half an hour or so. Can you come now?'

'I'm at the hospital in Magenta right now. How long will it take me to get there from here?'

'No more than ten minutes on foot. If you have a car, it's best to leave it where it is, because it's not easy to park here.'

He gave me the address and directions how to get there.

Following them, I walked down a long straight street, then turned left into the Via Pusterla: the name reminded me of a poet I liked a lot. Left again into the Piazza Indipendenza. On the corner, under the portico, a few North African youths were talking among themselves, with their backs against the wall, wrapped warmly in their down jackets. Further on there were other immigrants, Eastern European in appearance, in a group, and further still, another cluster of young men whose nationality I couldn't guess. I continued along the Via Garibaldi, took another couple of turns, and exactly ten minutes after I'd set out, there I was, facing Signor Gandolfi.

I introduced myself with the usual lie, which was starting to seem like the truth, and saw him turn pale. I hadn't even finished explaining my supposed ties of kinship to Patrizia when he started to apologise.

'I really don't know what could have happened. I've been in this business twenty-five years and I've never known anything like this before.'

Clearly the gravediggers hadn't kept quiet, despite Benedetta's cash. Taking advantage of his embarrassment, I pressed on with my questioning.

'Could you take me through the various stages of the funeral?'

'It was my partner who sealed the coffin, on his own. He went to the hospital about ten in the morning and I think he did what he usually does, in other words he soldered the metal part and then screwed on the wooden lid.'

'Is it normal for one person to do this on his own?'

'Yes, perfectly normal. We had another funeral earlier, at nine, so I assume the men arrived later, just in time to carry the coffin to the hearse. Unfortunately, there wasn't much money for Signorina Vitali's funeral, so it was all done a bit on the cheap, but I can assure you we followed the normal procedure.'

'Couldn't there have been a mix-up when the coffin was moved from the mortuary to the hearse?'

'What kind of mix-up?'

'Couldn't the coffin containing Patrizia Vitali's body have been confused with an empty coffin that had been put there to receive another body?'

'That strikes me as highly unlikely. Assuming there was an empty coffin there, the lid wouldn't have been screwed down properly, and the boys would have noticed that something was wrong when they got hold of it. But most of all, if another firm had left a coffin there and later found it closed and full, don't you think they would have said something? Believe me, my dear, this is a world where the competition is fierce. If anyone had discovered that we'd made a mistake, in less than an hour the whole of Magenta would have known about it, starting with us.'

'So what do you think happened?'

'I think it was the cemetery that made a mess of things. Do you know how many mistakes they make? Tons of them, believe me. A person thinks their son who died at the age of twenty in a motorcycle accident is lying under that stone, instead of which those people have mistakenly buried an old man who died in a nursing home. Do you remember what happened in the cemetery in Turin a few months ago?'

I did remember. I'd read all about it in *La Stampa*, the newspaper I continued to buy in order not to give up my old habits in one go, almost as if reading the news from Turin made Stefano seem a little less distant in time and space.

'Well,' Gandolfi went on, 'in Turin they dug up a whole section of the cemetery, mixing up the remains of dozens of people.'

That wasn't exactly what had happened. Things had been exaggerated for political reasons, and he was exaggerating them even more, to back up his theory that the mix-up had happened in the cemetery. But why on earth would there have been an empty coffin at the cemetery anyway?

'Assuming that the problem can be traced to the cemetery, how do we solve it?'

His embarrassment turned into something approaching fear. 'We'd have to exhume a certain number of bodies, at least those buried during that period, but I don't think it's something that can be done discreetly.'

He was certainly thinking of his own self-interest. The last thing he wanted was a scandal. But neither did Benedetta, though for different reasons. No exhumations, then.

I didn't have a lot more to ask him and, from the way he was tidying the papers on his desk and closing the drawers, I guessed he had to go. I stood up and made to leave. He, too, stood up and took the blue coat he'd slung over the back of a nearby chair.

'I'll see you out. I have to be somewhere, too.'

We left the building. When we were outside, he asked me, 'Did you walk here?'

'Yes, as you recommended.'

'If you like, I can give you a lift to the hospital. I'm going that way myself.'

'Thanks.'

We walked a few metres, to a large car parked near the pedestrian crossing. He held the door opened for me. As I got in, I noticed that it was identical to Marco Callegari's. Even the colour was the same. Or perhaps not: the grey of this one tended more to mother-of-pearl, whereas Marco's had a more golden tinge. Small nuances that helped the owner to stand out from the others, while remaining firmly within the group of winners: different yet equal.

'Nice car,' I commented, sure I would arouse his male vanity.

'It's my partner's,' he replied. 'I have one similar, but it's being serviced at the moment.'

The journey took hardly any time at all. As I got out, Signor Gandolfi handed me his business card.

'If you need me, this has my office number, though you have that already, and my mobile number.'

I thanked him and threw the card carefully into my bag, as I usually did.

It was almost three, not that you could tell the time from the light. When it's foggy, every hour, from eight in the morning to four in the afternoon, looks the same.

I set off for home, on the usual Route 11. No fields this time, no car showrooms, no discount stores: the grey mists had swallowed everything. You could barely make out the red lights of the car in front, and if that car risked a little forward spurt you found yourself floating alone in a thick sea.

Nerve-racking as the drive was, I started thinking about Patrizia's case. I remember it was the actual word 'case' that came into my head, not in a clinical sense, like the Case of the Wolf Man, but in the sense of a case to be solved. It was embarrassing, the way I was starting to take this job seriously. Especially as I hadn't yet achieved any results. My visit to the undertakers hadn't provided me with any new ideas about the disappearance of the body. I told myself I should have gone to the cemetery to ask a few questions, but I sensed that I wouldn't have heard anything I hadn't already heard from Gandolfi: they would have to exhume, but... About Patrizia I had only discovered things that Benedetta already knew or at least guessed. Patrizia, or 'poor Patrizia' as everyone called her, had been a simple, modest, reserved person – almost irritatingly simple, modest and reserved, in my opinion. In any case, nothing that could establish a connection between the last days of her life, her death, and the disappearance of her body. To find out more, I'd need to identify Patrizia's hypothetical 'boyfriend', always supposing he existed and wasn't just a projection of Signora Bono's wishes. Certainly, if he existed, he was a strange character, 'suspicious', a detective would have said. Someone who didn't bother to visit his own girlfriend after she'd been knocked down by a car, who didn't even go to her funeral, who perhaps didn't even know his girlfriend had been knocked down, was definitely a suspicious character. The one problem was that this person probably didn't exist.

God, what a fog! But of course, as usual, as the weather forecast always put it, it was patchy fog. Which meant that, from time to time, the real world suddenly reappeared in your field of vision. It was during one of these sudden bright intervals that I saw, on my right, the fork in the road from which the Strada alle Cascine started. On that corner between the main road and the side road, a prostitute, not in the first flush of youth, was waiting for customers, shivering despite the fur jacket thrown over a miniskirt that left little to the imagination – not enough, considering her age. Even the mist in my mind thinned for a moment and I remembered that, two days earlier, I'd made a mental note to consider the role of the prostitutes in the whole affair, as witnesses to the accident if nothing else. The thought of the supposed 'boyfriend' was niggling at me, making me imagine all kinds of dubious possibilities where there was probably nothing but blind fate. But it wouldn't hurt to find a witness.

I turned onto the side road, abruptly, getting myself insulted by the driver behind for my pains. I passed Imperiale's factory, and, despite the fog, which was again growing thicker, I had my confirmation that those discarded condoms and that camping stool hadn't lied. Every twenty metres, leaning against the trees or sitting on folding chairs, alone or in pairs, young girls were on offer, almost all blonde, almost all attractive.

I drove on as far as the spot where Patrizia had been knocked down.

As I passed, the prostitutes would step forward, peer into the passenger compartment, and withdraw: I wasn't a customer.

At the spot where the accident had occurred, a girl was standing. She was wearing a padded jacket and a long black dress with a slit all the way up to the groin. She had pale blonde hair and excessively heavy green eye shadow. She, too, approached then drew back, but I opened the window all the way down and called her back.

'Excuse me, can I ask you something?'

'Are you police?'

'No, this is something personal.'

I knew that might sound ambiguous, but I couldn't think of anything else. I wasn't exactly feeling at my ease.

I assume I didn't look like a policewoman, because she came to the door.

'I don't usually do things with women. Only men. But if you want me to do something with you it's a hundred Euros.'

'No, it's not about that.'

'What is it, then?'

'Do you…'

How on earth should I put it? Work? Practise? Strut your stuff?

'…always stand in this spot?'

'What's it to you where I stand?'

'I wanted to know if by any chance you saw the girl who was knocked down here, just where you are now.'

'The brown-haired girl who always rode a bicycle?'

'Yes, that's the one. Her name was Patrizia.'

'Yes, I saw her last summer and autumn. She passed here on her bicycle every evening, between six and seven. One evening she waved to me, just like that, like we knew each other, and I waved back, and after that every time she passed we waved to each other. Then I was told she'd been run down by a car, but I didn't see that. I'm here in the evening, and the accident was in the morning.'

'Do you think one of your friends might have seen it?'

'It's possible. There are girls here at all hours, even early in the morning, seven, eight. There are lots of customers in the morning, people going to work. Lots of family men come here for a quickie on their way to the office.'

'So someone could have seen her?'

'It's possible.'

'Please. Patrizia was my cousin. The person who knocked her down got away and they haven't caught him. Please, I beg you.'

'I didn't see anything, but if you come tomorrow morning about seven you're sure to find Alina. She has red hair, very red. She might know.'

'Thank you, thank you very much.'

'Don't mention it. I'm sorry about your cousin. She was a nice girl.'

'Nice.' I had never heard her called that before. Maybe it took a prostitute to hit the target – a 'nice' prostitute. Perhaps that wave they exchanged was a kind of bond between outcasts. For the first time I felt sorry for Patrizia, and for this other girl, here on the road, and for all the others.

I did a U-turn, very carefully because the sides of the road were almost invisible and I didn't want to end up in a ditch. I went to switch on the headlights, and by mistake switched them on full beam, in time to see a grey wall right in front of me. Startled, I slammed on the brakes. Luckily no one was passing. I set off again, at twenty kilometres an hour, with my nose practically stuck to the windscreen, as if that might help me see better. I don't know how I managed to get back onto the main road. There, everyone was driving at a snail's pace, wrapped in that fog that was becoming even darker as evening approached.

The girl's words echoed in my head. *If you come tomorrow morning about seven you're sure to find Alina.*

The next day at seven in the morning! If the fog persisted, that meant leaving home at four. If I could even get home. I remembered that billboard I had seen two days earlier: *Motel Rode, soundproof rooms, mirror and light effects*, or something like that. I'd never been to a motel and didn't even have any idea what they were like, if they all had rooms on the ground floor with cars parked outside, like the ones you saw in American films, or if they were like ordinary hotels, only not very clean. But if I really had to discover these dens of vice, I might as well take the plunge that evening and avoid having an accident on the way to Bergamo or coming back the next day at dawn.

The bright red neon sign of the Motel Rode did actually remind me of the Bates Motel in *Psycho*. I recalled that in ancient Rome prostitutes were in the habit of dyeing their hair red. And the next day I was going to meet a prostitute with very red hair.

I pulled up outside the entrance. I didn't have any luggage, I didn't even have a pair of pyjamas, just the toothbrush I always carry with me, but I didn't think they'd be surprised: I assumed people didn't usually turn up at such places with suitcases and trunks.

What did surprise them was that I was on my own.

'Isn't the signora with anyone?'

'No,' I replied sharply, 'I'm alone.' Then I felt the need to give an additional explanation. 'I stopped because of the fog. I have an appointment in the area very early tomorrow morning, and I preferred not to take any risks.'

'You did the right thing, signora,' the receptionist concluded obsequiously. 'Would you be so kind as to let me have your credit card?'

I handed it to him and he passed it through the little machine: payment in advance, of course.

'Here's your key. Room 107, first floor.'

The room was halfway between a boudoir and a bedroom in a Turkish brothel, not that I have much experience of Turkish brothels. Fire-red carpet, strawberry-red wallpaper, blood-red bedspread, and the ceiling in various shades of red. It took me a while to realise that the ceiling simply reflected what was underneath it. *Light and mirror effects.* I should have known.

The clock radio on the bedside table said 16.58.

I took out my mobile and dialled.

'Good evening, Signora Ghislandi, this is Anna, how are you?'

'Fine, and you?'

'I'm fine, too, thanks. Listen, I've had to stop near Milan because of the fog. I'm sleeping over at a friend's house. I'd like to ask you a favour. Could you go up to my apartment and give Morgana a few bites from the box? And a little water, too, she likes to drink with her food. Do you mind?'

'Not at all, I'm pleased to do it. You know how it is, I'm always on my own here in front of the television going soft in the head. At least this way I have a pleasant change. Would you like me to do anything else in your apartment?

Water the plants perhaps, do some ironing… I really don't mind!'

'That's very kind of you, but please don't put yourself out. You'd already be doing me a great favour feeding Morgana and giving her a bit of a cuddle. It'd be a great weight off my mind.'

'I'll go up there right now. Would you like me to do the same thing tomorrow?'

'No, just fill her bowl, that'll be fine. I should be back by midday.'

'Goodnight, then.'

'Goodnight, Signora Ghislandi, and thank you.'

I felt guilty about all the times I'd tried to avoid poor Signora Ghislandi.

I wanted to take a shower, even if the motel sign did remind me of *Psycho*. I went into the bathroom, and found there wasn't a shower, but a huge whirlpool bath. I dropped the idea and simply gave my face a quick wash.

I switched on the television: children's programmes, cartoons, old TV movies, shopping programmes, fortune tellers, lottery predictions, music videos, and three pay channels which, for thirty seconds, showed images of fellatio and penetration from every possible position before a caption appeared on the screen: *This is your hotel's Pay TV. To view the film, dial your room number on the remote control, followed by the OK key. The fee of €12.50 will be added to your bill under the heading "miscellaneous".*

I switched to one of the shopping channels. Among the items for sale were a set of pots, a bicycle and a sun-ray lamp. Lulled by the salesman's voice, I fell asleep.

I was woken by the sound of my mobile. The name

Callegari was flashing on the display.

'Hi, it's Marco.'

'Hi.'

'Listen, I'm still at the hospital, but I'll be finished in half an hour. That means I could be with you in Bergamo by eight-thirty. How about having dinner together?'

I had two conflicting reactions. My more 'conscience-led' half was indignant at the idea that, to males in the third millennium, the word 'separated' was still a synonym for 'easy prey'. The other half of me considered that a man who had the courage to travel more than a hundred kilometres in that hellish fog just to see me was a small boost to my self-esteem.

While he waited for my reply, I closed my eyes and saw the trattoria, the table in the corner, his hands moving as he spoke. I thought again of that ungiven caress: perhaps he was missing it, too.

'Dinner's fine, but I'm not in Bergamo. I'm staying in Vittuone, at the…'

Shit. How could I tell him I was in a luxury knocking shop? I took a deep breath and came straight out with it.

'At the Motel Rode. I stopped here because of the fog. I couldn't go on.'

'I'll pick you up at eight.'

He really was unflappable.

'Fog permitting.'

'Fog permitting.'

I shouldn't have agreed. Not that I'd been inundated with invitations since my separation, but there'd been a few and I'd always refused. Instead of which, on the one night when I couldn't even change my clothes, I'd consented to go out with a man.

I took a bath, using the scented salts the motel provided. It took me half an hour to fill that huge bathtub, and when I was lying in it, all alone, I felt ridiculous, halfway between a Hollywood star and an abandoned mistress.

With my hands, I tried to make my hair look as decent as I could: luckily the perm was holding. My hair was perhaps the thing I most liked about myself, or at any rate hated the least. It used to be brown, but over the past two years, with the increasing number of white hairs, I'd started to dye it a reddish colour. 'Have it wavy, not curly,' my idiot hairdresser had said to me. 'It'll take ten years off you.' That stupid hyperbole of his had forced me to think about how I was ten years ago, at the age of twenty-eight, how I was the day I met Stefano. The passing of those ten years hadn't improved either my appearance or my state of mind.

I looked at my clothes, which I'd thrown down on the bed. Jeans, denim shirt and blue sweater. I was still dressing the way I had when I worked at the hostel. There wasn't much I could do, these clothes didn't allow me a great deal of variation. I hoped Marco had chosen somewhere warm and decided to leave the sweater, undoing three buttons of my shirt to give a glimpse of my tiny breasts. Then I made myself up, with the two things I had in my bag: a little eye pencil and a touch of lipstick.

At five past eight the telephone on the bedside table rang.

'Signora, there's a man asking for you at reception. Shall I send him up?'

The customs of the house were clearly a little different

from those in normal hotels.

'No, I'll come down.'

That would have been the last straw, asking them to send him up before I'd even said hello.

Marco greeted me with a smile that immediately revived our bond.

'You did the right thing, not going back to Bergamo. You can't see a damn thing on the road. I think my colleagues in emergency will have their work cut out tonight. This area is full of idiots who say, "I know the fog, it doesn't scare me". And then they crash into a tree at a hundred kilometres an hour.'

'Is it still as thick as before?'

'You can't see more than three metres in front of you. I'd have liked to take you somewhere rather special, but it's best not to go too far. Do you like Indian food?'

'Yes.'

'I actually prefer Signora Maria's. Come, I'll take you there.'

I'd fallen for it. He had wanted to see if, for his sake, I'd have accepted something trite but fashionable: Indian, sushi, Mexican... For pulling that stroke, I should have dumped him there and then and gone back up to my room, but I tried to be charitable and tell myself that it had been a friendly move designed to reveal something of himself, to show me the kind of man he was: the antithesis of glamour. Apart from the tan and the car, of course.

Maria's Restaurant was very similar to the one where we'd had lunch, just slightly more elegant. Elegantly simple is how I'd describe it. The light was low, almost non-existent, and on every table there was a lighted candle. I guess that made it all a bit obvious, a bit schmaltzy, but as soon as we sat down I appreciated the fact that the little circle of light cast by the flame forced us to move closer together so that we could see each other as we talked. It was the same at the other tables: everyone was leaning forward and talking in low voices. Everyone, not only the couples. Actually, I noted that it wasn't really a restaurant for couples, a place of assignation for secretive lovers. Clearly, Marco had tact.

We skipped the starters and the first course we ordered arrived almost immediately: a fantastic barley soup served with a slice of bread and a generous dose of extra virgin Ligurian olive oil, so intensely yellow that it looked like honey.

'Have you ever noticed,' Marco said, dipping his spoon in the steaming bowl, 'how tastes change with age? Take this soup, for instance. Would you have liked it as much at the age of twenty as you do today?'

'No, until I was twenty-five I couldn't stand soup of any kind. For me, those dinners at home with the thick vegetable soup were always a chore.'

'Me, too. Then, when I got to thirty, I suddenly changed my mind, and now I love soups and broths. We change with time.'

I could have told him that there was just one taste men never lost, their taste for twenty-year-olds. At eighteen they go crazy for twenty-year-olds because twenty-year-olds give the impression of being experienced women, from twenty to thirty they go with twenty-year-olds because they're young but not too young, and from thirty onwards they seek out twenty-year-olds precisely because they're younger. I could have said all that, but the fact that he was here, having dinner with me, even though I was nearly twenty years past the age of twenty and was starting to have something more than character lines on my face, meant that his interests went beyond young girls. It was a good thing that men like him existed. No sooner had I finished thinking this than I realised how stupid I was being: why on earth should I find a man who'd give a second glance to a woman pushing forty exceptional in any way?

I heaved a deep sigh and calmed down: I was getting worked up over nothing, all by myself. There he was, sitting opposite me, watching me slowly eat, probably not even comparing me with other women, young or old.

He told me about a patient of his, a young man who had been involved in a car accident and who, in his opinion, should have been walking normally by now, after six months' treatment, but was still in a wheelchair. We discussed the psychological aspects of physical traumas, and then the problems of accepting artificial limbs and prostheses in general.

'I think there's still a lot to be done at the neurological level,' I said, 'at the interface between the body and its technological extension.'

'You're right. That's a problem my wife's fascinated by.'

'Is she a neurologist?'

'No, she's an electronics engineer and works for a company that produces prostheses.'

'My husband was an engineer as well. I mean, he is an engineer, with Fiat, only he's not my husband anymore.' How hard is to find the right words when we talk about our exes!

It was strange, but the references to his wife and my ex-husband had made no difference to the atmosphere between us, had done nothing to break the intimacy growing under cover of the shoptalk and the jokes and, above all, the silences, which were becoming increasingly long, increasingly intense. During these pauses, I think we were both trying to find an excuse to make an affectionate gesture, a delicate but unequivocal gesture. If he makes one more remark, I thought, about how women are taken in by commercials for beauty creams, I'll reply that men are just as gullible – razors with more and more blades, aftershaves for the man who has everything – then I'll stroke his cheek with the back of my hand, the way they do in the commercials. I'll do it with a touch of irony, I told myself, that way I'll see if he takes it as a joke or if he responds with something tender.

I can't know for certain, but I have a feeling he was thinking along the same lines as me, because after a while he found the right pretext, a doctor's pretext. He took my hand, which had been resting on the table, and separated the index finger from the others.

'What's this scar here, under the knuckle?'

You really did need a clinical eye to notice the two little spots on my finger.

'An accident in the kitchen, cutting the roast, at the age of twelve.'

'Traumatic?' he asked with a smile.

'Nothing that couldn't be overcome.'

I didn't take my hand away and he didn't let go of it. Instead, he gently took hold of the other fingers and started to caress the back of them with his thumb, slowly.

The silence grew deeper than ever. We were barely aware of the waiter bringing us ice cream with hot chocolate sauce.

And at last came the caress I had been longing for, with his left hand open, and his wedding ring leaving a cold streak on my cheek.

If you're over fifteen and not yet eighty, tenderness isn't easily contained, you can't keep it in check and you can't be content with it. But then, why should you be content with it? Going back to the motel together and climbing the stairs to the bedroom was the natural continuation of that caress. Perhaps Stefano was right: there are situations that inevitably lead on to a more intense moment, a moment, nothing more. But why had Stefano so often found himself in such situations?

While we were getting the keys from reception, Marco moved away for a moment to phone home and say he wouldn't be back that night. I don't know what excuse he gave but it didn't seem to cause any problems, a sign that at the other end there were few difficulties either. Misplaced trust or acceptance of the state of things? I thought of my own misplaced trust, my betrayed trust. Couldn't Marco's wife have felt betrayed, too? Humiliated by what Marco had done and was about to do? I'd recently read a book by an American psychologist, although in her case 'psychologist' was pitching it a bit high: it was called *Against Love* and was about betrayal as a kind of therapy for couples. Had Marco and his wife read it, and were they putting its suggestions into practice? Stefano certainly hadn't needed to read it! And yet I was starting to think that if I'd cheated on him, too, I might have understood him better – although that didn't guarantee we'd have stayed together.

We climbed the stairs in silence. Step after step, I imagined the moment when we would close the door of the room behind us and embrace, leaning up against the wall, tearing the clothes off each other.

Instead of which, as soon as he turned on the light, Marco burst out laughing at the sight of the mirrors on the ceiling and those pretentiously tacky fittings. I couldn't help laughing with him. And that laughter was more sensual, more erotic than any passionate embrace.

We threw ourselves on the bed, laughing like lunatics, kissing through our laughter.

He took off his jacket. Underneath it he was wearing only a white T-shirt. I embraced him and slipped my hands under the T-shirt. He opened my shirt and moved his hands over my back. Discovering each other's skin for the first time always gives you a frisson. It's a frisson that can't be repeated. From the second time onwards it's only a memory, but that first time its power is phenomenal. How wonderful to feel skin you've never touched before under your fingers!

I went into the bathroom. When I came out I was naked and I felt beautiful, for no other reason than that he was looking at me. Even the intoxication of being naked is a miracle the first time, the intoxication of displaying yourself rather than seeing. Men may be aroused by looking, but I'm satisfied by the dropping of the veil, the falling of the barrier.

He was still dressed. I took off his T-shirt, opened his belt and took off his trousers. As I did so, slowly, stroking his thighs all the while, I thought with a touch of exasperation of the moment when I'd get down to his calves and come to his socks. But they weren't there: he'd been lying on the bed waiting for me to undress, but he'd already taken off his socks, to avoid the most ridiculous moment, when the man is in pants and socks. He had on a pair of black stretch boxers. I took them off, too, caressing him with both hands.

We hugged, and at that moment a flash of anxiety stopped me. The condom. How should I mention the condom? If you make love to the same person for ten years, some things are part of a tried and tested procedure: touching, kissing, trying to arouse one another, thinking of someone else, perhaps a stranger, to become more aroused yourself, waiting for him to do the same so you can help him to put on the condom, trying to reach orgasm, faking it if you have to. Making love with a man you've just met is different, it's more beautiful and more difficult.

But he'd thought of that, too: looking at the table on his side of the bed I saw a condom, still in its packet, placed there in full view to spare me the embarrassment of asking him about it.

It felt strange, making love with all those mirrors. Actually, it was a nice sensation, looking at his broad back while he was on top of me. I saw my hands embracing him and it felt as if I was embracing him better, harder. His back was as tanned as his face and his bottom stood out clearly. I liked his bottom. That glance in the mirror lasted only a moment, then I saw my own face and felt ridiculous, as if I'd left my body and was gazing at myself. Thinking this, I was running the risk of losing all the sweetness of the moment, so I closed my eyes and forgot about the mirrors. Then he turned me over, gently, and I felt his legs on mine, his pelvis on my buttocks. And I felt many other things, long-forgotten things. And at the end I felt his weight softly resting against my back and his arms encircling my body, holding my breasts.

'At night lovers undress each other and kiss, but they never help each other to dress.' Those, more or less, translated as I went along, were the words of a song by a French singer named Benabar: '*Les amants le soir se déshabillent en s'embrassant, le matin c'est rare qu'ils se rhabillent mutuellement.*' And he was right.

We'd cuddled for a long time, the way you never think can actually happen in reality, and hadn't slept much. The alarm had been set for six: he had to do his rounds very early and I... I had to visit a whore.

Waking up with a man you've only just met isn't like going to bed with him. It's more embarrassing. I'd always thought that those scenes where the woman gets out of bed with a sheet wrapped round her were shot like that to satisfy the demands of the censors, but that morning I also felt like using the sheet as a bathrobe. Morning is the time for regrets, for the detritus that the thrills of the night before have left in their wake. But it had been worth it, I thought. I got out of bed naked, and he looked at me in such a way that if I'd actually been wearing a sheet I'd have thrown it on the floor and basked in the warmth of that gaze.

In the bathroom, I looked at the whirlpool bath, which had ample room for two. In the middle of the night I'd thought of taking a bath in it with Marco, but I hadn't had the courage, it would have been too much like something out of a risqué magazine. Maybe next time, if there was one.

We kissed goodbye just outside the motel. I don't know how I'd have felt if I'd had to go home to my husband. But that wasn't my problem, I had to visit a whore. I had to track down the elusive Alina and ask her about Patrizia.

Visibility hadn't improved since the previous evening. It was a good thing I didn't have far to go. The girl I'd talked to the day before was right. The road was busier at that hour than at any other time of the day, or so I thought – I know now that night is worse. On the way to the scene of the accident I passed at least four of those family men who grab a quickie before going to work. I was in luck: there, standing by the tree to which anyone other than Benedetta would have tied a bunch of flowers, was a girl with very red hair, wearing boots, low-cut jeans that left her midriff bare, and a very visible G-string. She was leaning in at the window of a car going in the opposite direction to me. I stopped, hoping the bargaining wasn't successful. It wasn't. The car left and she turned to me. I lowered the window and said, 'Alina?'

Without waiting to hear another word, she turned, crossed the road and ran off in the direction of the fields.

'Wait Alina, I only want to talk to you!'

But she was already too far away.

Shit! I'd blown the one opportunity I had to throw some light on how Patrizia had been run over. I wouldn't get the chance again.

I turned back, feeling more defeated than ever. I stopped at the bar where I'd had a sandwich two days earlier: it's incredible how quickly you become a creature of habit. I had a breakfast of cappuccino and brioche and a glass of water for the pill I took for my backache, my one true partner in life. I opened my bag to look for a paper handkerchief and saw that my mobile was flashing: I had a message.

At nine I finish my rounds, 30 minutes break, if you're

in the area I'd love to kiss you. Marco.

I felt better and started to press frantically with my thumb on the keys.

9 am hospital car park. I need to be kissed.

I took the *Corriere della Sera* from the next table and read it until it was time to leave for Magenta.

The car park was almost deserted: visiting hours hadn't started yet. I pulled up and waited. Outside the emergency department were a man and a woman. He had his arms round her shoulders, while her head hung in an image of pain and despair. After a few minutes, a siren blared and the couple had to step aside to let an ambulance go in. After that, in the short time I waited, there were others, grief-stricken couples or groups, holding each other tight in a futile attempt at consolation. At least they had each other. When Patrizia's stretcher had been taken hurriedly out of the ambulance, there had been no one for her.

At last I saw Marco come out. He'd thrown his grey overcoat directly over his white coat and his tan looked even more out of place in that atmosphere of seemingly endless winter. I wanted to run to him and embrace him, as if my adolescence hadn't been dead and buried for a couple of decades, but was a kind of dormant disease, ready to recur at the slightest stimulus. And yet I think he had the same urge as me, because he began walking faster. But then, after a moment, he came to an abrupt halt as a dark red car passed. The car turned into the area reserved for hospital staff and disappeared behind a hedge, and Marco continued on his way towards me.

'It was a colleague,' he said even before saying hello, as if he felt the need to apologise for that abrupt halt. 'You know how it is...'

'Male or female?'

Misplaced jealousy. Clearly a symptom that my adolescent disease really had returned.

'Male. Dr Maestri, as it happens.'

'The doctor who treated Patrizia Vitali?'

'That's right. There's only one, and one's enough.'

That was when the idea suddenly came into my head, the idea from which all the others – or almost all the others – were to spring. 'What kind of car does Maestri drive?' I asked.

'An old Lancia Fulvia. It must be nearly forty years old.'

'Is he a vintage car enthusiast?'

'Who, Maestri? No, just stingy. It's a car he was left by his grandfather. He uses it as little as possible and when he parks it outside the garage of his house he puts a grey sheet over the top of it, the kind they used to use a lot, with the licence number on it.'

The idea was growing in my mind, but now wasn't the moment. 'Shall we get out of here?'

'Yes, but I have to be back on the ward at ten o'clock on the dot.'

'You will be. Get in.'

We parked in a cul-de-sac, at the end of which was a concrete wall beside the railway line, and there we kissed. That hadn't happened to me since my last year of senior high school, when my then boyfriend would pick me up after school and we'd go to the outskirts of the city, to a deserted, unpaved street near the factories, and we'd kiss and kiss, nothing else, without speaking, for more than an hour – until we realised that the street was so deserted, we could actually make love there, even in broad daylight.

After that, the kissing came to seem less important. Strange things, kisses! They matter a lot at the start of a new relationship, then they pass, like something you've left behind you, and you catch yourself envying the kids you see kissing at bus stops or against the doors of night, in Prévert's words. When you start a relationship, you do it, too, you kiss passionately in public when you can, to annoy the passers-by, but after a while you're back in the role of passer-by yourself, someone who's already used up their stock of kisses. In those few minutes, though, it seemed to me that our stocks were inexhaustible.

At a minute to ten, Marco climbed the entrance steps and I watched him, filled with emotion. In love, no, but certainly filled with emotion.

A minute later, a phone call from Benedetta brought me down to earth.

'Any news?'

'Not at the moment. The undertakers blame the people in the cemetery and say the coffins must have been mixed up...'

'They don't know what they're talking about!'

That categorical rejection of the most logical theory struck a jarring note. Why was Benedetta ruling out the idea of a mix-up from the start? It was as if she knew more than she had told me.

'Anyway,' I replied, 'to be absolutely certain there was a mix-up, we'd have to have an exhumation, a mass one.'

'Out of the question.'

'Of course.'

'Is that all you have?'

'For the moment, yes.'

'And it's taken you four days to find that out?'

I managed to hold my tongue instead of telling her to go to hell. Hire a detective, I would and should have said, but I was getting into the whole case by now, because of the money, but not only that.

'I don't think I need to reiterate that our family wants this matter settled as soon as possible.'

I did, though, allow myself the pleasure of a parting shot. 'Did you know your sister had a boyfriend?'

'No.'

'Now you do.'

I left it hanging, as if the revelation of something which was not exactly unusual, given that Patrizia had been twenty-three, was of major importance. I know now that in fact it was. And I also know how important the other revelation was, the one I didn't make: that a redheaded prostitute might have witnessed the accident. I don't know why I didn't tell her that at the time, I think what stopped me was that unpleasant sensation that I was being taken for a ride, that I was only there to look for things that Benedetta already knew. It wasn't just spite, it was caution: almost as if, by demonstrating how much I knew, I'd have already felt in danger. Or maybe I didn't tell her in order not to have to add the second part, in order not to have to admit that I had lost my only witness. Although, as I realised at that moment, Alina was lost only to me. She could hardly change her pitch, so perhaps someone else…

I headed home with two fixed ideas in my head, two separate ideas I tried to combine in some way, even though I didn't know how.

I arrived just before midday. On the third floor I rang

the bell, smiling once again at my downstairs neighbour's naivety. Next to the bakelite doorbell, she had stuck a label cut out of some advertising circular: *Giovanna Ghislandi, 10 Vicolo Aquila Nera, 24100 Bergamo.*

'Good morning, signora.'

'Good morning, dear.'

'I wanted to thank you again for last night.'

'Don't mention it. It was a pleasure, and it made a nice change. What can I do, I'm always here on my own. It's not that my children won't come to see me, they're working.'

'Unfortunately, work does take up a lot of time.'

'Oh yes, especially the boy. Boy! I still call him my boy, but he's forty-two. He works in Dalmine, he has a good job…'

I let her tell me about her son, a mechanic, and her daughter, a dental nurse, hearing the words she would say in my head before she said them, then, when she got onto her husband, who had died of a heart attack twenty-five years ago, I found a way to interrupt her monologue.

'Could I ask you another favour?'

'Go ahead!'

'Do you remember that hat of your husband's that you showed me once? Would you lend it to me for a day?'

She looked a bit doubtful for a moment, then went inside her apartment and came out a few moments later holding a wide-brimmed hat.

'Look after it for me, it's a memento. I bought it for his birthday a week before he died.'

I swore to treat it with respect, said goodbye to her, and climbed the last flight of stairs.

I realised immediately that something wasn't right, or rather that it was exactly as I should have foreseen:

Morgana hadn't miaowed on hearing me arrive. That was the signal.

I opened the door and was overwhelmed by a bad smell I knew: on the kitchen rug Morgana had expressed her disapproval at having been abandoned all night, without warning.

I called her. She didn't answer, and didn't come to me. But I knew where to find her. I took the steps and looked on top of the mirrored wardrobe, behind the carved edge. We stared at each other, and the expression in her eyes was much sterner than in mine.

I made lunch for both of us and, smelling the smell of the meat spreading from the kitchen, Morgana agreed to make up. As a sign of her forgiveness, she rubbed her little nose against my calves.

When I'd finished eating, I sat down at my desk, switched on the computer and connected to the internet. I wanted to follow up at least one of the two ideas that had been obsessing me. I went to Google Images and typed in *Red Lancia Fulvia*.

The search for Red Lancia Fulvia has not produced any results.

Suggestions:

– Make sure you have typed all the words correctly.

– Try using different keywords.

– Try using more general keywords.

I tried being less specific: *Lancia Fulvia.*

This time I got fifteen results, at least two of which were very satisfactory, with a good view of the car from both the front and the side. A pity it wasn't dark red – though once

I had printed it, pushing the cartridge of my printer to its limit, the colour was completely different from what appeared on the screen anyway. It didn't matter, it would work just as well.

Then, still on the internet, I hired a car for the next day. I looked for one very different from mine and in the end opted for a Stilo. Reservation for 5.45 a.m., Orio al Serio Airport. Another ungodly hour.

The next day I would do what I could and, with a bit of luck, might get my two ideas to fit. I looked at the late Signor Ghislandi's hat and told myself it might actually work.

Seeing as I was connected, I checked my e-mail. Thirteen new messages: five advertisements for Viagra, four mails from an American site selling fake Rolexes made in China, two chain letters, and two identical mails from the Progetto co-operative: *We didn't see you at the meeting with the people from the regional education board. They approved the work done with Franco and Samantha, but insist that the results we obtained with Denis are poor, especially as regards his marks at school and his relations with his classmates. If you'd been there it wouldn't have been so bad. Are you still intending to work with us? Let me know. Laura.*

But how could they care about educational attainment when it came to someone like Denis, who would take out his handkerchief and spend twenty minutes waving it, staring into space and smiling, totally absorbed in the movements that damp piece of material was making in the air? Before thinking about school, they needed to understand what was inside him that gave rise to that compulsive behaviour, they needed to know where exactly his mind was. I decided to write a report and send it to the children's psychiatric service. They might never pay me for it, but it didn't matter.

And so the afternoon passed, and the evening.

For a while I let the cursor hover over the reply key, then once again dropped the idea and switched off the computer.

The afternoon had passed, and the evening.

I got ready to go to bed, but I felt that something was missing, a goodnight to someone. I picked up my mobile and hesitated for a long time. Would a message at this hour get him into trouble? In the end I decided that someone like Marco must always have an answer ready. Perhaps he'd tell his wife what Stefano always told me at times like that: it's the phone company ringing to let me know who called when my mobile was off. And I believed him every time. I wrote just two words – *Good night* – dialled his number and sent the message. Two minutes later the answer arrived, probably written in the bathroom, with the shower running to hide the noise of the keys: *Starting long weekend with family. Good night.* An elegant way of saying *Do not disturb*, of saying that for the moment he was a married man again.

To remember in order to forget, that's the necessary paradox. To remember the past in order to forget the present, in order to forget that he could come along the road at any moment, and if he did he'd certainly try to do to me what he did to the corpse I'm looking for.

I know what's happening inside me. My pupils have dilated, and my blood pressure has risen. From my internal organs, a large quantity of blood is rushing towards my brain and I feel my stomach knotting. It's all the fault of my 'limbic system', all the fault of my thalamus, my hypothalamus, my hippocampus and my amygdala. The 'limbic system' is one of the oldest parts of the brain: it's the starting point for the 'primal circuit of fear'. From the pituitary, which lies deep in the hypothalamus, a charge of corticotropin has started off and turned into a cascade, beginning the secretion of neurotrasmitters. I know some of my synapses have gone into action and are working through the mediation of noradrenalin. My 'primal circuit' has analysed the situation briefly and compared it against the innate fears: fear of the dark, fear of animals, fear of death. What has emerged from the comparison is that I have good reason to feel afraid, not so much a rational reason as a primitive one: my 'primal circuit' has accumulated these age-old fears and is reacting to external stimuli exactly as it would if I were one of the first *homo sapiens*.

But, for the moment, the 'rational circuit' still has the upper hand over the primal one, and so I keep digging. With small thrusts. Gradually I descend. Into the earth, into hell. From time to time I measure with my eye the depth I've reached. Twenty centimetres. It's very little. I have to concentrate my thrusts in a restricted area, go down until I find something, something horrible, something which has conserved nothing of its original beauty, its warm human essence, except the traces of another person's abuse, and yet something which will indicate to me that my psychologist's hypothesis is right. After that I'll widen my digging, go further, reveal more details.

The prostitutes are there, more of them than ever, behind the flames rising from the paint pots they use as braziers. They go off, get laid, and come back, without respite, without hope. They come back to their spot, the usual spot, the same spot they, or perhaps others, were in, that morning just under a week ago.

Saturday, 19 February

No sooner had I shut my front door than I looked at the thermometer on the wall of the landing: six degrees, below zero of course. Then, too, like now, I wondered who was making me do this, what was making me leave home on an icy dawn. This wasn't my life, it was some other woman's. But hadn't I become a different woman? I'd found the courage to say I'd had enough of Stefano's betrayals, I'd moved to another city, I'd made love with a married man. I was definitely a different woman, but I didn't know if I liked this new identity.

Well before these doubts had disappeared from my mind, I found myself at Orio airport. I parked my car, after getting the keys from a clerk who was even colder and sleepier than me, and took the grey Stilo I'd booked.

Although it was Saturday, and only just after six, there was a fairly continuous stream of traffic on the road: vans, lorries and even tractors. That damned plain wouldn't hear of taking a break, having a bit of fun, stopping all those sacrifices to the god of work. Better for me, though: at least this way I'd be more likely to meet Alina again, the red-head who did the early shift, who specialised in morning tricks with the tireless workers of the Po Valley. Did they, even during those moments, during those hurried fucks fitted in between the kiss to the wife and the opening of the shutters of the shop, did they, those tireless workers of the Po Valley, care about Alina's residence permit and think to themselves that illegal immigrants ought to go back to their countries? Perhaps they did, perhaps they even thought that about Alina, but not straight away, perhaps after ten minutes, if it lasted that long.

Eight below zero, according to the thermometer on the dashboard. The wind that had brought all that cold had done at least one good thing: it had cleared away the mist. In the still bleary light, the fields appeared, completely covered in frost. Stopping at a red light I looked at myself in the rear-view mirror: a dark coat, distinctly unfeminine in style, unisex they'd have called it once, the collar turned up, Signor Ghislandi's last hat on my head to hide my hair. As a disguise, the image in the mirror was reassuring, from any other point of view it was grotesque, but, as usual, I didn't care.

The usual route: Dalmine, Agrate, Milan ring road, exit seven, Route 11, Vittuone, turn left, Strada alle Cascine, paved road, unpaved road, first prostitutes, the wider stretch where the accident occurred. Alina wasn't there: day off or work commitments? I hoped she was busy with a customer, otherwise my dawn awakening, my change of cars, my Lieutenant Kojak disguise would have been completely pointless. I drove on without slowing down, past Signora Bono's farmhouse. About two kilometres further on, the road crossed another nameless unpaved road at an acute angle. I had the impression this would also take me to the main road, and in fact I actually needed to go that way to get back to Alina with the left side of the car towards her. I turned onto it. Before long I saw the farmhouse in the middle distance, on my right. This was the first time I'd noticed this small wood in the middle of the fields, beside which the road I was on passed. The branches of the tallest trees hung out over the road, forming a kind of canopy.

I continued the detour and, as I'd predicted, came back out onto the main road near the first houses in Corbetta. Another turn to the right and here, after a while, the sign I was now used to: Vituon. I looked at my watch. The detour had taken about a quarter of an hour. Assuming that the average length of a quickie was no more than fifteen minutes, I headed confidently for the lay-by. As I came level with the factory, I saw Giovanni Imperiale's black car coming in my direction and turning rapidly in at the entrance, practically cutting me off: another tireless denizen of the Po Valley.

I spotted Alina from some distance away, because at that point, and for quite a stretch before and after, the road is straight, so straight as to make you wonder how it was possible that the hit and run driver hadn't seen Patrizia. I slowed down to the speed of someone getting ready to check out the merchandise. I took a last glance in the rearview mirror to make sure that, from a distance anyway, I looked like a distinguished, somewhat elderly gentleman. A few metres before I pulled up by the redhead, I lowered the window and lifted my mobile to my left ear, as if to make a phone call, then stopped the car and turned my head slightly towards Alina.

She approached, ready to supply information, something like 'blowjob thirty Euros, all the way fifty euros' – assuming those were the rates. When she was a few steps from me, I pressed the key in the top right-hand corner of the phone's keypad with my thumb and took a photograph of her, then set off again slowly, without any screech of tyres, like someone who's decided that the goods aren't to his taste. Alina hadn't noticed a thing, I was almost certain of that.

I drove on for a kilometre and stopped in the usual open space near the farmhouse: the moment had come to confirm my other idea, too. Before getting out, I took off the hat, lowered my coat collar and debated whether it was a good idea to visit Signora Bono at that hour. But surely, people who worked on the land woke up early, even on Saturday. So I took a folder from the passenger seat and got out.

I found her in the kitchen, of course, wearing the same floral printed dress, brown cardigan and apron as the previous time.

'Good morning. How nice to see you.'

'Thank you, I'm sorry to disturb you again.'

'You're not disturbing me, go on.'

From the folder, I took the photographs of the Lancia Fulvia I'd printed the previous evening and showed them to her.

'Is this by any chance the car of the person who used to pick up Patrizia?'

She went to the table, picked up the glasses she'd left there and put them on.

'Well, at a first glance I think so, but the thing is, I don't really know much about cars. They aren't really a woman's thing, are they? Now if you ask me about cooking, or mending, or looking after the hens or the pigs, fine, but cars...'

I was getting ready to leave without having found out anything new, but Signora Bono had a flash of inspiration.

'Come with me. I'm not the only one here.'

We went out into the yard and she started calling, 'Abdel, Abdel.'

The young Arab I'd seen working on the tractor the previous time emerged from one of the sheds and crossed the yard in our direction.

'Abdelkader,' he said, holding out his hand and smiling.

'Anna,' I replied.

'Listen, Abdel, the signora here has brought some photographs of cars, but you know I don't know much about them. You'd recognise if this is the car of that fellow who used to come for Patrizia. You know, the one we never saw, who waited for her at the end of the drive.'

The young man took the papers I held out to him and looked at them for barely a moment. 'This is the one, a 1965 Lancia Fulvia 2C. Only this one is blue, while Patrizia's boyfriend's was dark red.'

He spoke Italian with a marked Lombard inflection, in a voice that could easily have echoed from the platform at a Northern League meeting.

'Are you sure?' I asked.

'Absolutely. It was one of Lancia's least successful cars. Quite unlike the coupé, the Fulvia HF, which won a lot of rallies before it was replaced by the Stratos...'

'I told you our Abdel was an expert!'

'I studied mechanical repairing to professional level, cars are my passion.'

'And tractors,' Signora Bono cut in.

'Yes, but cars even more.'

'One day he's going to leave us and open his own workshop.'

'And did you ever see Patrizia's boyfriend?'

'No, it's like Signora Caterina says: he never came into the yard and never got out of his car.'

'And did Patrizia ever talk to you about him?'

'No. She was always very kind, but she never talked about herself. Just normal things. "How are you", "What would you like to do if you had more money", things like that.'

'It's like I said,' Signora Bono added, 'she was a very reserved girl.'

Any discussion of Patrizia always seemed to end with the word 'reserved', but at least one thing was clear: Patrizia's mysterious boyfriend had a Lancia Fulvia identical to the one owned by Dr Maestri, the doctor who had treated the young woman so lovingly. Unless there was a sudden flood of Lancia Fulvias into the area, it must have been the same car, and the same man.

On my way back to Bergamo, I weighed up my little haul of successes: I had identified Patrizia's boyfriend and I had a photograph of Alina, which I wouldn't be able to do anything with on my own. During the seventy-four-kilometre journey, I continued to speculate about Patrizia and Dr Maestri. Were they girlfriend and boyfriend? He was small, a bit hunchbacked, homely, completely devoted to his patients, she was pleasant enough but dowdy, and quite demure, almost a nun. The two of them together? It was possible. But then something else occurred to me. Why hadn't anyone in the hospital mentioned that Patrizia was Dr Maestri's girlfriend? Didn't anyone know? Well, he was apparently as reserved as she had been. But then, when he got back from the United States and saw her there, dying, why hadn't he shown the slightest emotion? The slightest mark of desperation? When Patrizia regained consciousness in front of him, and then he lost her forever, how could he remain impassive? Impassive to the point of not even going to his girlfriend's funeral? Wasn't that taking reserve to extremes?

There were starting to be too many things in this affair that didn't make sense. The body vanishing, Benedetta belatedly discovering an interest in her little sister, the boyfriend treating Patrizia's death like that of any other patient.

I should have listened more to these doubts! Instead of which, still weighing up my fleeting triumphs, I thought about how best to find answers to these questions, how to use Alina's photograph to move on and find out more about Patrizia's death. Move on at the very moment I should have been dropping the whole thing. Actually, I knew perfectly well how to use the photograph, except that it didn't just depend on me, I needed someone else, and I didn't have the courage to make that phone call, to admit, once again, that I needed him, perhaps not only because of Alina's photograph.

But in the end, back at home and with Morgana finally lying affectionately on my knees, I did phone him.

'Hi, did I wake you?'

'No, of course not, it's nearly eleven.'

But his voice sounded thick and sleepy.

'Are you alone?'

'Yes.'

This time the answer seemed genuine, or at least I wanted to believe it was.

'How's the weather in Turin?'

'Cold.'

I assumed he hadn't yet raised the blinds in the bedroom of what had been 'our' home.

'If you can spare five minutes, there's something I need

to talk to you about.'

'Of course, let me just make myself more comfortable.'

I imagined him in his dark blue pyjama trousers – only the trousers, because he felt hot at night, even in winter, and always slept bare-chested. The noises that reached me through his cordless phone told me all about his movements through that space I remembered only too well. I heard the squeaking of the sliding door in the living room, and in my mind's eye saw the room, the red sofas, the bookcase, saw him walking barefoot on the cold floor – he never remembered to put his slippers on – to the wooden chaise longue, the one a 'rich' uncle had bought him in Trieste from an antique dealer who dealt in salvage from the breaking up of ships. I heard, or thought I heard, the creaking of the wood under the weight of his body as he sat down and I prepared myself to tell him everything before I got to the request I really needed to make.

'I'm ready, go on.'

I told him about my encounter with Benedetta, the misunderstanding, the work I was carrying out and all the things that had happened. He listened, interrupting me only from time to time to clarify some detail, then, when I had finished, he asked me, 'Have you gone mad?'

'Listen, Stefano, if you're going to be like that let's stop right there. I know you think I never do anything right...'

'All right, perhaps I used the wrong tone of voice, as usual. But naturally I'm a bit surprised. I married a psychologist and now I find my wife is a detective.'

'Ex-wife.'

'If you prefer...'

'And besides, I'm not a detective, I'm just helping someone in difficulty, someone who has serious problems expressing her emotions, and who pays well.'

I lied, knowing now that I was lying, knowing that he was right and that all this was increasingly revealing itself to be exactly what it was: pure madness.

'All right, then. Let's say you're a psychologist with a rather flexible remit. But could you explain why you've told me this whole story after a month when we've hardly spoken, apart from that brief call on Valentine's Day when you almost slammed the phone down on me.'

'It's just that I need to...'

'What?'

He knew perfectly well what was coming after 'I need to...', but he wanted me to be the one to say it.

'It's just that I need to ask you a favour.'

'I'm listening.'

'It's about Alina, the prostitute who saw the accident.'

'What about her?'

'Well, she doesn't want to talk about it. The other girl must have told her I was looking for her to ask her about Patrizia's death and she runs away if I try to approach her.'

'Perhaps she's afraid you want to force her to testify. She probably doesn't have a valid residence permit and doesn't want any trouble.'

'I'm sure that's true, but I need to meet her and talk to her somewhere quiet.'

'And how are you planning to do that?'

'You...' I hesitated one last time. 'You have to bring her to me.'

'Me? My wife, sorry, my ex-wife is asking me to pick up prostitutes for her. Don't you see how crazy that sounds?'

Put in those terms, I had to agree with him, but I insisted, 'It's not a question of picking up prostitutes, all you have to do is bring the girl to me in a motel near there.'

'That's all, is it? With my luck, I'm sure to end up in a police swoop. I can already see the paragraph in the newspaper: "Among the customers detained was a forty-two-year-old engineer from Turin…".'

'I beg you.'

There, I'd said it. I'd sworn I wouldn't stoop to begging him, instead of which it had only taken a few minutes.

'And how am I supposed to recognise her?'

'I told you: I took a photo of her, I can send it to your mobile.'

'That's all we needed. So now you're collecting photos of prostitutes on your mobile.'

'Better collecting photos than collecting affairs.'

It had slipped out. It might have cost me dear, but in fact he became more compliant.

'Touché,' he said. 'Tell me what I have to do.'

'On Sunday evening we take a room in a motel I know…'

'You know motels? Since when?'

'I only know this one, and not for the reason you think.'

Actually that reason was part of it, too, but I acted as if nothing had happened. 'We spend Sunday night at the motel,' I went on, 'then about seven on Monday morning, you go out, pick up the girl, and tell her that instead of doing it in the car you want to take her to a hotel. It'll cost a little more but I think it's possible. When you get to the motel, bring her up to the room and I'll talk to her.'

'What if she refuses? What if when she sees you she starts screaming and runs away? What if she calls the police?'

'An illegal immigrant working as a prostitute calling the

police? Come on!'

'But they might make trouble for us at the motel.'

'You must be kidding. If they made trouble for everyone who took prostitutes to their rooms, they'd have closed down a long time ago. We may need to give them a little tip, but I don't mind.'

'But it's Monday, I have to work.'

'You can be at the office by eleven. Do you have any appointments that can't be postponed?'

I knew that on Mondays he had a commitment he couldn't drop, but that was at seven in the evening: his five-a-side football game.

Reassured about the time scale, he finally yielded. 'All right. With you, I thought I'd seen everything, but I was wrong.'

There was affection in his voice: a way of reminding me that many of the things we'd seen together had been really beautiful. Before I got a lump in my throat and couldn't speak, I told him how to get to the motel and fixed the appointment: the next day, Sunday, at ten at night, make sure you have dinner first.

I felt touched by the memory of his Monday evenings spent playing five-a-side football: it was another of those areas of the male world I couldn't penetrate. On Mondays from seven to eight, come rain or come shine, I knew that Stefano was there on the pitch and I knew he wouldn't miss it, not even if the youngest and prettiest of the secretaries in his office had made him the most exciting of propositions. For him, for his friends, and I think for millions of men between the ages of twenty-five and fifty, the weekly match was much more than a mere game: it meant solidarity, camaraderie, male bonding, the kind some people used to find in a gentlemen's club. When Stefano and I were first together, I'd tried to understand that world, tried to understand what fascinated him about it. I hadn't succeeded. Seen from outside, from behind the fence that marked the boundaries of the pitch, the match seemed to rest on an incomprehensible logic. No, it wasn't that the game was especially complex – a match between forty-year-olds played at the end of a day's work wasn't the place for technical subtleties – it was rather the dynamics between the people, the variety of human types. There was Gianni, who was always pissed off, who, every time he lost, left the pitch before the end, angrily taking off his shirt and telling his companions to go to hell. There was Luciano, who encouraged the weaker ones, shouting 'bravo' at every barely acceptable kick. There was Paolo, who was always cheerful and would collapse on the ground, shaking with laughter, at every clumsily missed shot at goal. And there was Stefano, who ran up and down with a constancy and tenacity he didn't have in any other situation, who put his heart and soul into it, as if his reputation – or the fate of the world – depended on it. And all of it, all that anger, that running, getting worked up, exaggerating in one way or another, seemed to me, watching from behind the fence, to be heavy with a meaning I couldn't grasp. That was exactly what I was missing, the ability to grasp the meaning of that game of football, the sheer enjoyment of being together, like children who were too grown-up for the playground. But perhaps the real meaning lay in what happened after the game, in the student-like spirit of the changing room. It seemed to me that, for Stefano, that changing room had become the one place where he could talk about men's things. In summer, when they insisted on leaving the door open to let out the steam from the show-ers, you saw them naked if you passed by, not caring a jot about the outside world, absorbed in endless conversations, interrupted at times by noisy bursts of laughter, or shouts of praise or encouragement. They probably weren't telling each other their latest adventure, or discussing that Sunday's matches. According to my husband, they talked about life, happiness, work, health, their impending mid-dle age, and a whole lot of absolutely normal things, but in a way, and from a viewpoint, that was deliberately male, as if without women around they felt freer, more authentic.

According to a female scholar, courage is the ability to look rationally at those things whose cause escapes us. Courage is the awareness of what we have to fear or hope. But if I look at things rationally, my fear turns to terror. As long as I don't think about it, as long as I remember, as long as I go back through this mental diary, I limit myself to my innate fears and delude myself that my trembling, my nerves, the throbbing of my temples, is the direct, uncontrollable consequence of what's happening in my cerebral cortex and in other areas of my brain that preserve the memory of infinite nocturnal dangers in the depths of prehistory. But if, instead of that, I linger over the events, I understand perfectly well that what's freezing my membrane isn't the dark, or the atavistic fear of the wolf in the wood, or the lethal appearance of these skeletal trees, or the toxic smell of the earth and the fertiliser, or the barking of the dogs. If I look rationally at Patrizia's death, at the corpse I'm about to dig up, at the danger I'm running, I can't help feeling crushed, stifled, by the weight looming over me.

That's why I'm not thinking rationally. Or rather, I'm using all my common sense to interpret the noises produced by my shovel: the liquid rustling of the earth as it's penetrated, the metallic crash of the blade against some stone, the pregnant silence when I lift it. What will the noise of the corpse be like?

Sunday, 20 February

It was almost half-past ten at night and, of course, Stefano was late. When we were together I got used to his constant lateness, I stopped worrying, didn't even get angry: I just accepted it or, rather, endured it. Now, though, it was different. What if something had happened to him? What if he'd had an accident in the fog because of me? What if he'd crashed on one of the thousand building sites along the Turin-Milan autostrada on his way to help me? But it wasn't only worry, it was nerves, too. I was nervous at the prospect of seeing him again. It was seven months since we'd last met. How would he be? Would he turn up in one of the shapeless sweaters he must have started wearing again, with the loose sleeves that would have swallowed up even a champion body builder? He'd look dishevelled, sloppy. And I'd feel guilty.

The situations in which I was starting to find myself seemed increasingly paradoxical, increasingly surreal: alone, in the foyer of a dubious motel where two days earlier I'd had a passionate encounter with a married man, waiting with trepidation for the arrival of… my husband, or rather, my ex-husband.

At last, at twenty to eleven, he arrived. He was wearing a new, short overcoat and a well-cut dark grey suit I'd never seen him in before. Beneath it, he had on a very high-necked black T-shirt. Some female hand more resolute than mine must have thrown away his collection of old shirts with their collars shiny from too much ironing. I hated him. I hated him because I realised he was changing, because, lateness apart, he was becoming the way I'd wanted him to be, but he was changing to please another woman, or perhaps other women in general. It was as if he hadn't needed to please me, having already pleased me once and for all many years earlier.

I hated him, but I smiled as I walked towards him, beneath the malicious gaze of the receptionist, the same one as three days before, who, as soon as I'd arrived, had handed over the key to No 107 before I'd summoned up the courage to say that I would have preferred another room.

'Hi.'

'Hi, squirrel.'

He'd never stopped calling me by that nickname. We approached each other, and force of habit sent our lips on a collision course. There was a moment of indecision, with our mouths a centimetre apart, and then a rapid swerve to channel that lingering trace of love into a chaste, friendly kiss on the cheek.

'Shall we go up?'

'Of course.'

It was strange to climb those stairs with Stefano, and very different from the way it had been with Marco: no heart in my mouth, no all-consuming desire, only a sense of disorientation and unreality. Had it taken less than a year of separation to extinguish all traces of excitement, even in such an equivocal situation? Or had it been the years of marriage that had deadened everything?

As soon as we were in the room, Stefano had the same reaction as Marco: he burst out laughing.

'Mirror effects,' he said through his laughter. 'Do they have the ones that make you look bigger or smaller? You have to make sure you reflect the right places in the right mirrors, otherwise you end up looking like Ken.'

'Ken who?'

'Barbie's sexless boyfriend.'

'Stupid!'

He took off his coat and jacket. His black T-shirt made the muscles of his arms and chest stand out, muscles I didn't even remember: he must have been going to the gym.

He glanced at the bedside table and saw the book I'd put there earlier. 'Haven't you read it yet? I bought it for you when we were still together!'

'I know, I always say I'm going to start it, then I start another book and this one gets left behind.'

He sat down on the bed, and I took a chair. 'So you really want me to pick up a prostitute and bring her back here?'

'Yes, it's vital.'

Together, we went over what to do the following day, like a couple of small-time crooks going over the plans for a risky robbery: we wake up at six-thirty, Stefano goes out, looks for Alina on the basis of the photograph, drives Alina to the motel, brings her up to the room, I question her, he drives her back. Estimated time: one hour.

'Do you think it'll work?'

'I don't see why not, even though I feel quite embarrassed about it. I've never been with a prostitute.'

I'd have liked to retort that the women he went to bed with weren't much better, but then the thought struck me that Marco's wife could have said the same thing about me and that there was no point in making such fine distinctions.

Anyway, we ended that discussion by wishing each other good luck. Then silence fell, not the silence of people who don't have anything to talk about, but the silence of those who've gone over the same things too many times and know it would be pointless to start all over again.

In an attempt to make small talk, I asked, 'How's Turin these days?'

'There's more building work going on than when you left.'

'That means they're finally going to finish the underground.'

'Yes, the underground, four ice rinks which won't be any use after the Olympics, an unspecified number of sports facilities, and a couple of new dormitory suburbs.'

'Where?'

'One where the old markets were and the other where the Teksid foundries used to be. They've built these horrible hives, with balconies so close together you think you're in the apartment opposite. The city's been sold out to property speculators.'

Despite the new muscles under his T-shirt and his air of a Casanova who's taken early retirement, his civic passion was clearly still as strong as ever.

'One of these days,' he continued angrily, 'I'm dropping everything and moving to France.'

France was an obsession with the Turinese, the dream of the Piedmontese middle class: an apartment in Nice or Menton and the certainty of always having a refuge for when times got really bad in Turin.

'Is the situation really so grim?'

'Look, right now the city's in a state of artificial euphoria in preparation for the Olympics, but they're using this thing as a smoke screen to hide the real ills.'

'Such as?'

'Such as Fiat. Some areas of Mirafiori are like a ghost town. There are huge factory buildings, completely abandoned, still with the machinery inside and the papers on the desks. It's like one of those science fiction films where there's a disease that wipes out human beings but leaves things untouched. That's what the productive heart of Turin has been reduced to. And they're still building apartments.'

'But who's going to live in them?'

'They've started saying that with the creation of the high-speed line between Turin and Milan, the Milanese will move to Turin because apartments are less expensive there but still work in Milan because the train will only take forty minutes.'

'That's nonsense! I don't know anyone in Milan who'd move to Turin!'

'Nor do I, and besides, even if they did, is that the height of our urban ambitions: to turn Turin into a dormitory of Milan? I know all about Piedmontese modesty, but that's ridiculous.'

I'd never before known him to be so disenchanted with his city. 'His', not 'ours', because I'd been a Turinese by chance, taken there at the age of fourteen by my father's job and kept there, even after my family had left, by university and by Stefano.

Now that Stefano had let off steam, the silence returned.

Stefano switched on the TV and started channel hopping. I sat down next to him, hoping to watch something, anything, just to help me get to sleep. Everywhere the remote control took us, the subject was the same: commentary on the day's football matches. Slow motion replays, arguments, unconceded goals, non-existent penalties, disputed offsides, counter-attacks, offensive full-backs, player ratings and the whole repertoire of Sunday night television. Stefano jabbed nervously at the controls.

'Aren't you interested in football anymore?'

'No, I'm sick to death of it.'

'Even Juventus?'

'Especially Juventus.'

'Then let's go through all the channels. Maybe we'll find a film.'

He pressed the arrow-shaped key and we ended up among the local shopping channels: sets of pots, gymnastic equipment, robot lawnmowers, water purifiers, and experts who promised to eliminate negativity. He went through all of them and came to the last area of all, the forbidden one, the porn channels. The image of a woman being fucked by two men appeared on the screen. The men were neither particularly young nor particularly slim.

'How about this one?' he joked.

'Maybe not.'

The following channel offered two women entertaining each other with tubular contraptions that looked like huge gumdrops.

'Or this one?'

'I don't think so.'

On the third pay channel, the lovers were a man and a woman, lying on a sunbed on a terrace by the sea, not doing anything too weird. Not that the film was clean – it was pure pornography, a series of penetrations from different angles – and yet it seemed less lurid, less anatomical than the others. However exaggerated the gestures and moans, the bodies exuded something sensual, a feeling of genuine, intense pleasure.

After the standard thirty seconds, the image of the couple on the terrace faded and gave way to the caption I had seen the previous time: *This is your hotel's Pay TV. To view the film dial your room number on the remote control, followed by the OK key. The fee of €12.50 will be added to your bill under the heading "miscellaneous".* In the background, the couple could still be heard panting.

'Do you want to see it?' Stefano asked.

Something in his voice told me he wanted to see it, and to be honest I didn't mind.

'Why not?' I replied.

Stefano started to fiddle quickly with the forward and back keys on the remote.

'What are you doing?'

'Wait and see. I don't know if it'll work. It usually does.'

'Do you usually watch porn films in hotels?'

'I watch films in general, and try not to pay for them.'

'How?'

'Like this,' he said, continuing to go back and forth from the pay channel. All at once, the caption disappeared and the couple appeared in sharp close-up. Now the girl was leaning over the parapet of the terrace and he was taking her from behind. What hadn't changed was the atmosphere of the scene. We started watching the film, in silence. In the past, we'd watched a few porn films, finding them fairly ridiculous, laughing at the men's oversized organs, the women's massive breasts, the moans, the cries, the length of time everything lasted, and the speed with which perfect strangers agreed to have sex with each other. This time, though, it was different, perhaps because of the quality of the film, or perhaps because we were no longer husband and wife and were gradually coming to resemble perfect strangers.

I realised that Stefano was getting aroused, not only in his groin, but above all in his head. I also felt turned on, and I didn't know if it was because of the film or because of the fact that I was watching it with him. I took off my blouse and sat down astride him, on his lap. He switched off the TV and laid his cheek on my breasts, embraced me, then kissed me on the mouth and, with his usual slight clumsiness, fiddled a bit to loosen my bra, the blue one with the little metal hooks, then…

After making love, some people smoke. I don't. I think. I think of poems, songs, other people's words that describe what I'm feeling at the moment, what I've just felt. That night, with Stefano already asleep beside me, I thought of a song by Gaber and sang it in my mind, skipping the words where I didn't remember them exactly: *It's Saturday, it's Saturday. There's something, you can feel it, something strange in the air: we haven't made love for a week.*

It hadn't been a week, it had been more than a year, a year and a half perhaps, since before we separated. When you stop making love, it's the first symptom that things are going wrong.

I take off her belt and stand there a while, the line of her neck, the curve of the hips, look so tired and familiar.

That was the point, that was how we'd been that night. I was tired and familiar to him, he was tired and familiar to me. I looked at him as he slept, naked, on his stomach. I looked at his broad back, his firm buttocks, his long, not especially hairy legs, all of which were impressive in a man past forty. Impressive, but tired and familiar. How different Marco's skin, back and bottom were. Would they be that way one, two, three more times and then become tired and familiar? If that was the case, Stefano was right to look for 'distractions' and come back with a clean conscience, convinced he hadn't taken anything from me. But was that really the case? Always? With everyone?

It's all so natural really, just a little effort at the start, then everything happens by itself, no sweat at all, no sweat at all.

Gaber was right, everything had happened by itself that night. It had taken only a little initial effort at the start, helped by the film, an effort to overcome the awkwardness, the detachment, then everything had happened by itself. No sweat, no passion, rhythmical and predictable, easy but inoffensive. With Marco it hadn't happened by itself, Marco and I had pushed things to their limits. It hadn't been natural, which meant it hadn't been obvious. It had been a journey of discovery, from his skin to the way he had caressed me to the moment he had entered me. I'd started to feel dizzy at the end, from hyperventilating too much. With Stefano it hadn't been like that at all. With Stefano it could never be like that, that was clear to me now. All that was left were a few listless caresses, and a little tenderness. A lot of tenderness, actually, but it wasn't enough. Stefano had realised that before I had: his affairs had taught him that. It wasn't true that his betrayals had taken nothing away from our marriage: they'd taken away the illusion that things could be fresh and new every day, and without that illusion our relationship hadn't resisted. We'd told ourselves we were too young to surrender to routine, we'd told ourselves that life could and should still have something amazing in store for us. And here we were, making love wearily, after watching a porn film, out of a kind of nostalgia.

The alarm went off at six-thirty. Six-thirty on Monday 21 February, according to the display. Stefano got up immediately, rested, clear-headed. He was a good sleeper and never had any difficulty waking up. If we'd had children, he'd have been the one to make them breakfast and take them to school. But we hadn't had any. We'd waited, and then it had been too late. At least we hadn't made the mistake of trying to solve our marital problems with a child. In a moment, he was ready to go out.

'I'm going and may someone help us.'

Someone, not *God*. Stefano was a complete atheist.

'Are you sure you know where to find Alina?'

'I think so. I take the Strada alle Cascine, go past a factory, carry straight on and come to the stretch where the road widens. That's where Alina should be.'

'Do you have the photograph?'

'Yes, I have it, and I've looked at it a thousand times.'

'Good luck, then.'

He smiled at me.

I let him get to the door, then remembered something basic. 'Thank you.'

There followed twenty-seven minutes of nervousness. Not so much the first twelve minutes, which I spent washing and dressing, but the other fifteen. Spent slowly, staring at the luminous numbers on the alarm, which seemed reluctant to move. 6:59, 7:00, 7:01, 7:02. At last that fateful 7:14, when I heard Stefano insert the key in the lock and I ran to hide in the bathroom.

I heard the muffled noise of steps on the carpet, the door closing, the key turning again and then voices.

'Give me the money, please.'

'Here.'

'If you give me another twenty euros, I'll undress.'

'Twenty euros?'

It was the moment to come out in the open.

As soon as Alina saw me, she had a moment of panic, but I didn't have the impression that she recognised me as the woman who'd tried to ask her questions, let alone the man in the hat with the mobile stuck to his ear. It was just the surprise of seeing a third person that had set alarm bells ringing.

'I don't do threesomes, and I don't do things with women.' Then to Stefano, who was leaning against the door, 'Let me out of here or I'll scream.'

I remembered her friend, the one who'd greeted me with the words 'I don't usually do things with women', but who would have agreed to entertain me for a hundred euros, if I'd wanted her to. I opened my handbag and took out a hundred-euro note – I'd claim it back off Benedetta, I told myself.

'What if we add this?'

She took it, still suspicious, but a little more willing.

'So shall I start undressing?'

I had no particular desire to see her naked, nor was I keen on giving Stefano a strip-tease for free, but, for the first time, I had a detective's cynical reflex: if she had to collect her clothes to leave, she'd be less inclined to run away.

'Yes, of course.'

Stefano looked at me questioningly, and I frowned

slightly by way of response.

Alina started to undress, quickly, without a hint of sensuality, as if she was undergoing an army medical. She threw her padded jacket over the back of the armchair, took off her T-shirt and, before it was even over her head, dropped her jeans. Underneath, she was wearing a bra and a bright red G-string. She took them off, too. When she was completely naked, I realised that she couldn't be more than twenty. Her figure didn't seem fully formed yet, her breasts were taut and her bottom small. I felt even worse, but there was no stopping now.

She lay down on the bed, and looked up at the ceiling, again without a modicum of sensuality, only a silent invitation to do what we wanted and quickly.

I sat down next to her and took her hand. 'Listen, Alina…'

She gave a start and sat up. Customers didn't usually know her name. It set off her internal alarm system again. There was fear in her eyes, the fear of someone who feels trapped. There was one of her against two of us, she was naked, probably illegal, and there was no way out.

'Listen,' I went on. 'You don't have to have sex with us, but we'll pay you all the same. You can keep all the money we've already given you.'

'Are you police?'

'No, don't worry. I'm the cousin of Patrizia, the girl who was knocked down on her bicycle near where you always stand.'

She said nothing. There was a puzzled look on her face.

'A colleague of yours told me you saw the accident and I'd like you to tell me what you saw.'

'And then I have to repeat it to the police?'

'No, just tell me what you saw, and we won't bother you again, I promise.'

My tone must have been quite reassuring, because she relaxed a little.

'It was morning. It might have been about seven-fifteen, seven-thirty, because I'd already done one customer. I saw the girl coming on her bike, like she did every day. She sometimes waved to me as she passed. She was kind, she always smiled. I saw the girl coming and on the other side I saw the car also coming, fast, very fast. At first I thought the man in it was doing things with a girl, because it had been parked for a while.'

'You mean the car was already there before Patrizia arrived?'

'Yes, it was parked there. Then, as soon as the girl started to come closer, the car set off, fast, very fast. I think the girl realised and got scared, because she stopped. But the car kept going and hit her, without stopping. I thought it was going to hit me, too, and I ran behind the tree, but the car drove off. It drove off just as fast, on the other side, the side the girl was coming from.'

'So it knocked her down deliberately? It wasn't an accident?'

'If it was an accident the man must have been drunk, because there was no fog that day and good visibility. So good that I saw the car go right to the end, where the road turns, and then stop. It started to turn as if it wanted to come back, but then another car arrived and the one that had knocked down the girl didn't come back, it went away.'

An execution, it had been an execution. It wasn't just a question now of finding a missing body or reconstructing, for emotional reasons, the last days of a young woman's life. Despite myself, I was investigating a murder. I was interrogating a naked, frightened young woman, but now that she'd started to talk she seemed eager to unburden herself.

'The girl was in the ditch and I didn't know if she was alive or dead. I just looked to see that she didn't have her head in the water, then when the other car came near I asked the driver to call for help because a girl had been knocked down. He told me to get in, and I got in because I was scared that the other man would come back and knock me down, too. So we went to a phone booth and he told me to go and phone 112, but I was shaking and couldn't speak, so in the end he phoned and said a girl had been knocked down and where she was.'

'And then?'

'Then he made me get back in the car and said, "I did you a service, now you have to do one for me", so we went to a road nearby and I had to give him a free blowjob.'

It must have been one of those good family men, one of those honest workers of the Po Valley, so honest they would never infringe the iron laws of the market: If I do something for you, I want something in return. And perhaps he'd been thinking: So, poor little Eastern European girl, you wanted to come to the free world? Now pay the price.

Stefano, who'd been silent so far, asked, 'Did you see what car it was that knocked down the girl?'

'It was a grey BMW X5.'

'Are you sure?'

'Listen, I see hundreds of cars every day, the ones I get into, the ones where the driver stops to ask the price, even the ones that slow down and the driver looks and then insults me. You have to know about cars if you want to know something about the customers. Whichever car I'm in, I know where to find the lever to lower the seat back. Lorries never have seats that go back, except on the ones that... Anyway, if I tell you it was a BMW X5, it was a BMW X5, a grey one. And I can also tell you that when it left, I saw that it had this thing on the back...'

'A dent?'

'No, something stuck on, yellow...'

'A sticker?'

'Yes, a yellow sticker on the rear window, shaped like a man swimming with, what are they called…?'

'Flippers? Like a scuba diver?'

'Yes, a yellow sticker shaped like a scuba diver, the people who go under the water.'

I must have been getting accustomed to the environment, because the question that next occurred to me was the kind that someone who knew that world well might think of.

'Had you ever seen that BMW before? Was he a regular customer?'

'Yes, he often came along the road, but he never looked at me. It's obvious he doesn't like redheads. But he went with other girls.'

'Did you ever see the driver?'

'No, like I said, he never approached me, not even to ask the price. He didn't like me.'

'Have you seen him recently?'

'No, I never saw the car again after that day. A lot of X5s go by, but the one with the yellow thing on the back I never saw again. I always check because I'm still scared.'

I looked at her. She was sitting curled up now, with her breasts hidden behind her knees. She seemed lost. On impulse, I stroked her hair in a maternal gesture, which she took as such.

'Can I get dressed?'

'Of course. My husband will drive you back.'

In a moment, she was dressed again. Stefano put his coat on and opened the door.

'Wait for me, I'll be right back.'

'Of course.' Then I said goodbye to Alina and added, 'Thank you, I really mean that.'

She smiled, with a touch of gratitude: perhaps the extra she'd earned from this unusual performance she'd be able to keep out of her pimp's greedy hands, though she'd have to hide it well, of course.

It was as they were going out, as the tension of that improvised interrogation drained away, that I started to feel afraid, not the terror I feel now, but a deep sense of anxiety and the usual dilemma: retreat or attack? Under the stimulus of fear, a young chimpanzee looks for comfort by running to his mother and rubbing himself against her fur, but I didn't have any such possibility of comfort. I could surrender, I could retreat, but I wouldn't find any loving arms to shelter in. I was on my own. Marco wasn't yet a presence, and Stefano wasn't a presence anymore, despite that lingering tenderness there still was between us. So I chose to attack and see it through to the end. To attack without weapons, without claws, even more impractical than Morgana when she fluffs up her fur and arches her back. The only strength I had was that I was used to digging into other people's forgotten past.

And it was in Patrizia's past that I needed to dig in order

to find out who had a motive to kill her and then get rid of her body, because the two things weren't unconnected. The reason for the disappearance of the body was linked to the method of her death. Something in that body might still give a clue to her killer. And in the meantime, the one thing I had was two cars: one, the Lancia Fulvia, surely led to Dr Maestri, the other, the BMW X5, belonged rather to Benedetta's world, but also Marco's, or the undertakers'. Yes, Signor Gandolfi's partner, the one who'd sealed the coffin, had a silver-grey BMW X5! A phone call wouldn't be out of place. I grabbed my handbag and emptied it on the bed. In among the mountain of keys, paper handker-chiefs, sweet packets, pens, lip glosses and other assorted objects, I found Gandolfi's business card: La Pace Funeral Directors, proprietors Gandolfi and Maestri.

Gandolfi and Maestri.

Maestri like Dr Maestri?

I put off the phone call: I had to think.

In the meantime, Stefano arrived.

'Everything all right?'

'Of course. I drove her back to work, if you can put it that way.'

'How did she seem?'

'I felt sorry for her. And I have to say that making her undress to question her did seem a bit like Gestapo tactics.'

I didn't know what to say. Perhaps I really was turning into a monster.

'Sorry to speak to you like this,' he went on, in a more conciliatory tone, 'but it seems to me you're doing things that aren't really you, things you don't know anything about, dangerous things. Are you planning to hunt down a murderer now?'

'Actually that was the first time in this whole affair that anyone's mentioned a murder. It took me by surprise.'

'Or maybe you've been taken for a ride. Are you sure someone isn't taking advantage of your good faith to poke around in some very murky waters?'

'That did occur to me a couple of times, but I'm thinking on slightly different lines now. I've realised something important. I think the key is the grey BMW.'

'I beg you, let it go. If it's about the money you know I have some savings. When we separated you didn't want anything, but – '

'When we married we agreed to a separation of property. The apartment was yours, so I'm not entitled to anything and I don't want anything.'

'We're not talking about what you're legally entitled to, but what you need in order to keep out of trouble.'

'Don't worry, I'll pull through.'

It had become a matter of pride and strength. I wasn't going to achieve anything by running away.

'Now have a safe journey back,' I said, adjusting the collar of his jacket.

'Aren't you coming?'

'I'm going to stay here for a while and think about what Alina told us.'

We said goodbye, with another embarrassed kiss, half on the lips, half on the cheek, both feeling somewhat ashamed that, despite our best efforts, the miracle hadn't happened.

'Have a good game,' I said, when he was at the door. 'It *is* still Monday evenings at seven, isn't it?'

'Yes. I see you remember!'

How could I forget?

*

I sat down in the armchair and picked up the business card of La Pace Funeral Directors, proprietors Gandolfi and Maestri. I dialled Gandolfi's mobile number. The answer came after one ring.

'Hello.'

He was speaking in a low voice, as if he was just outside a church where a funeral service was taking place.

'This is Anna Pavesi, Patrizia Vitali's cousin. We met last week…'

'Yes, I remember.'

'I need to ask you something. Is your partner, Signor Maestri, by any chance related to the Dr Maestri who works at the hospital in Magenta?'

'Yes, Riccardo, my partner, is the uncle of Paolo who's a doctor at the hospital. Why do you ask?'

I didn't really know why. My head was a jumble. Gandolfi's answer threw some light on the matter, but was very far from providing a solution.

Like a coward, I rubbed my bracelet over the microphone of the mobile, to make it sound as if the line was cutting out, then hung up and switched off the phone.

I started walking up and down the room, talking to myself in a low voice, telling myself things and refuting them, asking myself questions and coming up with the answers, then correcting them, changing my mind, gesticulating to convince myself first of one hypothesis and then, immediately afterwards, its opposite. This went on for a good half-hour, until the picture was sufficiently clear and credible, at least to me, and I'd decided to go on the attack, the real attack, even though not everything fitted yet. It would later, I told myself, when everyone made their inevitable confession.

I took my handbag, went out and locked the door. On the way downstairs, I looked at the tag with the number 107 attached to the key. It wasn't big and heavy like those in other hotels, and lay easily in the pocket. Obviously people had to be very careful not to take it home with them, but always to hand it back to that unctuous man who, this time, looked me up and down with an even more sardonic look than before, a look almost of contempt, as if to say: See these respectable ladies? They're more depraved than whores. But of course he kept all that to himself and said instead, with a saccharine smile, 'See you soon.'

'I don't think so,' I retorted. After all, I could always see Marco at my apartment. I was a free woman, although I still found that hard to remember sometimes. But would it be the same in my apartment? Surrounded by my everyday things, wouldn't Marco feel a bit trapped? Wouldn't he be afraid that I might want to force my way into his life and destroy his settled existence and his long family weekends, like the woman in *Fatal Attraction*? Would I want to do that, or would I be content with romantic restaurants and hot nights that got more and more lukewarm as we went along? Would we love each other forever, would we say goodbye, or would we meet less and less often until we forgot to phone each other?

Ah, yes: I had to make a phone call.

The first phase of the attack. A phone call to Benedetta.

'Hello Benedetta, Anna here.'

'I'm in a meeting. If you can possibly be quick about it...'

'Your sister was murdered.'

Silence. A very long silence. Surprise or the fear of being discovered? Because Benedetta's role in this whole affair was one of the things that didn't quite fit yet.

She recovered. 'Are you sure, or is it just a theory of yours?'

'I'm sure.'

'Do you know who it was? Do you know why?'

I counterattacked. 'Do you have any ideas?'

She absorbed the counterattack. 'No, absolutely not. It's up to you to... No, I'm sorry, I know it's not your job. Perhaps it's best if we stop right here. Let's make an appointment for the end of the week, I can't before then. You can tell me what you've found out, I'll pay you, and we drop the whole thing. Obviously, you mustn't say a word to anyone.'

'I'm carrying on.'

Again silence. Was she stunned? Scared? The same doubts as before.

'Why?'

Again, I attacked. 'Because I feel as if I'm being taken for a ride.'

'By me?' Her voice seemed to shake, imperceptibly.

'By someone.' It was better not to be too specific, better to let her think that...

And then there was that matter of pride, that demonstration of strength I felt I had to make to myself, perhaps to Stefano, perhaps even to the world. As if a woman had to constantly prove herself, at least a woman without a double-barrelled upper-class surname.

'Now I really have to get back to my meeting. Keep me informed.'

I would keep her informed, and I would watch my back. But she hadn't come out in the open. My attack had failed, or at least looked as if it had. Now it was time for the second phase.

*

I set off, through those same villages strung out along the road, bumper to bumper with thousands of other cars, each with a single person on board, a person who, in order to get to work, had learnt to exercise the virtue of patience and to fill in the long waits between one lurch forward and the next: making up in the rear-view mirror, reading in the newspaper about what was happening beyond the windows, calling phone-in programmes on the radio to supply traffic information, listening to cassettes to teach themselves English, picking their noses.

Road signs: Vittuone 1, Corbetta 4, Magenta 7.

A vaguely pleasant morning, pale blue sky, with a sun that hadn't yet made up its mind whether or not to penetrate the high layers of thin cloud, temperature below zero, risk of ice on the road surface, as signalled by the light on the dashboard, puffs of grey smoke from the exhausts. Stop, go, stop, go.

I looked in the rear-view mirror. No, not to make up, just to see my face again, to see if my eyes still had that gleam they'd had when Marco caressed me, to see a strand of that reddish hair in which he'd buried his face.

Road signs: Corbetta 2, Magenta 5.

Lorries and trucks. Small vans full of packages, express parcels, wrapped cheeses, household appliances, supplies of drinks. Bricklayers' vans, with rubble in the back and brooms tied behind the cabin. Vans driven by artisans, plumbers, electricians on their way to bring relief to those who'd been waiting for them for days. Big lorries, articulated lorries, moving merchandise from one side of the globe to the other, because merchandise is the most important thing: produced where the costs are low, sold where the costs are high. The new creed tearing the world apart depended on these containers with their roaring engines.

Facile observations, the kind you make when you're in a traffic jam, on the lookout for new signs: Magenta, town centre, railway station, hospital.

I followed the directions that said 'hospital'.

The usual itinerary. Car in the car park, next to the area reserved for hospital staff, front steps, lift to the fifth floor.

Dr Marco Callegari wasn't in the corridor or by the coffee machine, but he wasn't the one I was looking for. I went straight to the nurses' room. Margherita, the head nurse, was there.

'Good morning,' I said, smiling in an attempt to ingratiate myself.

She returned my greeting without enthusiasm.

'I'd like to speak to Dr Maestri. Is that possible?'

'I'll go and look for him. Hopefully he'll have finished his rounds, if not you'll have to wait a bit. You can go in the lounge for the moment.'

I sat down in the lounge. I picked up a magazine and read a few easy tips: how to get rid of stress, how to make sure your children go to school willingly, how to make a quick dish of chicken with almonds when your mother-in-law invites herself over for dinner unexpectedly.

After twenty minutes, Dr Paolo Maestri arrived, with a face as black as thunder.

'I thought we said everything there was to say to each other last time.'

We were off to a bad start.

'I wanted to talk to you again about the funeral and the transfer of the body…'

'I don't recall seeing you or your cousin at Signorina

Vitali's sickbed, nor do I remember seeing either of you when the funeral needed arranging. I arranged the funeral myself with her employer, Signor Imperiale. Quite frankly, all this concern about her now that she's dead makes me a bit sick!'

He was right, I could have endorsed every word he said. But his tone was far too aggressive. It wasn't the resentful tone of the upright person lambasting other people's wickedness. No, it was the tone of the bully, the pupil forced to repeat a year jeering at the teacher who's just given him yet another bad mark in front of his classmates, the tone of someone who knows he's in the wrong and therefore goes on the attack. And at that particular moment, I could have taken many things, except being attacked. I felt anger rising from deep inside me, from my intestines, my chest, my heart. I felt it sweep over my brain, like a hot wave. I don't often get angry, but when I do, anger blots out everything else, every common-sense consideration, every rational thought. My jaws first close spasmodically, then open suddenly, and a torrent of malice spews from my mouth.

'Now listen to me…'

Damn, my voice was already shrill and unsteady, two things I can't stand, but can't control when I'm angry – and at that moment I was really angry.

'Listen to me, and listen carefully, because I'm going to tell you some things you already know, things that mean you don't have the right to play games with me.'

I paused for breath, then launched into my lecture.

'Patrizia had a boyfriend and this boyfriend used to pick her up from the farmhouse in a red Lancia Fulvia. Now, you drive a red Lancia Fulvia and there aren't many cars like that in this area. Conclusion: you were Patrizia's boyfriend.'

'What if I was?' For all his drooping shoulders, he'd lost nothing of his arrogance.

'If you were her boyfriend, then your behaviour would seem suspicious, to say the least. Patrizia turns up on your ward, dying, and you don't show the slightest distress, you treat her with professional detachment, then you sign the death certificate, have her packed up in a coffin, and don't even go to her funeral! I hope I never have a boyfriend like that.'

'Then obviously I wasn't her boyfriend.'

He was still making fun of me, calmly and insolently.

'Well, I think you were, and I also think you murdered her. Because Patrizia was murdered, wasn't she?'

I paused, to see what effect my surprise announcement had had. It hadn't had any.

'If you say so…'

'It's not me who says so, it's the person who saw a BMW X5 just like your uncle's car knock the girl over and then drive off. It's the body disappearing from the coffin which your uncle made sure he sealed on his own. It's the unusual amount of care you took of that patient – '

He interrupted me. 'You're a psychologist, aren't you?'

'Yes.'

'Then I'd advise you to do a bit of self-analysis, or better still, see a psychiatrist, because your condition seems quite serious to me.'

I regretted that I wasn't a man, the kind of man who reacts to something like that with physical violence, because I felt a strong desire to smash his face in. Instead of which, I had to try and crush him with words.

147

'If you like, I'll tell you the story from the beginning. You meet Patrizia and get together. She's no great beauty, but you're no Adonis yourself. Together you're more like a friendly society than a couple, but that doesn't matter. Except that after a while Patrizia starts to get bored. I don't know why, but she gets bored. And you're desperate. Yes, of course, the nurses worship you, you're their idol, but going to bed with you is another matter. In addition, you may actually be in love, madly in love with Patrizia. So one morning you borrow your uncle's 4x4, an X5, the kind of car that's quite common in this area, and run her down. You're sure you killed her, but a few hours later you see her here in the hospital, on your ward. Although she's seriously hurt, she regains consciousness, so you sedate her and over the course of the next week you poison her with drugs. The doctor who ordered the CAT scan says that the trauma in itself wasn't the cause of death. But Patrizia has to die, otherwise she could talk, reveal who'd run her over. You kill her and even sign the death certificate. Then you come to an arrangement with your uncle, the undertaker, to fake the funeral and get rid of the body. While an empty coffin is being buried in the cemetery, you dig another grave somewhere else and put Patrizia's body in it, in such a way that it can't be recovered, in such a way that no one will ever find those traces of poison that remain in the bones and hair even years later.'

'Then why didn't I have her cremated? That would have been the simplest way to get rid of the body.'

'Cremation requires a waiting period during which the body remains in the crematorium before being incinerated. That would have been too risky for you.'

'Fair enough, but the day Patrizia Vitali was knocked

over by a hit and run driver in a car you say was similar to my uncle's, I was on a plane on my way back from the United States.'

'That's what you say.'

'Then go to the police and report me, if you're so convinced. They can check it out. At the same time, I'll report you for slander. Shall we do that?'

That was the point: I had nothing, and, above all, I was nobody. I was a poor woman who'd made a wager with herself, and was about to lose. I'd assumed that, confronted with my reconstruction of the murder, he would crumble, but he had strong nerves, much stronger than mine.

'Now I think you should go. I never want to see you here again. The same goes for your cousin.'

The spell of Benedetta's double-barrelled name had no effect on him.

He went out without even putting on airs. He'd wiped me out.

I left, too, with my tail between my legs, hoping not to meet Marco. And luckily I didn't. I didn't know if he was at work, if I could hope to take refuge in his arms. Back in the car park, I entered the area reserved for staff. His BMW X5 was there. I noticed for the first time that it had a yellow sticker on the rear windscreen, shaped like a scuba diver.

I couldn't breathe. It was as if my lungs didn't want to dilate, didn't want to let air in. I closed my eyes and held onto the railings around the parking area. Twenty seconds, thirty.

A BMW X5 with a yellow sticker on the rear windscreen. This really was a story about cars. Alina had seen a silver-grey BMW X5 with a yellow sticker on the rear windscreen knock Patrizia down, deliberately, to kill her.

Marco had a car exactly like that. Why would Dr Marco Callegari murder a girl who, as far as I was aware, he didn't even know? But was it true that he didn't know her? In the provinces everyone knows everyone else, more or less. And besides, in all probability, Patrizia was his colleague Dr Maestri's girlfriend.

There was a kind of spider's web growing in my head, a web of interconnected thoughts and vague relationships, a nasty, sticky spider's web: Patrizia Vitali, Benedetta Vitali, Paolo Maestri, Marco Callegari, and me. Yes, even I had a thread of my own in the spider's web now, connecting me to the others: to Benedetta through work, to Marco through passion... Only through passion? On my part, yes. But what if it had been different for him? What if his principal motive had been to find out what I was looking for, what I knew about Patrizia's death?

Again unable to breathe. Nausea, and the desire to vomit. A pain in the stomach, and lower – as if my period pains had suddenly started.

Was Marco a murderer? Had he used me?

I didn't know what I felt more: shock at the fact that I'd shared a table and a bed with a murderer, or disgust at having believed that what Marco felt for me was, if not love, then at least attraction.

I summoned up the strength to move away from the railings, get in my car and drive off.

I drove in a trance. Buried in confused thoughts and memories, hypotheses and fears.

Marco Callegari and Paolo Maestri. Two colleagues. Two rivals, perhaps? In work? In love? Marco met Patrizia through Maestri. Marco seduced Patrizia, easily, as he'd done with me. Patrizia wasn't beautiful, but Marco might be one of those compulsive womanisers who are more interested in the quantity of the prey than the quality. Patrizia, though, wouldn't let herself be loved and then dropped, Patrizia made claims on him, threatened to tell his wife: a classic situation. And Marco killed her, to save his family, his peace and quiet, his position: a classic situation.

The tollbooth on the A4 Milan-Venice autostrada. Entering, taking the ticket, still in a trance, moving mechanically.

But how to account for Maestri's silence? How to account for his acting as if nothing was amiss, his absence from the funeral, his lack of emotion? Was Patrizia his girl-friend or not? What if Marco had killed Patrizia to punish Maestri? Or to scare him? Yes, to scare him. Maestri was his accomplice in something, and wanted out. Trafficking in expired drugs, or organs taken from South American babies. Defrauding the health authorities, or performing euthanasia on a series of wealthy old people, or carrying out unauthorised drug trials. You heard so much about doctors and hospitals! Even the most horrible things could be true. But why get rid of the body? To carry on, to make the intimidation even more cynical.

Agrate Brianza exit, no more tailbacks towards Venice.

What if those unauthorised trials had been conducted jointly by Callegari and Maestri with Patrizia as their guinea pig? Maestri seduces her, the two doctors together subject her to their experiments. Then something goes wrong: Callegari kills her and Maestri, with the help of his undertaker uncle, gets rid of the body. And was Benedetta mixed up in all this somehow? Was she only acting out of posthumous love? Or did her family's holdings include a pharmaceutical laboratory involved in unlawful experimentation? And what about me? How much at risk was I? Would they kill me, too? All the self-confidence I'd shown in front of Stefano was ebbing away, overcome by these fantasies, this confusion. Yes, it was the confusion more than anything that made my temples throb.

A4, Bergamo exit, turn right, Via Bonomelli, Viale Papa Giovanni, Via Camozzi, Via Pignolo, Pignolo Alta, Sant'Agostino: end of the trance.

The cold air woke me and the winter serenity of the square in front of Sant'Agostino, with its lawn and its trees and the old houses in the background, cheered me up. The old city seemed to protect me: a return to the womb, to the streets where I'd played as a little girl, during the summers I spent here with my grandmother, far from my parents' quarrels, far from the unknown towns where my father's work took us every two or three years. I set off along the sloping Via di Porta Dipinta, gazing at the buildings on my right, imagining how life must have been in those houses when the families who had built them were at the height of their glory. Once past the long balcony that constituted the only view from the street onto the Lower City, I started to hear the powerful notes of a piano, or perhaps two. It was said that in one of the last houses before the Via di Porta Dipinta comes out into the Piazza Mercato delle Scarpe, there lived two twins who were exceptional pianists. I didn't know them, I'd never even seen them, but it was true that music often came from those windows, music that made you want to stop right there in the street and sit on the ground to listen. And on that late morning, with the milky light pouring down from the sky, those notes of music helped to make the return to the great womb of the mother city particularly pleasant.

I bought a couple of things at the mini-market in the Via Gombito and at last headed for home. On the stairs I remembered that I'd just spent another night away from home and prepared myself for Morgana's anger, as if I didn't already have enough problems of my own.

Instead of which, my cat was waiting for me behind the door, happy to see me. As soon as I entered, she started circling me, rubbing against me and miaowing. I put down the bags, threw my coat on a chair and took her in my arms, hugging her to me.

Morgana. The warmth of her body, the softness of her fur, the deep vibration of her purring. She seemed to understand when it was the right time to give me her affection. Some people find the affection of a cat or a dog a small thing. After all, it's only an animal, they say, it's because you feed it, they say. That's not how it is, a dog, a cat, a mere beast, as they say, is capable of a love that's total, even possessive sometimes, but always freely given. I needed Morgana, I needed her completely genuine affection. I needed it in order to forget for a moment the risks I was running, Patrizia's body, Dr Maestri's equivocal behaviour, the road with the prostitutes emerging from the fog like scantily clad ghosts, Stefano and our tender inability to love each other, Marco who had perhaps used me and might even decide to kill me. It was the first time my life had been in danger, or the first time I knew that it was. We're in danger every day, every time we step off the pavement, take a plane, go to the bank: we might never return home. And yet what I was feeling was different: darker, more imminent, more threatening.

I was tempted to phone Benedetta and tell her that there was nothing more to be done, and then to call Stefano and reassure him: you can stop worrying, I've dropped the whole thing. But would giving it all up be enough to keep me safe?

If Marco really was the killer, would he be content not to see me around anymore? Haunted by the suspicion that I'd discovered something, would he leave me alone? He knew everything about me: where I lived, what I did, what car I drove, he even knew the stifled scream that escapes my lips when I reach orgasm. He knew too much about me, and I felt ashamed that I'd granted him all that knowledge so easily, that I'd put myself in danger through my own actions.

But now I really was in danger, an about-turn wouldn't be enough to make me safe. So no phone call to Benedetta, no phone call to Stefano. Just keep going and watch my back. Keeping going had become a necessity, to see if I'd made any enemies, to put a face to them, to figure out what had happened and then get out, whether with my head held high or my tail between my legs didn't matter, but get out intact and resume my life, my real life, my normal life. I thought I could do it, but once again I was wrong.

The afternoon passed slowly, and I found it impossible to do anything other than watch the daylight gradually fade over the roofs of Bergamo until it turned into a darkness punctuated with lights.

A simple, almost poverty-stricken dinner, with a little cheese and a pasta soup: a cuckold's soup, as a friend of mine used to call it, because she said that wives who were too busy with their lovers made it in the evening, hurriedly, for their husbands. Water, a stock cube and a little pasta of your choice, cooked in an instant. And Morgana on the table, a h

now, with a plastic plate containing a little minced, slightly burnt meat. Two old maids.

Then television. Nothing interesting to watch. A little channel hopping and in the end, for no particular reason, I switched to RAI3. *Have you seen them?* was on, a pro-gramme filled with stories of wives who run away from home, old people who lose their memories and vanish dur-ing a train journey, men who leave for the fields or a build-ing site and never come back, perhaps murdered, their bodies never found. Hundreds of people vanishing into thin air every year. And there was the female presenter, giving news, reconstructing cases, showing photographs to the viewers in the hope that someone may have seen them. I followed all this distractedly, my head still buzzing with dark, frightening thoughts. Then I dozed off.

I was woken by the ringing of the phone.

'Are you watching television?' Stefano's voice was strangely agitated.

'Actually, I fell asleep.'

'Then wake up because RAI3 Channel is showing an item about someone who disappeared in Vittuone.'

'I'll have a look. Bye.'

'Bye.'

I turned up the volume.

'...and this is the village, on the outskirts of Milan, where Pasquale was last seen. We have a short interview with the witness who contacted us after watching our pro-gramme two weeks ago.'

They cut from the studio to an exterior shot. Below a grey sky, there was a street, with a lot of traffic, and on the other side a low building bearing the sign *Bar – Snacks.* I recognised the place. It was where the Strada alle Cascine crossed the main road.

'It was in this bar,' an off-screen voice said, 'a bar patronised mostly by workers and clerks from the local companies, that Pasquale Avvisato was last seen. The young man from Sicignano degli Alburni had last contacted his family on 22 November, calling them from a phone booth, since which time they had heard nothing more from him. But Signor Carmine Gammella, owner of this bar, claims he saw him here on 29 November. Let's hear what he has to say.'

Now they cut to inside the bar, and a close-up of a man in his sixties, leaning on the counter.

'I remember the boy well. He used to come here on Mondays, at lunchtime.'

The interviewer interrupted him. 'Every Monday?'

'Every Monday from the end of October, four Mondays in a row. He'd sit there in the back, take the *Gazzetta dello Sport* and read all the football pages.'

'Did he come alone?'

'The first couple of times, yes, but the last two times he was with a girl, a brunette, young, who spoke with a strange accent, French I think. He'd look at the paper, they'd chat a bit and then leave.'

I started paying more attention.

'Did you think the girl was his friend, his girlfriend?'

'Hard to say. They certainly didn't seem to dislike each other, but I couldn't say if they were friends or if...' He gave a weak smile and spread his arms.

The interviewer, who was still off-camera, persisted with another question. 'Are you sure the last time you saw him was 29 November last year?'

'Yes, I'm sure, because he was a Salernitana supporter, like me, and I remember we talked about the game the day before with Vicenza: Salernitana 3, Vicenza 1. And Salernitana played Vicenza on 28 November. I have a good memory for football matches, we do the pools here…'

'And did he seem restless, nervous?'

'Not at all, he was the calmest man in the world.'

'Are you sure it was Pasquale Avvisato?'

'He never told me his name, but when we talked about Salernitana for the first time, he told me he was from Sicignano. And the face you showed on TV is definitely him. I have a good memory for faces, too.'

The interview ended there, and they showed his mother's appeal, indicating that it was a repeat.

'Pasquale was as good as gold,' a devastated-looking woman said to camera. 'Everyone liked him, everyone. He studied chemistry and even found a job, only he said they weren't putting him on the books and there wasn't any security, so he quarrelled with the boss of the factory and after that no one would give him work. That was why he went up North, because he said things were different there, they respect people's rights there. I beg you, Pasquale, tell us where you are, tell us if you need anything. We're all here, me, your father, your sisters, we're here waiting for you. Phone us, all we need to know is that you're well.'

Then they went back to the studio and the presenter gave the address of the programme's website, where further details and photographs of Pasquale Avvisato could be found. I sat staring at the TV set for a moment or two longer, but they went on to another disappearance. So I switched off, went to the computer and connected to the internet. After a few moments Pasquale's face, with its long thick beard, was looking at me from the screen. I printed his details:

PASQUALE AVVISATO
Age (at the time of his disappearance): 25
Height: 1.60m
Build: slight
Eyes: brown.
Hair: black. Thick black beard.
Disappeared from: outskirts of Milan
Date of disappearance: 22 November
Clothes: details not available
Broadcast: 7 February

Pasquale Avvisato, a young man from Sicignano degli Alburni (SA), left his home town in September last year to look for work in Lombardy. According to his parents, Pasquale was having difficulty finding work and with his chemistry diploma he was sure he would find a good job in the North. About the beginning of October, he telephoned his family to say that he had found a job but was unable to tell them anything further. Pasquale did not own a mobile phone and called home once a week from public phone booths.

His last phone call was on 22 November, after which the family received no further news from him. During the broadcast of 7 February, the young man's mother appealed to him to contact his family and let them at least know that he was well.

Update, 12 February:

The owner of a bar in the municipality of Vittuone (MI) claims to have seen Pasquale Avvisato on several occasions, the last of them on 29 November, in the company of a young woman with brown hair. The young man seemed calm. An interview with the witness will be broadcast on our 21 February edition.

The girl with brown hair, Vittuone, the bar close to where Patrizia worked: coincidence, or was there a connection? There was now a new figure in the already confused picture swirling around in my mind. Pasquale Avvisato. He had last been seen on 29 November, and the very next day, 30 November, Patrizia was mown down by a grey BMW X5 with a yellow sticker on the rear windscreen. It was hard not to think that the two events were linked. But then I would also have to establish a link between Pasquale Avvisato, Marco Callegari and Paolo Maestri. That was a lot of men involved with a girl as nondescript as Patrizia!

I still couldn't figure any of it out, and couldn't see a way through. There I was, on the sofa, thinking, shuffling the images of the people involved like cards in a game of solitaire. Tiredness gradually overcame my reflections: I felt it descend like a veil over my eyes, making me woozy and gently wafting me to sleep. Completely lethargic now, I got ready to go to bed. Around me, everything was silent. No one in the streets, no cars, even Signora Ghislandi's television was off. I switched off the bedroom light and in the dark I saw something flashing on the bedside table: there was a message on my mobile. I picked it up, without switching it on, and read:

I want to see you again, I need to see you again. Marco.

Goodbye lethargy, goodbye sleep: I knew now I was going to have a restless night, tossing and turning in bed, with no chance at all of dropping off.

The thought of Marco was more painful than my back. I could feel his presence, close to me, and it made me feel nauseous. Alina had said she had seen lots of girls get in his car. He was not only a murderer, he was also a regular customer of prostitutes. Marco had a family, a wife who was an engineer, and quite likely had other affairs, and yet he wasn't averse to the idea of paying for the occasional fleeting thrill, doing things a doctor like him should have known were risky. Why did someone like him go with whores? True, Hollywood stars did it, too, but to me it didn't make sense. Perhaps it was a desire for domination, for total and absolute possession, but that seemed equally strange to me.

The feeling of disgust wouldn't go away.

It was an ambiguous sensation, an outburst of self-righteousness.

That same morning I'd seen Alina, I'd talked to her, I'd even felt some affection for her, and yet the fact that Marco went to bed with me and with women like her made me feel degraded, soiled. I was ashamed to realise that, deep down, I was just as prejudiced against whores as anyone else.

I'm digging faster now, with more energy. The action of the adrenocorticotropic hormone, ACTH, has stimulated the medullary area of the surrenal glands, and adrenalin has also entered the circulation. That means my body is able to react appropriately to fear. But it isn't courage, it's only desperation.

I've made a first hole. At last forty centimetres deep. The noise of the shovel has been rhythmical, regular: the liquid rustling of the earth as it opens, the pregnant silence as that same earth is lifted and dumped a bit further away. Rustling and silence. Rustling and silence. Nothing else.

Two cars come along the road, travelling together. They stop by a group of three women. It could be a police swoop, I think, but no one gets out of the car, nor do the girls try to run away. I have a sense there's a small amount of haggling, then they get in: two in the car in front, one in the car behind. The cars seem full. An orgy?

They drive off. And the silence returns.

Another car. It doesn't even slow down. Probably it's already got its load. I try to figure out what car it is, to see if I'm able, from that distance, to recognise the 4x4 that might lead to my death. Although they're not called 4x4s, they're called SUVs, but they're basically the same. The car that's passing doesn't look like an SUV. As it passes the fires, it looks more like a long saloon in shape, a Mercedes, or something like that.

Will he come here tonight? Or is this a night off, to be spent with his wife and family? If he does come, will he see me or will he only be thinking of getting down to the nitty-gritty, screwing whichever girl's on duty?

I abandon the first hole, in which there's nothing but earth, and doggedly start a second one, a few centimetres further on.

Another car stops by the girls, this one could be it. It's big, high, rather square at the back. But I can't see the head-lights. It's the shape of the lights that distinguishes that model from all the other SUVs.

A girl gets in and the car sets off again, disappearing into the distance. Whatever it was, the driver didn't see me.

I start digging again. And remembering.

Tuesday, 22 February

A slight noise like the ticking of an old wall clock. Then a breath and a little flop on the mattress: Morgana had jumped on the bed. No, she wasn't demanding her breakfast yet, it was her way of getting the day off to a good start, and it was a good start for me too: her nose under my chin, her body stretched out against mine, her purring. Light was filtering between the slats of the closed shutters, a weak, cold light. It must have been about seven: too early to really get up, too late to find the sleep I'd been pursuing in vain all night. I freed myself for a moment from Morgana's embrace and went to the kitchen, to light the wooden stove. My grandmother had never wanted to have central heating installed: she said it made the air too dry and gave you a cough. So she'd warmed herself all her life with that exact same stove, exactly like Signora Ghislandi downstairs. With the poker I removed the cast iron rings and put in two pieces of wood, then put the rings back in their place. Through the small door at the bottom, I slid in a lighted piece of newspaper and stood watching as the magic of fire slowly enveloped the wood. I liked those gestures, that ritual. When I was in a hurry in the morning, I contented myself with the electric radiator, which only came on at the preset hour, but whenever I had the time I allowed myself the luxury of that complicated, archaic procedure. When I clearly heard the noise of the fire inside the stove I went back to bed, and slid in under the duvet, where Morgana was waiting for me.

While the apartment gradually warmed up, I thought again about how to proceed, what to do to extricate myself as quickly as possible from that situation where everyone, Marco, Maestri, Benedetta, seemed like deadly enemies. I had to find some scrap of evidence I could take to the police in order to accuse one of them, or even all of them. Right now, as Dr Maestri had reminded me, I had nothing. So I'd have to carry on, make more inquiries, formulate new hypotheses. Like a detective, but without a gun, without a repertoire of judo moves, without the slightest idea of how an investigation was carried out.

The new lead to follow was Pasquale Avvisato. Was he a friend of Patrizia's? Her lover? Was the little Cinderella capable of betraying her prince in the white coat? Was her prince capable of killing her in a jealous rage? Could anyone feel so strongly about a girl like Patrizia – hardly your average *femme fatale* – as to kill her in a jealous rage? What was hidden behind her demure façade?

As usual I lost myself in a maze of conjectures, forgetting the hypothesis that was the basis of everything: was Patrizia the girl who was with Pasquale Avvisato in that bar?

'I get the idea,' I said to myself. 'I need to spend another day in Vittuone.'

I finally got out of bed and opened the shutters. It was foggy, even in the Upper Town, which meant that out in the Po Valley it would be like swimming in a glass of water and pastis, with not much water and a lot of pastis.

I went into the kitchen and Morgana followed me. I emptied some bites into her bowl, but she didn't seem to appreciate that: she wanted the tin and I knew it, even though I'd pretended to ignore it. Our tastes in the morning didn't coincide: she didn't find those little balls of dried food very appetising, while I found the smell her stewed morsels spread through the apartment quite nauseating, especially before coffee. But she had won.

To get away from the stench, I took refuge in the bathroom: I had time that morning, time to take a shower, to massage my thighs with anti-cellulite cream, to count my white hairs in front of the mirror, to feel a little older, though perhaps not yet ready for the scrapheap.

I decided I even had time to leave the car in the car park and go by train. I got the railway timetable, which I always kept around through force of habit, or perhaps as a curious memento of my father, Ernesto Pavesi, who, after many transfers and promotions, had risen to become deputy head of repairs for the State Railways. When I was a child, my father would take me to see the trains, regretting perhaps that I wasn't a boy and didn't want to become an engine driver. We would watch from the bridge as the trains passed and he would point out the different kinds of carriages and their serial numbers. Then he would tell me about the routes those trains took, where they were going, what time they would arrive. And I would listen to him, not sure why he was telling me all this, but fascinated anyway, entranced by the names of the towns, which seemed so distant and exotic.

I noted the times on the back of an old photocopy: the 2620 Bergamo-Milan express, departing at 9.48, arriving at Central Station in Milan at 10.35, then the 11.20 train to Rho, arriving at 11.36, and finally the local Rho-Vittuone train, leaving Rho at 11.58, arriving in Vittuone at 12.06. I'd think about how to get back once I'd got through the things I had to do.

I put on a pair of jeans, just for a change, a polo shirt, a sweater and trainers, knowing I'd have to do quite a bit of walking. Then I put my mobile, my purse and a few other things in a rucksack and left. I set off for the funicular station in the Piazza Mercato delle Scarpe. When I was on board and waiting to depart, I exchanged a few words with the driver, not so much for the pleasure of making a comment on the cold, foggy weather, but to feel like a genuine inhabitant of Bergamo, a fully paid-up member of that little world, marked by tradition and custom, of the old city on the hill. The funicular descended silently, as if ploughing a furrow, between the gardens of luxurious, inaccessible mansions. Then I took bus number 1, which crossed the centre of the Lower Town to the railway station.

The train was one of those double-decker ones which fill up with commuters in the morning. At this hour it was almost empty. I took a seat on the top deck, to enjoy a view of the frost-covered fields, even though I knew the dirty window panes and thick fog wouldn't let me see much. On the other hand, as was often the case, the most interesting view was inside, in the faces and the gestures of the few passengers. What about that old man, who was sitting next to the stairs, Turkish I guessed, his face so still and furrowed it looked like stone? Where was he going with that case full of cigarette lighters, small sponges and paper handkerchiefs, which was slung around his neck with a cord from a roller blind?

And what about those two young girls, who surely should have been at school at that hour? What were they going to Milan for? Window shopping? Dreaming of a future as models? As usual, I wasn't sure whether to feel envy or compassion for that age of hope. At their age, I was wearing an orthopaedic corset and my one hope was that I could take it off. I was actually quite a pretty girl and could probably have allowed myself more frivolous dreams, but we didn't have frivolous dreams in my family, and besides, with that corset coming all the way up to my neck… Anyway, I'd been spared the disappointment of getting within a hair's breadth of my goal and then falling down: getting to be almost a ballerina, almost a beauty queen, or almost an actress. I couldn't even imagine getting close to my goal and when, at the age of seventeen and a half, I finally took off the corset, it seemed too late to chase after adolescent dreams, too late for anything except a quiet life, an interesting profession and a man who loved me. But not even someone who's content with that is totally safe from illusions.

At Cassano d'Adda a girl got on, probably a university student. Before she sat down, she cleaned the seat with a napkin and, with a disgusted air, moved a free ads magazine that some inconsiderate traveller had left there. From her bag she took an orange wrapped in a paper napkin, spread the napkin on the seat facing hers, and as she peeled the orange placed the peel on it. Instead of a wrapped brioche full of saturated and unsaturated fats, this health fanatic was eating a wholesome, juicy orange, segment by segment. When the train pulled in to the station and the girl stood up to get off, she left the napkin with the peel on the seat.

Central Station, a crossroads of trains and destinies, sounds and announcements, endless delays and departing trains, people running, ticket checkers on platform twelve, groups of Japanese, Sinhalese cleaners, rolls served with natural bad grace, kiosks with windows full of porn cassettes, little models of the cathedral, either phosphorescent or lying on a bed of shells, and other unlikely souvenirs.

For once, I didn't miss either of my connections, and I was in Vittuone barely twenty minutes after the scheduled time.

By the time I'd crossed the village and found myself on the main road, I regretted coming on foot. The roads of the Milanese hinterland are not made for solitary walkers: the cars seem constantly to brush against you and the lorries appear to want to throw you to the ground just by displacing the air. I walked on the edge, in the thin strip between the asphalt and the low walls that marked the boundaries of properties, amid clumps of grass, waste paper, tin cans and cigarette packets. It was like walking in a very narrow no man's land.

After lots of frights and curses, I finally reached the crossroads, which I knew well by now. On one side was the bar where Pasquale Avvisato had been seen, on the other, the unpaved side road. I stood there for a moment, undecided as to what to do, then looked at the time and saw that it was nearly one. I hoped I'd still be able to find Patrizia's employer, Signor Imperiale. I took the side road and then, at the first fork, the short path that led to the factory. Before I even went in, I threw a glance at the outside canopy to check that Imperiale's car was there. And there it was, the Porsche Cayenne, symbol of wealth achieved and displayed, shiny, black, new, with its tilted oval headlights which made the front look like the face of a smiling Chinese man.

I repeated the same route as on my first visit, and again met no one in the corridors or on the stairs. I peered in through the open door of the owner's Spartan office and, seeing him busy on the phone, knocked. The expression on his face was halfway between surprise and annoyance. He motioned me to sit down.

It wasn't a long phone call. Replacing the receiver, Imperiale held out his hand, cordial once again. 'Nice to see you.'

'Sorry to disturb you again, but this'll only take a few minutes.'

'Go on.'

Before getting to the point, I made the usual excuse of wanting to pay the funeral expenses.

'Like I already said,' he replied, 'I did it willingly.' Then, lowering his voice, he continued, 'Anyway, part of the money was what I owed Patrizia as her salary for November, which we pay at the end of the month, so let's not talk about it anymore.'

'Well, thank you again. I'd just like to ask you another question. Where did Patrizia eat lunch?'

'Usually here in the office. Her landlady made her a roll, or put some vegetables in a plastic container, and she'd eat it here.'

'Never outside, in a bar, for example?'

'That may have happened a couple of times, no more than that.'

'I'm sorry, one more thing, and it really is the last one. Did you know Pasquale Avvisato?'

The tone of his answer was polite but firm. 'Can't say I've ever heard the name. Was he a friend of Patrizia's?'

'Possibly. He was mentioned on *Have you seen them?* last night. He's disappeared.'

I showed him the information about Pasquale I'd print-ed off the internet. He looked at it, somewhat hurriedly, then handed it back.

'And why are you looking for him here?'

'I know it seems a bit odd, but last night on TV they said he was seen in Vittuone in the company of a girl who, from the description, could well have been Patrizia. Of course, there must be millions of girls like her. Patrizia was nothing special to look at...'

'I thought she was a nice-looking girl.'

It was strange that someone like him, who the previous time had revealed his embarrassment with women, should let slip a comment about Patrizia's physical appearance, a comment I agreed with purely out of politeness.

'Yes, in a fresh-faced kind of way, I suppose.'

'Anyway, that's all I can tell you, I'm sorry.'

'Not at all. You've already been too kind.'

I stood up, shook hands with him and left. It was the turn of the bar.

I asked for a toasted ham and cheese sandwich and a small beer and sat down at a little round table by the window. Outside, the procession of lorries continued, and inside, so did the procession of office workers who, once their quick meal was over, went to order their coffee from the counter. The regulars were clearly split between people who ate at the square tables and people, like me, who picked at something at the little round tables. From the square tables, covered with paper tablecloths and dishes heated in the microwave, rose laughter, political debate, loud gossip. At the round tables, silence reigned. They were occupied by people on their own, reading the newspaper while biting into indigestible rolls. Or else, though in smaller numbers, they were occupied by clearly furtive couples. Colleagues who'd become lovers after being friends, finding a common bond through a smile, or a warmer tone while saying, 'Could you pass me the Federzoni file, please?' I couldn't help imagining them, in their offices, exchanging increasingly tender glances: she has a problem with her computer, he goes to help her, stands behind her, one hand on the desk and the other on the back of her chair, then an error message appears on the screen, he leans forward, towards the monitor, to read better, and their cheeks almost touch, they can feel the warmth of each other's face. Until one day, helped by the absence of two colleagues laid low with flu, they're alone in the office and they kiss: that first long kiss. And then the rest follows: the passion, the lies, the emotion of meeting again, the guilt feelings, the apartment of a friend of his who's away on a long journey, the excuse of a girls' night out. And those lunch breaks, those oases of tenderness and drama: 'I love you', 'I can't stand this anymore', 'If it wasn't for the children...', 'We have to come to a decision'.

I waited until all those people had swarmed out and back to their bills and files and the premises were virtually deserted before approaching the owner – Signor Carmine Gammella, if I remembered correctly.

'Good afternoon. I saw you on television last night and I'd like to ask you something.'

'Please, go ahead.'

He was a small man, with excessively tight-fitting black trousers and a flowered waistcoat.

I took Patrizia Vitali's identity card from my bag and showed it to him. 'Could you tell me if this is the girl you saw with Pasquale Avvisato?'

'Oh dear, it's not a very good photo, and so small...

Salvo, pass me my glasses, they're next to the coffee machine.'

The boy at the counter gave him a pair of glasses for long sight, the kind you can buy in pharmacies. The man looked closely at Patrizia's face and finally concluded, 'I'd say that's her. I notice it's a French identity card, and that girl, the one who was with the boy, spoke with a French accent. Has she disappeared too?'

'No, unfortunately she's dead.'

He crossed himself, completing the gesture by kissing the hand with which he had made it. 'And this boy, this Pasquale, does he have something to do with her death?'

There was a hint of the inquisitorial in the man's voice, as if he was hypothesising not only a connection between Pasquale's disappearance and Patrizia's death, but also the possibility that Pasquale was guilty of it. Yes, Pasquale kills Patrizia then disappears to throw everyone off the scent. Why hadn't I thought of that? Perhaps because of Marco's X5. That was the fly in the ointment, the thing that complicated what was otherwise a very straightforward story: Patrizia is friendly with Pasquale Avvisato, the latter misunderstands and asks for something more, but Patrizia is already involved with Dr Maestri and is faithful to him, leading to a fit of homicidal madness.

But that was it: Pasquale seemed more like the kind of person who'd use a knife, who'd act suddenly, in the heat of the moment, not the kind of person who'd cold-bloodedly lie in wait in the fog, on board a large car, what's more a car that wasn't his. We were back with Marco's X5.

What if Pasquale had stolen it? What if he *had* been much more cold-blooded than I thought? He steals a car and uses it to kill the woman who's rejected him.

I came back down to earth. 'Did you see the girl at other times, or only with Pasquale?'

'I saw her twice and both times she was with Pasquale.'

'Did you hear them arguing or quarrelling?'

'Oh, no, not at all, they seemed to get on like a house on fire.'

'Has anyone else asked you about this girl?'

'No, signora, you're the first.'

'What was your impression of her?'

'I don't know, she seemed very well-bred, very kind, a bit sad but kind.'

The same old story. I didn't know what else to ask. So I thanked him, paid and left.

I had the impression that every new piece of information merely served to confuse my ideas even more. A new character would appear, and that character might be a victim or a killer, or even be completely uninvolved, but had the effect of increasing the chaos and indecision in my mind, and throwing a new light on facts I'd so far taken for granted, like Marco's role in the murder for example. I didn't know why the idea that his car had been stolen hadn't occurred to me until the figure of Pasquale had put in an appearance, but now I couldn't get it out of my mind. Marco's car is stolen, then he gets it back, blithely unaware of the fact that it's been used in a murder. Marco innocent: that would be wonderful! But what about the Marco who uses prostitutes? The theft idea didn't explain that, just as it didn't explain Dr Maestri's curious behaviour, or tell me all I needed to know about Pasquale.

Chaos, chaos, nothing but chaos.

Once again, I had the impression that everything revolved around cars, which really weren't my scene: the fact that I'd been married to an engineer for Fiat had merely increased my lack of interest in cars. But there was someone living nearby who seemed to live for engines: Abdelkader. Perhaps he'd noticed the movements of cars in the area. If Marco's BMW X5 really was the key to everything, Abdel might be able to tell me more. I set off along the unpaved road again. It was so much easier to walk here, I said to myself, without lorries brushing against you and threatening to run you over every two minutes. A moment later I realised how stupid I was: the only reason I was here, on this road, was precisely because a girl had been knocked down and killed in this very place. So much for feeling safe! And in that fog! You could feel it sticking to you, streaming through your hair, getting inside your clothes. Even the tall trees lining the path were hidden by the cold vapour until you got close to them. At ten paces, they were simply grey lines, blurred and dark. At five paces, they were black columns, the bases of which were visible, but which disappeared as they rose so that you couldn't see the tops at all. At one pace, they revealed their true nature, the rough, bare bark, but as soon as you passed them and you happened to look back, they were again swallowed by the whitish cotton wool. You couldn't have said if you were in the third millennium or the Middle Ages. The only signs of civilisation the eye could make out were my trainers and the refuse thrown in the ditch or snagged in the brambles: waste paper, pages torn from porn magazines, plastic containers, and a few iron drums. But forgetting those objects, you felt like a pilgrim, a wayfarer in an unknown land, haunted by brigands or evil spirits. And my brigands, my evil spirits were called Marco, Patrizia, Benedetta, Paolo, Pasquale. It was in their company that I walked the two kilometres that separated me from the farmhouse, and anyone who saw me would probably have thought I, too, was a ghost.

When I got to the farmyard, I ran straight into Signora Bono, who was carrying a big plastic bucket full of burnt polenta. She greeted me and, perhaps thinking me so unaccustomed to country life as to be unable to understand what she was doing, she carefully explained, 'I'm taking the polenta to the hens, they go mad for polenta, so whatever's stuck to the pot I give to them.'

Trying to hold my own in the conversation, I replied, 'Yes, whenever I went to see my in-laws in the country, I always gave leftover polenta to the neighbours' hens.'

'That's a pity. We usually only give hens the polenta that's stuck to the pot, the leftovers are for human beings. Fried in a pan in the evening, then bathing in milk the next day.'

It was true, one of my happiest childhood memories was the polenta and milk my grandmother used to give me: I would leave some polenta just so that I could have it again at the next meal in a bowl drowning in warm milk. But now wasn't the time to get carried away by memories.

'I'm sorry, Signora Bono, but do you think I could have a word with Abdelkader? It's about a car. He knows a lot about cars and he may be able to help me.'

'Have they found the car that knocked Patrizia over?'

'It's possible. Someone says they recognised the kind of car it was.'

'God be praised. When they catch him, they ought to shoot him, and I mean shoot him. A lovely girl, young, beautiful, fresh as a rose… What a terrible end. We need the death penalty!'

She paused for breath, letting her anger subside in a long sigh that continued her words in a different form.

'I'll call Abdel.'

She put down the bucket and walked to the shed where the agricultural machinery was kept. After a few minutes, she reappeared with the young Moroccan and a thickset man who, despite his white hair and lined face, seemed to exude brute strength.

Signora Bono picked up the bucket again and with her free hand pointed at the man. 'My husband.'

'Pleased to meet you.'

I held out my hand and he shook it without a word.

'I'm going to see to the hens. I'll leave you to talk.'

There was something about the three of us standing there at the edge of the yard that seemed somehow timeless, just like my walk. It was cold but they didn't invite me to come inside and sit down.

'Have you ever seen a silver-grey BMW X5 pass by on the road?' I asked Abdel.

He looked at me in astonishment. 'Only one? There are dozens of them, morning, noon and night. There are a lot of rich people around here. Everyone's rich except us Moroccans.' He laughed, and even his laughter seemed to have a Lombard inflection.

'What do they come this way for?'

It wasn't that I didn't know, but I wanted to be sure how much he knew.

'Obviously, they come for the girls. Haven't you noticed how many there are?'

Signor Bono hadn't said a word, but seemed to be listening to everything with great interest. It took me a moment to realise that what he was most interested in was me. He was staring at me, undressing me with his eyes, or it might be more accurate to say that he was tearing the clothes off me. What I saw in his eyes wasn't so much desire as a kind of animal hunger and all the mental pictures that conjured up: foaming at the mouth, physical violence, possession, mauling. I tried to ignore him.

'But among all these X5s, did you by any chance notice one in particular? One with a yellow sticker in the shape of a scuba diver on the rear window?'

'Ah, yes, the seven o'clock minibus!'

'What?'

'That was what I called it, because last autumn, when I was doing the last part of my mechanic's course, I used to see it every morning when I was on my way to school.'

'And did you ever see the driver?'

Signor Bono took his eyes off my thighs for a moment and looked straight at Abdel.

'No. It was too dark in the morning and I was too sleepy. Sometimes I saw it parked near the girls, but I didn't look inside, people don't like you looking them in the face when they're with whores.'

Bono sniggered in a kind of grimace: he'd started staring at me again. In the meantime, I was seething inside. So, I really had been special for Marco: a free fuck instead of all those paid ones!

'One morning,' Abdel went on, 'I even saw it parked on the other road, the one that leads to the main road but further over, towards Magenta. It was parked next to that small wood and there was no one in it.'

'Perhaps the owner was in it with one of the girls.'

'I don't think so, it was too early. I was taking the hay to the cows on the Malpensata farm, so it must have been five-thirty. At that hour the girls aren't there yet. And besides…' – he lowered his eyes, almost embarrassed – 'when the girls are on board the cars never park, they keep moving. But the BMW was actually parked next to the wood.'

At the time, I didn't know how much weight to give this information. Now, unfortunately, I do. But in any case, I decided to dig a little deeper.

'Was that before or after Patrizia's death?'

Abdel did not have to think about it for long. 'It was the same day. Now I come to think about it, I realise it was the same day Patrizia had the accident. I remember because I was at the Malpensata farm until eight and when I got back here it had just happened. And I don't often go to the Malpensata farm, it's usually Mohamed who goes.'

On the one hand, what he'd just told me seemed like a vital piece of information, on the other it made me suspicious: I had the impression that what Abdel was saying was being tacitly dictated by Signor Bono, and that he was lying, as if Bono was only there to supervise his lies – apart from thinking disgusting thoughts about me, of course.

But if it was all true, it meant that the day Patrizia was killed, Marco's car had been in the area, ready and waiting. And now there was an extra witness: not only Alina, but also Abdelkader.

Despite the doubts I harboured on the young man's credibility and his landlord's role, I couldn't help asking one last question, about Pasquale. 'Do you know this man by any chance?'

I handed him the sheet of paper with the photograph. He looked at it and shook his head. 'I've never seen him before, but if you leave this paper with me I'll ask some friends from my country and let you know.'

'Of course.'

I thanked Abdel and took my leave of both of them, even Bono, who muttered 'Goodbye', shaking my hand firmly and looking me in the eyes like a hunter sizing up the prey.

Wondering again why on earth I hadn't taken my car, I set off once more. The landscape hadn't changed, but I noted that new ghosts had appeared, the usual ones: the prostitutes. Clearly the lunch break was over and the afternoon shift was starting. The first one I saw looked like a little girl who's stolen her elder sister's dress, the loud one their mother doesn't like: under her open black coat, she was wearing a very short dress, acid green in colour and very tight-fitting, practically a second skin that barely covered her private parts. I'd have liked to ask her the question I considered crucial, but too much time had passed since I'd harassed Alina, and my conscience wouldn't allow me to give another adolescent let down by life the third degree. I walked past and let her vanish in the fog behind me. I noticed that some of the plastic stools were still empty and assumed they would be filled only for the evening shift, when there was more traffic.

The second girl had such transparent skin and such light blonde hair that if it hadn't been for her short red dress I wouldn't even have seen her stand out against the pale grey of the background. I didn't have the courage to talk to her either: she looked so fragile, I was afraid my questions might break her in two, although I was sure she was used to far worse trials.

For a while I walked alone, tormented by my spirits, but without any ghosts on the road. It was only on the last stretch, when I was no more than a few hundred metres from the main road, that I saw a big, burly, almost fat girl, sheathed in a white polo-neck sweater that emphasised her decidedly ample breasts. I pretended that I was going to walk straight on, then, just as I came level with her, I asked, 'Excuse me, do you know a man who often comes here in a silver-grey BMW X5 with a yellow sticker on the rear windscreen?'

'Go away!'

'Please, just tell me if you know him.'

'I told you to go away!'

'Do you know him, yes or no?'

I might have seen it coming, I should have seen it coming, but I wasn't alert enough. She bent down, picked up a stone and before I'd even grasped the meaning of that movement, I felt a sharp pain in my cheek. I realised what was happening and started running, but couldn't avoid getting another stone in my back. I continued running and stopped only when my feet hit the asphalt of the main road. I was breathing heavily, my heart was pounding, and I had tears in my eyes: tears of anger. Anger at her and at myself, anger at Benedetta and even Patrizia, poor Patrizia, not to mention my anger at Marco. As if by conditioned reflex, I thought of Stefano, of his arms consoling me: but Stefano wasn't there, wasn't even at home, and would never be again.

I crossed the road and went into the bar where I'd had lunch, hoping my face wasn't swollen or purple.

I asked the owner if he knew where I could call for a taxi to take me to the station. He called it for me. 'It'll be here in five minutes. But what on earth did you do to your cheek?'

'I hit myself with a car door.'

'I'm sorry,' he replied, but I assumed he'd noted my answer as one of the worst excuses ever pleaded by a battered woman.

The taxi arrived, and half an hour later I was sitting on a train bound for Milan, where I changed to a train for Bergamo.

On the Milan-Bergamo train, I sat down on the upper deck, as I had on the outward journey. The nasal voice of a loudspeaker announced that the train would leave twenty minutes late. The seats around me were empty, but the heating, unusually, was on. After all the cold that had seeped into my bones during my walk, the heat that gradually overcame me was the one pleasure in a day that had gone badly, like so many others, though perhaps worse than most. I took off my jacket, folded it to make a pillow, and laid my cheek on it, the bruised one, so that it couldn't be seen. The voices of the station became ever more distant and muffled: the announcements, the screeching of brakes, the clanking of departing trains, everything grew softer. I took off my shoes and pulled my feet up, hugging my legs with the knees against my chest, in the childlike security of the foetal position, and fell into a deep sleep, the kind I only achieve on trains.

A noise woke me, a clamour of people suddenly entering the carriage. Instinctively I put my shoes back on and grabbed my bag, ready to get off, sure I'd reached my destination. I looked out. Milan Lambrate station. Only four kilometres travelled, another fifty-two to go.

The sweetness of sleep had faded. I decided to at last start the book I'd had with me for a while: Dürrenmatt's *The Pledge*. Before I knew it, I'd devoured the first twenty pages. I don't believe in destiny, but sometimes it seems as if books lie in wait for us, waiting to be read at a specific moment. I know that's not true, but I like to think it is, I like to think that the words with which Dürrenmatt begins his story were written precisely for my state of mind at that moment. 'You people construct your plots logically,' the character of the policeman was saying to the writer of detective stories, 'but in your novels chance plays no part.' The policeman was complaining about the lack of attention crime writers paid to chance, and about their senseless love of logical murders, knots all tied up, complex plots. Reading those lines I had the feeling that the policeman was right, that in Patrizia's story chance had played an important role. I wondered why I had that impression, that idea that the event had been basically a banal one, but couldn't find an answer.

By the time the train got into Bergamo station, I was on page thirty-eight and was reluctant to close the book.

Leaving the funicular station I found myself back in the warm embrace of the Upper Town, with its smell of burning firewood, its lights that still seemed like Christmas lights, even though they hadn't been Christmas lights for a while now, not since the light-hung fir tree that had occupied the entire front of the Agnello d'Oro hotel had been taken down. In passing it, I took a glance in that direction: I was right, it was no longer there. In compensation, an intense aroma of buckwheat polenta was coming from the restaurant opposite. I was tempted to go in, but the memory of the rough welcome the lady owner and the waiters usually reserved for their customers held me back. No, I would eat at home, a nice polenta with sausage, and it didn't really matter if it was a precooked polenta, ready in eight minutes, it didn't really matter if it didn't leave that thick burnt crust in the pot that Signora Bono gave her hens, it was still hot polenta.

If I were a well-built man, how deep would I dig the grave that's meant to keep my unmentionable secret? No less than a metre and a half. To avoid the rain, the scratching of a dog, the constant movement of the tree roots or some other banal accident which might bring to light a body that ought to be forgotten by everyone. But what if, apart from being a well-built man, I'm also in a hurry? In that case I might be content with a metre. Or even less.

But I'm not a well-built man, I'm just in a hurry and I have terrible backache.

My second dig has now reached more or less sixty centimetres and the shovel has just produced a muted, stifled noise.

I aim the torch, but again can't see anything. I switch it off immediately, out of fear.

I resume digging, but again that liquid rustling as the blade goes in is missing: something's blocking the shovel, and it isn't a stone. Instead of planting the shovel in the ground, I widen the hole, then shine the torch again. The bottom is no longer brown, it's pale blue: a fragment of material emerges from beneath the ground, a piece of denim.

I stop. I can still hear that muted noise in my head, but worst of all I can still feel the tactile impression of the moment when the shovel touched the body. Now I know exactly how a shovel sinking into a dead body sounds and feels and that sensation enters my memory, joining my list of gruesome recollections, like using scissors to cut up a lung for the cat, or placing my tongue on one of those porous cardboard discs that pastry cooks put under cakes.

I shine the torch again.

And I'm forced to walk away a few paces and rest my head against a tree.

I don't want to throw up. I don't want to throw up.

My God. And I thought the hardest part would be locating the corpse.

Are you happy now? I say to myself. You have your body now, the body you've been looking for all this time is within reach. Aren't you happy? Dig it up, bring it to light, confirm your psychologist's hypothesis. You know that little piece of leg that's peeking through isn't enough for you. You know that if you want to be really sure you have to get to the face, or what's left of it.

I approach the hole again. With my gloved hand, I move the earth that's still covering the material. I want to see if it's a pocket, or part of the trousers. That way, I'll have an idea of which direction to dig in so as to get to the face.

I mustn't throw up, I mustn't throw up. Not here. Not now.

But what I find under my fingers isn't a pocket, or a zip, or a belt. It's a piece of leg. Just a piece of leg.

And under the material I can also feel the flaccid texture of decomposed flesh.

I mustn't throw up, I mustn't throw up.

I must let my thoughts wander as I continue. Memories, I need memories.

Wednesday, 23 February

That morning, the mirror test was more tragic than usual. It wasn't just the white hairs to be counted, the skin of the face to be scrutinised for signs of sagging, large or small, the expression lines to be stretched with meagre results. It was also the very conspicuous bruise on my right cheekbone. On seeing it, my anger returned, and I almost choked with suppressed tears.

I was a grown-up woman, almost old, certainly too old for a whole lot of things. I should have been having a quiet life, with everything mapped out: husband, home, children to be picked up from school and taken to their judo or dance classes. Instead of which I was alone, childless and penniless. So penniless I'd had to accept an absurd job, a job in which prostitutes threw stones at me. I really had hoped for a better life than this. My anger showed no signs of abating. I decided to let off steam by attacking someone: someone in particular, the person who could well have been responsible for all of this. I grabbed my mobile and found Benedetta's number.

'Hello Benedetta, Anna here.'

'Who?'

'Anna Pavesi, the psychologist…'

'Oh yes, of course, I'm sorry, it's hard to hear you, I'm at the airport. Actually, I have to hurry because they've already called my flight.'

'Bullshit. Yesterday, when I was asking questions about your sister's murder, a prostitute threw a stone at my face and now I have a purple cheek.'

'I told you to drop it.'

'Aren't you interested in knowing who killed Patrizia?'

'No. All I wanted was to get her body back and avoid a scandal, but now it seems we risk uncovering something even more compromising, so I repeat: it's over. Finding a body is one thing, finding a murderer is another.'

'But what if whoever's blackmailing you for Patrizia's body is the same person who killed her?'

'No one's blackmailing me. Don't go getting such strange ideas.'

'I can't drop it, it's too late.'

'Why?'

'Because I know who killed her and that person knows that I know. So I'm in danger, too.'

There was a long silence, so long I thought we'd been disconnected. Then I heard Benedetta's voice again, as hard as ever, perhaps even more so.

'You're bluffing. Perhaps you think you can extort money from me with these sensational revelations, but I'm sure you're bluffing. In the next few days, I'll have a cheque sent to your address. Cash it and that'll be the end of it. Don't call me, don't come to see me, forget everything. Is that agreed?'

'You haven't understood a thing,' I said, and hung up.

I sat down and rested my head on the kitchen table. Well, I'd let off steam. That was the one positive result of my phone call to the woman with the double-barrelled name. The rest was just growing confusion. Each time I heard her voice, I had the impression she was involved somehow, but I could never figure out in what way. Above all, I could never figure out why she would have killed her half-sister. And yet I felt it, inside me, which was precisely the reason it didn't mean anything.

I switched on the radio, and, between one song and the next, heard the DJ who always imitated the Lombard businessman in his Porsche Cayenne. 'Here I am in my Cayenne,' he was saying, laying the accent on thick, 'looking at the people in a tailback on the ring road. It's my morning entertainment, then I go and play golf. Cayenne Turbo, go! Any other kind is for losers.' Businessmen from the Brianza region weren't the kind of people I usually rubbed shoulders with, but the two or three I had known really were like that: rich kids with expensive toys and an even bigger sense of their own power than the scions of the great families, families like Benedetta's. Northerners with lots of money, the kind of people who'd filled Romania with Italian factories and were now raking it in, in China or wherever else the global market led their recklessness.

I kept myself busy with housework, vacuuming the apartment, much to Morgana's annoyance, washing and even polishing the floors, but the thoughts kept niggling at me. Had Marco really killed Patrizia? How did the others – Pasquale, Dr Maestri, Benedetta – fit into the jigsaw? And above all, did one of them want to kill me? Thinking about it now, I tell myself that if I'd been more afraid then, I'd be less afraid now, I wouldn't even be here now. Instead of which, my unconscious gained the upper hand: I told myself I was exaggerating, that I'd be able to keep Marco at bay, and that when I had my answers about Pasquale, everything would be resolved. I should have run away, thrown them off the scent. But that seemed too melodramatic, too much like something you read about in a novel, a mystery novel. To convince myself, I picked up the Dürrenmatt, with its admonishments to see things clearly. I turned to page eleven and found a sentence that had struck me earlier: 'Forget about perfection if you want to get closer to things, to reality, as men should do, otherwise just keep quiet and do your stylistic exercises.' I shouldn't be scared by the fact that the characters didn't fit into a perfect criminal system, simply because, in all probability, there was no system, but only chance.

The afternoon was no different from the morning: an alternation of anxiety and reassuring lethargy.

But then, at six, the phone rang.

'Hi, it's me.'

I'd have liked to provoke him and ask, 'Me who?', but for the moment Stefano was still the only person who had the right to say just 'It's me'. He was still my point of reference, despite everything.

'Hi.'

'I wanted to know if you've managed to keep out of trouble.'

'It's not over yet, but I'm not in any trouble for the moment, apart from a bruise on the face.'

'Did someone hit you?'

'No, but a prostitute threw a stone at me. The prognosis is good, though. Two days, possibly less if treated with face powder and foundation cream.'

'You're making a joke of it, but I'm really worried. You're dealing with dangerous people.'

How could I tell him that the most dangerous person was the one I'd slept with? Was it more embarrassing to tell him about my newly-revived sex life or the fact that I'd let myself be fucked by a supposed murderer? Yes, fucked, because for him that was obviously all it had meant.

I tried to change the subject. 'I finished *The Pledge*. You were right, it's a terrific book.'

'Yes, it is. If you think about it, the story's nothing special, but it turns into a great tragedy.'

'It's tragic precisely because it doesn't need a particularly complicated plot. It's just the tragedy of life.'

'Ah, yes, the tragedy of life…'

'You sound tired. You always drawl like that when you've been sleeping badly.'

'I haven't slept at all for two nights, three if you count the one we spent together, which wasn't exactly restful.'

'Why's that?'

'Here at Fiat they've been laying people off. They only told me about it on Monday.'

'And how are you involved?'

'In the worst possible way: I have to decide who to let go. Do you know what that means? I have to go down on the shop floor and say, You won't be working for the next six weeks, starting next week, and you won't receive any salary.'

'Can't it be done in rotation?'

'No, they've decided not. It's their usual way of getting rid of the people they think are too disruptive. And it's my job to be their spokesman, their strong-arm man.'

'In other words, it's a dirty job but someone has to do it!'

'More or less. How do you choose between a family man with three children to support, but whose wife works, and a twenty-six-year-old woman who lives alone and barely manages on her salary? On what basis do you choose who to condemn to a six-week nightmare?'

'And is that why you've been losing sleep?'

'Of course. If you have the slightest conscience, you can't sleep at night because of something like that. But they don't have a conscience, all they know is how to cut, nothing else. At least if they knew how to make cars! At least if they had a revival plan. No, their one slogan is: cut expenditure. Cut and sell. Let's sell off the factories that make us a ton of money! It's all good building land, according to the town planning project – the project we ourselves drew up! But they don't come and tell the workers themselves, they send me and people like me.'

'Do you remember what Brighetti used to say, the engineer who lived with your family?'

'Of course. I didn't want to believe him, but it's true. Doing a job like that drives you mad.'

'For him, it was even worse.'

'Well, he had to organise that whole wave of sackings in the Eighties. And he did have to undergo psychiatric treatment for quite a while.'

'If you need therapy,' I tried to joke, 'we can come to an arrangement.'

'That's why I phoned you.'

'Because I'm a psychologist?'

'Because you're … because you were my wife, because you've always understood me.'

It was the kind of sentence that can wipe out years of humiliation in a flash, that can make all the lies and betrayals disappear. It was one of the most dangerous of sentences and I knew it was, but I still felt like hugging him, like taking his head in my lap and caressing him. To him, too, I was the only person who could say 'It's me', just 'It's me'.

'And what are you planning to do?'

'For the two most tragic cases, I've asked Michele and

Giorgio for help.'

'The guys who play five-a-side with you?'

'Yes, Michele has a repair shop, so I got him to hire this really good mechanic with a five-year old son who's always in hospital. And Giorgio, as you know, has that plastics company, and he's agreed to take on another guy who has a lot of problems at home.'

I wasn't the only one to lend him an ear, then, his friends from five-a-side were also there to help him out. He'd once told me that in the first few months after our separation one of the few things that cheered him up, apart from the company of his three oldest friends, was that Monday date, that insubstantial source of merriment, it was the thought that there would be at least one good thing in his week.

'What about the others?'

'I can only hope they don't hate me too much, that they understand it isn't my fault. As if finding someone to blame helped anyway.'

'I'd like to be there, with you.' I, too, had let slip a sentence meant for effect: it had escaped from deep inside me, from the uncontrollable region where affections lie.

'Why aren't you? Why did we separate?'

'Because you can't stay with only one woman.'

'That and a dozen other reasons, all perfectly valid. But doesn't it ever happen to you that you remember only the good times and forget the things that drove us apart?'

It did happen, but it was the last thing I would have admitted to him. 'I try not to let that happen,' I said. 'Some things aren't easily forgotten.'

'You know, I've never told you this, but there were four or five occasions, while we were still married, when it occurred to me that I was really happy. Which, when you get down to it, is something people almost never think. We always think of the things we're missing, but it's hard to think, "I'm happy". But I was happy and I did think it.' That was when he came out with it: 'Do you think we'll ever get back together?'

It was a quite a broadside, but I was ready for it. 'I don't think so, Stefano. I think it's too late for that.'

'You may be right.'

But was I? Would we ever find a way to stop mattering to each other?

We ended the call with a few pleasantries and a few marks of that difficult affection that still existed between us, then the evening continued and faded out with dinner and listlessly watching a film on TV.

Horror. From the Latin *horrere*, 'to have your hair stand on end'. When fear becomes horror, it's accompanied by a feeling of revulsion for what seems cruel or disgusting. Horror is a fear that goes beyond fear, beyond a point of no return.

Right now, the three forms of fear are coexisting in me: innate, socialised fear, horror and terror.

Innate fear is fear of the night, of the moment when, under cover of darkness, predators go into action. The fear of wild animals and storms, of ghosts, evil spirits, the dead.

Fear of the dead becomes horror if you have the dead person in front of you, under your nose. With his stench mingling with the odours of the countryside and the miasmas of the nearby city. With his body gradually revealing itself as the shovel continues its work.

To tell the truth, I'm trying to remove only a thin strip of earth, from the legs to the face. I go past the waist and what I see, however horrible it is, starts to confirm my theory. I try to remember the kind of clothes Signora Bono had taken to dress the dead girl: jeans, pullover and blouse, probably the only things Patrizia owned. Yes, the clothes that appear when my hand shifts the last layer of earth support my hypothesis.

And the more my hypothesis is strengthened, the greater grows the third form of fear, terror. Terror, the manuals say, is caused by the inevitability of pain linked to a certain threat. The terror of death is an emblematic example of that.

The threat terror provokes in me has four wheels and a solid body. At any moment I expect to see it stop beside one of the prostitutes, I expect to recognise it and to freeze. I expect that from that point the worst will begin. If there is something worse than all this.

And yet I thought I'd already seen the worst, I saw it yesterday. Only yesterday, but it already seems such a long time ago. Fear digs deep furrows in the line of memory.

Thursday, 24 February

Telephone.

'Hello?'

'Hi, it's Marco.'

Consternation. Why hadn't I left? Why hadn't I got away? What to do with Marco? Attack him as I'd attacked Maestri? The result might have been even worse.

'Can you hear me?'

'Yes, Marco, I can hear you, but it's a bad line.'

'Then of all the things I'd like to say to you, I'll say only the main one: shall we have dinner together tonight?'

Dinner with a killer. It was like the title of an American film. And he was still playing at being the lover: 'Of all the things I'd like to say to you…' Why not tell me everything – all the things I'd have liked to hear, the whole truth, as they say in court?

'All right. Just tell me where and when.'

The brain acts according to processes that are still largely unknown to us. Some areas put together thoughts, formulate hypotheses, make conjectures, handle feelings, without the other areas realising it, and the most rapid, most efficient areas abuse their power over the others. That was what had just happened to me: while part of me was still trembling at the idea of meeting a murderer, the other was already putting together a plan, a counterattacking strategy that wasn't limited to averting danger, but would remove it once and for all. Yes, the most efficient area of my brain had established that only the truth, the whole truth and nothing but the truth, about Patrizia's death, could save me. It had established that I had to confront Marco, I had to go to that dinner.

'Do you want me to come to your place in Bergamo?'

Good idea. Dinner in the Upper Town, at Bernabò's in the Piazza Mascheroni, a full restaurant, people in the square, people along the Via Colleoni, no dark side roads, no isolated trattorias deep in the countryside, no hidden spots.

'That's perfect.'

'Shall I pick you up from your place? Where do you live exactly?'

'It's a small street that's a bit hard to find. You can park in the Piazza Mercato del Fieno: it's a paid car park and every now and again you find a spot.'

Then I thought it over for a moment: better to be even safer.

'No, I tell you what. Do you mind parking in the Lower Town and coming up by funicular? I can meet you in the Piazza Mercato delle Scarpe at about eight-fifteen.'

'Great.'

'I really want to see you.'

'Me, too.'

Actually, it wasn't even a lie, even though my motives were different from his. Or perhaps not. Probably not. We almost certainly both had Patrizia's death at the centre of our thoughts, although we were looking at it from two different sides.

As soon as I put down the receiver, a salvo of chimes exploded: at least a dozen bells were tolling midday. At such moments, I always felt I was experiencing the true essence of the Upper Town, its charm, which had hardly changed since medieval times. The few cars that drove through it didn't disturb it, Japanese tourists photographed it without contaminating it with the present day. The people greeted each other in the streets, the carpenter's dog, full of woodshavings, stood as a sign outside his shop, while Bartolomeo, drunk as usual, shuffled the whole length of the Corsaiola, with his hands behind his back, yelling curses. That was Upper Bergamo beneath the bells of twelve o'clock.

Not quite at twelve, but just a few minutes later, Signora Ghislandi rang at my door.

'I have home-made casoncelli. Would you like to come down and have lunch with me? If not, I'll cook them and bring then up to you.'

'Thanks very much. Is it all right if I come down in a quarter of an hour?'

'Of course it is. But are you sure it's no bother coming down? If you'd rather eat alone, I'm happy to make them for you.'

'Not at all, Signora Ghislandi. I love eating in company.'

Basically we were two women alone, and it was a good idea to keep each other company, however sad the thought of that was. If nothing else, lunch with her would keep me from obsessing about my date that evening.

Signora Ghislandi's apartment was identical to mine, only the furnishings differed. Mine still had the furniture my grandmother had inherited from her mother, while hers had suffered the hunger for innovation of one of her children, who'd fitted out the living room of her apartment in nasty fake dark wood, all too reminiscent of the Seventies.

On the round table, which was too large, too cumbersome for the room, there was a blue tablecloth, close-stitched by the woman herself, the tablecloth she put on it for special occasions.

'Please sit down, doctor.'

She called me 'doctor', with that exaggerated deference old people have for those who have studied.

I took a chair, the cushion of which still had a plastic cover on it that stuck to your bottom when you sat down. She brought to the table a steaming tureen filled with casoncelli drowning in a sea of melted butter. My doctor had told me that, now that I was approaching forty, I needed to start keeping an eye on my cholesterol, but I tried not to think about that. If Signora Ghislandi could live to over eighty on dishes like that, so could I.

I started eating with gusto, while she told me, probably for the twentieth time, about the grief her daughter had caused her, separating from her husband.

'You know, doctor, I think about it every day. I still can't believe it. I never thought something as terrible as that would ever happen to me. I never had that in my life, not even when my poor dad died in the bombing of Dalmine, not even when I lost my husband. But now that I'm old, Giovanna gives me this grief.'

From time to time I made a slight movement with my head, neither nodding nor shaking it, simply participating silently in what I knew wasn't so much a conversation as a monologue. That, too, was a way of keeping someone company.

'It's not so much because of Giovanna, she's grown up, but because of Giacomo, the baby. I call him a baby, but he's already fourteen. But he still suffers, even though he pretends he doesn't. The other day he said to me, "You know, grandma, it isn't anyone's fault, I understand them. People change, even grown ups. Mum and Dad changed in different ways and now they can't be together." You see what a head he has, what a heart. But they didn't tell him the whole story, they didn't tell him his daddy had found himself another woman, a woman who, forgive me but I have to say it, is a bit of a whore. Because freedom's fine, but to do that…'

I almost felt implicated, both in the role of Giovanna, the betrayed wife, and in that of the whore. If Signora Ghislandi had seen me with Marco, she probably would have thought I was a home-wrecker, too.

'…I tell myself, there are so many single men, why go for a married man. I say, so you're separated? Because she's separated, that one. So go with a man who's separated, there are plenty of them. But what can you do, that's the way things are these days. People spend too much time away from home and don't think about their family anymore. This woman works with him, and seeing so much of each other every day they started getting ideas. It's because there's not enough hunger anymore, because when I went to work I didn't have either the time or the inclination to look at men. Life's too comfortable now. Just think, I used to walk from the Upper Town, because I've always lived in this building, and I used to go down to the station and there they'd come and pick us up and take us to the factory. Then ten hours at the loom, and you had no time to look at men, not even if Amedeo Nazzari passed in front of you. Too comfortable, life these days.'

Poor woman, deep down I understood her. At the age of over eighty, I imagined she might have some difficulties accepting such things. And yet she wasn't the only one to divide the world into watertight compartments: the separated with the separated, the others, the normal, with the normal. For those of us who'd made the mistake of failing, the third millennium hadn't quite started yet. And so all we could do was put up with Signora Ghislandi's complaints, the pitying looks of those who tried to understand, the arrogant looks of those who didn't even try to understand, and the stupid looks of men who thought that separation, in a woman, generated only an insatiable desire for sex. Fortunately Stefano and I hadn't had children, otherwise I'd also have had to stand the endless parade of all those devout women who asked at every opportunity, 'What about the children, did they suffer?' and wouldn't find peace until you admitted that yes, they had suffered. Even though it wasn't true, because when the adults are intelligent, the children manage wonderfully. But confirming that fictitious suffering gave the charitable ladies the certainty that they'd done the right thing spending their whole lives with men they'd married but didn't love any more, that they'd done the right thing staying together for the sake of the children, because that way their children had grown up well, without traumas, without problems, not like the children of separated people! In the words and false politeness of these bigots, the hypocrisy was so concentrated you could touch it.

And yet I continued to listen and to smile at my neighbour. After all she liked me. With my mother it was worse. Ah, yes, my mother. Since my father had died, she'd developed the ability to go out of my head completely for weeks. I absolutely had to call her.

*

I quickly finished my lunch, not without drinking a little glass of Rosolio that made me think of a poem by Gozzano. Then I went back upstairs to my apartment, picked up the phone, took a deep breath, and dialled my mother's number.

'Hello,' I said.

'Nice to know you're still alive,' she retorted, without giving me the chance to continue. 'Assuming you *are* alive: there are dead people who communicate with their loved ones at séances more often than you do.'

My mother was one of those people whose telephones don't seem adapted to making outgoing calls: they demand to be called regularly, daily even, but are completely incapable of lifting the receiver and taking the initiative. Perhaps if she'd phoned me every now and again, if she'd taken the trouble to find out how I was, our conversations would have been a little less tense. Instead of which, every time I called her she told me off, and every time I let more time pass before the next call. It was a vicious circle.

'It's been two weeks since I last heard from you. You know I'm getting old. One day you'll see my obituary in the newspaper. No flowers, please, give something to charity instead.'

'I'm sorry, mother, but I've had to work like crazy.'

'Oh, yes. If you'd remained with your husband, you wouldn't have these problems. He has a good salary, you had a home. But you wanted to leave.'

'Mother, how can I make you see that being happy in a marriage is about more than having a good salary and an apartment without a mortgage…'

'Happy! That's a big word. Your father and I weren't even happy on our wedding day, but we kept going, each with our little faults, we kept going, every day.'

'But Dad never cheated on you.'

'How do you know? Are you sure? Lucky you. I certainly wouldn't bet on it.'

But she was right, they hadn't been happy: a life of grudges and quarrels, but a life maintained, inexplicably, as a couple, until the end, when the tumour left my father with barely any voice to answer my mother's reprimands.

Why was it so difficult to live together?

'Anyway, I just wanted to tell you that I'm fine.'

'What about your back?'

'It hurts from time to time, but I'm used to it.'

'If you want to be seen by someone good, come here to Iseo, Luigi has found a chiropractor who performs miracles and also gave him an exceptional homeopathic treatment.'

Luigi's ailments came and went with his mood. He was a widower, she a widow, and they'd known each other forever. They'd got together not out of love but to have someone to talk to about rheumatism and cholesterol.

'Unfortunately for me homeopathy isn't enough: do you remember what the doctors said? That I'd have the condition all my life, and that's what's happened.'

The tone of my reply had been sharp, and deliberately nasty. Another of my mother's abilities was that of not understanding, not wanting to understand, what had really happened to me that day on the rocks. She'd continued to downplay it, to treat me like a capricious child. And that really annoyed me.

Our call lasted barely a few minutes, just short enough for us not to get as far as mutual insults. I put down the receiver angrily and the phone immediately started ringing: my mother must have felt the irrepressible desire to have the last word. 'Hello,' I said, ready for battle.

'Hi, it's Marco. I have to talk quickly because I'm in a bit of a rush. We're short-staffed at the moment, one of my colleagues is sick, and I can't get away from the hospital before eight. Would you mind coming to Magenta? I'll take you to eat in a little place round here.'

I was caught off guard. The previous conversation had taken away my ability to react, and I was silent a moment too long.

'Is that all right? Eight o'clock, here in the hospital car park?'

'All right.' It was the only thing I managed to say.

But it wasn't all right. It wouldn't have been all right if he'd been simply a slightly too selfish lover, the kind who loves having you at their beck and call, let alone a murderer who probably couldn't wait for me to meet the same fate as Patrizia.

I cursed myself. Once, a hundred times. And, as usual, I extended my curses to Benedetta and Patrizia, gradually extending them to take in the co-operatives which had stopped giving me work, the local authorities which weren't paying the co-operatives, the minister who had cut off the funds and even the prime minister – it was never a bad idea to curse him. And despite everything, at six I started to get ready, though in a completely different frame of mind from the first time. That first time, Marco's invitation had aroused my vanity as a woman of nearly forty, but now I knew that highlighting what remained of my beauty wouldn't be any help. I looked in the drawer for my bra with the wraparound cups, which made my breasts look like two smooth, firm bowling balls – exactly how I'd wanted them to look in that motel. I took one look at it and chose another, one bought at the hypermarket. While I was making up in front of the mirror, I felt a sense of nausea growing inside me that was anything but metaphorical. I even retched a couple of times, which sent me rushing for a glass of water, but in vain: I vomited, a nervous vomiting, like a victim preparing to be sacrificed. And yet I got ready, because I couldn't do anything other than meet his challenge.

At eight, punctual in his lateness, Marco emerged from the hospital and came straight towards me. I lowered my window and made an effort to smile, while little drops of cold drizzle bathed my face.

Without speaking, he gave me a kiss on the lips, quickly, like a snake that decides to go straight onto the attack, then said, 'Come on, get out, we'll go in mine.'

'Isn't it better if we take both cars, then I can go straight back to Bergamo?'

'But we still have to come back this way. And besides, in this weather we'd run the risk of losing each other.'

I wasn't well enough prepared, I wasn't ready for an eventuality like this. I was falling headlong into the trap I was sure he'd prepared for me.

As I got in his car, I couldn't help turning to look at the rear windscreen. There was the sticker with the scuba diver, it hadn't been a dream, or a nightmare, there it was, lit by the headlights of the car behind us, back on that damned road.

'Did you really want to see me?' he asked.

I tried to lie. 'I couldn't wait.'

'Because over the phone you didn't sound so keen to go out.'

'And how do I seem now?'

'Doubtful.'

Was it my voice that had betrayed me? Or my long face? Or perhaps the fact that I hadn't dressed up?

I took his hand off the gear lever and put it in my lap and stroked it. His skin beneath my fingers gave me a sense of revulsion I found hard to overcome. I thought of those hands on the thighs of young prostitutes and wondered how they managed to overcome their disgust at that contact, that violated intimacy. And yet, for all the compassion I felt, I realised that it was because of them that those hands seemed so repulsive. Those hands that had lightly stroked my back and made me quiver with pleasure now seemed to me unclean, only because they'd touched other women who did it as a job: dirty women, sick women, women soiled inside and out, said an irrational voice I couldn't silence, the voice of prejudice. Even the fact that they were the hands of a murderer seemed to fade into the background compared with the graver sin: they were the hands of a man who went with whores.

I tried to change the subject. 'What kind of place are we going this evening?'

'I've never been there. It was recommended by a friend. Apparently it's part of a farm, and they serve only their own produce... Ah, yes, this should be the road.'

He turned abruptly onto one of those unpaved roads with which I was by now sadly familiar.

I shuddered. In an instant, the lights of the other cars had vanished, the illuminated signs, the windows of the car showrooms, the people. We were alone, he and I, in the darkness of the countryside, in a place just like the one where he'd already committed a murder. We were in the situation I'd sworn never to find myself in. And yet that was where I'd ended up, without even protesting, without forcing him to make any effort other than to lie, to surprise me with his supposed chores at the hospital, his mysterious farm/restaurant.

No, my whole life didn't pass in front of my eyes, the way they say it does. The only thing that came into my mind was Stefano's face when he'd realised the kind of trouble I was getting into and I'd told him not to worry. Fear, which drives you to be vigilant and clear-headed, had given way to the kind of melancholy that deadens your reflexes and makes it easy to just give up. I'd already gone beyond the fear of what might happen to me, my sorrow was entirely focused on what would happen afterwards, Stefano's sadness, Morgana's miaowing as she waited for her mistress. I was already taking my death for granted, it was the others I felt sorry for.

All at once, in the cone of light cast by the headlights there appeared a small open space with a few cars parked in front of an old building with a dim light over the main door. This was the end of the road, the farm/restaurant.

I heaved a sigh of relief. If Marco had wanted to kill me he could have done it before we arrived. Much more sensible to do it sooner rather than later, after people had seen us dining together. But a moment later I started worrying again: perhaps it was only because he hadn't had all the answers he was expecting from me, and couldn't tell how much I knew and who I'd already told the things I knew. That was it, of course: the dinner was meant to probe the terrain, murder was for later. It was no coincidence that he'd chosen a place where nobody knew him!

He parked and got out. I made to open the door, but he

stopped me. 'Wait, I'll come and get you.'

A second later, there he was, with his umbrella open to shelter me from the drizzle.

We went inside. Under the brick vaults of what seemed to be the former kitchen of the farmhouse, there were no more than ten tables, of which only one was free: ours. The wall at the far end of the room was more than half occupied by a huge fireplace with a blazing fire in it. I would have liked to wipe everything I knew from my mind, everything that made that dinner abnormal, and savour all the good, beautiful things I saw around me: the walls, the linen tablecloths, the polished furniture, the wooden partitions, the fire in the fireplace, even Marco's smile.

We approached the table. He moved a chair away for me, waited and pushed it closer as I sat down. Pure gallantry: at any other time I would have appreciated it.

The owner, a woman, soon arrived, welcomed us and informed us of the customs of the house: no orders, just a long succession of small courses. The only thing we had to choose was the wine. Marco asked what the first courses were and ordered, to start, a Franciacorta white from a producer he seemed to know well.

Why couldn't I be wrong? Why wasn't Marco simply Marco and not Patrizia's likely murderer? The question continued going around in my head until, just as the tarte tatin of shallots with raspberry purée arrived, I connected it with another that had preoccupied me for a while in the past few days. What if Pasquale Avvisato had stolen Marco's car to kill Patrizia? Was that another biased assumption, or did I just want to see Dr Marco Callegari restored to normality?

When he apologised once again for not having been able

to come to Bergamo and thanked me for agreeing to join him, I found a way into the subject.

'I'm glad it worked out. My neighbour's car was stolen yesterday, and it was parked not far from mine. If the thieves had moved a few metres, we wouldn't have been able to have this dinner at all.'

He laughed. 'I'd have sent a taxi for you.'

'Have you ever had your car stolen?'

'You must be kidding! I've always had old crocks that thieves wouldn't touch with a bargepole.'

'The one you have now doesn't look like an old crock to me.'

'No, I agree, but that was a piece of luck. I bought it a month ago, used, from that dealer on the main road, after Corbetta, or perhaps it's already the municipality of Vittuone, I don't know. The price was very good and I told myself that for once in my life it was worth going a bit crazy for a car. Although my passion for cars continues to be almost nil. You know, I did it more than anything for the family, so we could travel in a bit more comfort…'

But I'd stopped listening, overwhelmed by my sudden awareness of how obvious it all was. My rational mind had been deceived by appearances and clichéd ways of thinking. Not for a single moment had it occurred to me that a well-known, tanned, successful doctor might buy a second-hand car, not for a single moment had I thought that, at the time of Patrizia's murder, that BMW X5 might have belonged to someone else.

'So you didn't put that sticker on the rear windscreen?'

'It really made an impression on you, didn't it? You spent the whole journey looking at it. Why?'

'I don't know. Just because it didn't seem like you.'

'You're right. The sticker was already there when I bought it and I didn't even bother to take it off. That gives you an idea how much I care about cars.'

In an instant everything had changed, I was seeing everything in a different light. I felt agitated, tense, confused. So Marco wasn't the murderer, the man who went with whores, the monster I had thought he was. But nor was he likely to lead me to the truth about Patrizia's death. Or perhaps he might.

I abruptly picked up my purse, opened an outer pocket and rummaged in it for a while, then asked, 'Could you give me your car keys?'

'Of course, have you lost something?'

'My mobile. I always keep it in this pocket but it's not there.'

'Do you want me to go and look for it?'

'I wouldn't hear of it! I'm almost certain it fell in the car, the pocket was slightly open. I'll go. I won't be long.'

He handed me the keys and I went out. I checked that I had my mobile in my pocket, as usual, to avoid it ringing at an inappropriate moment in front of Marco, then, from the shelter of the little canopy outside the farmhouse I opened the car door with the remote, and ran to it. Once inside, I opened the glove compartment and looked for the registration document. Keeping my head down, as if I was looking for an object on the floor, I unfolded it and read the name and address of the original owner: Giovanni Imperiale, 12 Via De Gasperi, Vittuone.

All at once I realised the truth, or at least part of it.

The details of the second owner were less illuminating: AutoEuropa, 121A Route 11, Corbetta. But the date of the transfer of ownership let a little more light in on the truth:

the first of December, the day after Patrizia was knocked
down. Imperiale had got rid of the murder weapon the day
after the murder. Of course, a car isn't like a knife, you
can't throw it in the bottom of a lake. Selling it doesn't
mean getting rid of it completely, but at least it's a way to
distance yourself from it, to avoid anyone who might by
chance have seen the accident linking the car to the driver.

The registration document also showed that on 12
January the BMW X5 had been purchased by Marco
Callegari, the very same doctor who'd been on duty when
Patrizia had been admitted to hospital. I thought about
how chance played with the plans of men, but I had to
admit that chance had also been helped along by
Imperiale's ingenuousness, or perhaps by his need to do
things in a hurry. Selling the car to a local dealer greatly
increased the likelihood that it would be bought by someone who spent time in the area, someone who had dealings
with local people.

Why had Imperiale killed Patrizia? An indecent proposal rejected by the girl? Or else the opposite. A proposal
accepted, followed by threats to tell his wife everything?
The other face of adultery, the less inviting one. And what
did Dr Maestri have to do with all this? Perhaps nothing.
Perhaps the baleful obviousness of chance had provided
Imperiale with a second car, a dark red Lancia Fulvia, identical to Maestri's, which he used to pick up Patrizia from
the farmhouse, to avoid attracting too much attention with
the bigger car.

But at that moment the one thing that really mattered
was Marco, and the fact that he was in the clear, that he
hadn't used me, that he didn't go with prostitutes. I was

euphoric as I went back inside, my only regret being that I couldn't tell him why.

I sat down, holding up the mobile.

'You're lucky you found it. I lose two a year, on average.'

We went back to talking about this and that, while the courses succeeded one another. I don't know if he noticed, but I started to lean forward, as if to invite that hand which had previously filled me with horror back to my cheek. Now I really could enjoy everything, starting with him. And yet the worm of rationality continued to work inside me: you're still missing something, it was saying, something you can discover tonight, something you can ask Marco.

Listening to that worm, I asked suddenly, 'Does your colleague Dr Maestri have a girlfriend?'

'Are you trying to make me jealous?' he joked.

'Oh, sure! A handsome, friendly man like him is every woman's dream.'

'So why do you ask?'

'Because I think he was having a relationship with Patrizia. Maybe a relationship on the side that he didn't want his regular girlfriend to find out about.'

'A relationship like ours?' His tone had become serious again.

'Do we have a relationship?'

I'd regained my ability to chill the most romantic situation, the most passionate request with a single line – my ability to ruin everything.

Somewhat mortified, he returned to the subject of Maestri. 'I assure you, nobody's ever seen Maestri with a woman. Actually imagining him with two, one regular and one on the side, is almost like science fiction.'

I decided to come out in the open. 'And yet, at the farm where Patrizia lived, they say they saw Maestri's car come and pick her up several times.'

'Did they see the car or Maestri?'

'The car.'

'At one time, they at least needed to see your face to identify you, now all they need is your car. We've become identified with the four wheels under us.'

He was right, damn it, how right he was.

'Do you think there are still many cars like that around?'

'I've no idea. It's just that it's so hard for me to think about Maestri with a woman, or with a man, or even with a pet. Everyone in the hospital assumes he's always alone.'

'Although I get the impression the nurses worship him.'

'That's possible, but I assure you that if his colleagues could catch him out in a mistake they'd fall about laughing.'

'And you?'

'Me first.'

'Why's he so loved?'

'Because he's a pain in the arse, he's arrogant, he's like the class swot, and he can't even play football. We needed a fifth person for the game against the male nurses and he wouldn't play, not even in goal.'

So the virus of five-a-side football had affected Marco, too! The only people spared seemed to be the various 'Dr Maestris', but they weren't so desirable.

'You don't think he might have a skeleton in the closet?'

'If he does, it's probably to do experiments with. Joking aside, I think that as far as that's concerned he's beyond reproach. You can say what you like about him, you can't cast doubt on his honesty.'

I insisted. 'Would you help me to try and find out if he really was having a relationship with Patrizia? He might keep a photo of her in his locker, or a letter.'

'Are you asking me to look through his things?'

'To all intents and purposes, yes.'

'I can try, but I can't guarantee anything. I don't think I'm cut out to be a spy.'

I still wasn't sure how exactly Maestri was involved, I just knew that his behaviour felt wrong.

'In any case, I don't think I'll find much. He's always been reserve personified. In the five years he's been working with us, he's never gone out with anyone, never talked about anything that wasn't work.'

'Let's try anyway.'

We were interrupted by the owner.

'Here are the cheeses,' she said, holding out two platters on which a dozen small portions of different cheeses were arranged in a circle, accompanied by honey and fruit compotes. 'You should start with this one, which is a soft cheese produced here, and then continue in a clockwise direction, towards the fuller-bodied cheeses, keeping the herb-flavoured ones for last.'

'Thank you,' Marco said. 'Thank you for your advice.'

She walked away, pleased with herself, and Marco immediately set about changing the positions of the various cheeses with his fork until he had completely subverted the order so carefully established by the chef.

'I'm starting to be sick and tired of these fads. Fast food, slow food. Why can't it just be food? Why can't we eat as naturally as we talk, for God's sake?'

This time, too, his letting off of steam ended in a smile which drew broad lines on his still tanned face.

'Were you being serious when you said we don't have a relationship?'

What could I reply? That everything had been spoilt because of a car I'd thought was his? Because of a suspicion? That the night we'd spent together had been wonderful, but that now we had to rebuild something that had been broken because of me?

I looked again at his face, the blazing fire, the linen tablecloth, then said, 'If we make love now we can start to consider it a relationship.'

'A relationship that lasts?'

'That will last until one of us says "I love you".'

It just came out like that, stupidly. I ought to devote myself to writing little mottoes inside boxes of chocolates, I thought. And yet there was a basis in truth.

He placed his forehead against mine, and the images of Maestri, Imperiale, Patrizia and Benedetta all went out of my mind.

We devoured the desserts, all different from the standard panna cotta with amaretto, all belonging to a near, very near future. We hurried out of the restaurant and ran to the car, but not because of the rain. Once inside, we kissed for a long time. He slipped his hand inside my blouse and caressed my breasts.

'Shall we get out of here?'

'Yes, let's go somewhere darker.'

Marco started the car and we went back along the side road, which was deserted now, empty even of prostitutes. At a fork, the only one before the main road, we turned left onto a path that led into the fields.

He switched off the engine.

'No, just turn off the headlights, but leave the heating

on.'

'Are you cold?'

'I will be.' And I started to undress, completely. When you make love in a car, you don't usually go that far, you take off just the main things. But I wanted to be naked again beneath him.

Now my back is hurting. A lot. The adrenaline has kept me going until now, it's helped me to dig and keep digging. But now it's abandoning me. And I start to remember again that day by the sea: playing among the waves, close to the rocks, on the rocks, unaware. Then a stronger wave than the others. It takes me, lifts me up, and slams me down. And the pain is strong, total, instantaneous. Then only the terror. The terror of legs that can't move. The pain seems to have gone, only the frantic fear of not being able to move, of not even being able to escape from the next waves. And then nothing.

And now the pain and the terror have returned. Pain in my back, made worse by the effort and the cold. Terror at all the rest. Terror, horror, fear, anguish, anxiety.

I've opened a line in the ground that runs along the thorax of the body. Even if I overcame my revulsion and tore open the clothes, the putrescence I'd find under them wouldn't give me the confirmation I need. I have to carry on, hoping that the face has conserved that one element I need as irrefutable proof.

I must be brave. I'm almost at the end of my efforts and I recall the last events, those that don't seem so distant, things that happened today, the day that's now coming to an end.

Friday, 25 February

I woke up, still with the sensation of Marco's body on mine. Perhaps it was the memory of the previous night, in the car, or perhaps I'd dreamed during the night, or at dawn, one of those dreams which take a while to fade and which, with your eyes half-closed, you try your best to hold on to. I tried right to the end not to lose the taste of that dream, but it was pointless. I found myself thinking again about that strange constellation of men that had formed around Patrizia: Giovanni Imperiale, Pasquale Avvisato, Paolo Maestri. Did they know each other? Were they rivals? Accomplices? Were all three of them in love with Patrizia? Were they competing for her?

The same old questions, the same old names, now with a new one: Imperiale, the killer. Assuming he really was the one who'd killed her – the car had already misled me once. I'd granted Marco the possibility of a theft, the possibility that there'd been someone else at the wheel, I had to grant Imperiale the same possibility – although that sale, the very day after the accident, was highly suspicious.

But the crux was still the relationship between the three men. What linked them? What pitted them against each other? I was convinced now that everything lay there, that only by understanding that strange network of people would I understand the motives that had driven the murderer. Even though the question that had brought me into this affair – the missing body – remained as obscure as ever. And I assumed that Benedetta would be very disappointed

218

to have the culprit, but not the body. Honour, reputation, discretion: that was what mattered to her, not the truth.

By now, these thoughts had ruined my awakening and driven Marco's taste from my mouth. I consoled myself by stroking Morgana, who was lying next to me as usual. But the questions wouldn't go away.

I got out of bed and found the envelope with Patrizia's things, hoping they might suggest something. I looked again at the photographs: the mother, the father, the strange house on concrete stilts... I lingered over that one. Once again, I had the impression I'd seen it before. Where could I have seen such a weird building? Definitely on a screen, but I wasn't sure if it was on TV or at the cinema, in a documentary or a feature film. Wherever it was, I didn't find any inspiration in the photos, or the other objects. But what they made me realise was that I'd completely forgotten my original intention: to reconstruct the girl's personality in order to understand what connection there might be between her death and the disappearance of her body. That, along with the question of the three men, was the crux of the matter, but I'd tended to dismiss it, perhaps for the simple reason that it was what Benedetta most cared about. Why get rid of the body? Only once, in all this time, had I tried to come up with a convincing answer. I fished it out of my memory: something in that body could still give a clue to her killer. In my confused accusation of Dr Maestri, I'd raised the question of poison, theorising that the body might indicate the way she'd been killed. But there was another explanation: the body might indicate directly *who* had killed her. What if Patrizia had been pregnant? That would provide a motive. She has a relationship with a married man and gets pregnant. She won't hear of an abortion, he refuses to leave his wife, with whom he has already had a child, perhaps a very young child, just like Imperiale. She threatens him, he kills her. But if someone, even belatedly, starts to get suspicious, they could have the body exhumed and, by analysing the DNA of the foetus, could identify the father, in other words, the killer. Anyone who watches television today knows, or at least believes, that they can perform miracles with DNA. And in this case, believing could be more dangerous than knowing – dangerous for Patrizia, of course.

So I reconstructed the sequence of events, putting Imperiale at the centre of everything. Imperiale knocks down Patrizia with his BMW. Alina said the car actually tried to turn back. To do what? To make sure the girl was dead? Not only that. To do something more appalling, more macabre: to take the body and get rid of it. But where? I didn't just have Alina's account, I also had Abdelkader's. 'When the girls are on board the cars never park, they keep moving. But the BMW was actually parked next to the little wood.' The car was parked near the little wood a couple of hours before Patrizia was knocked down, with no one in it. There was no one in it because Imperiale had got out and gone into the wood. To do what? It seemed obvious to me now: Imperiale was in the wood digging the grave where he would put Patrizia's body. When the hole was ready, he just had to wait until the body became available.

But then why kill Patrizia with a car, why simulate an accident if he was going to hide the body afterwards anyway? Perhaps he was just being over-cautious. If for some reason it wasn't possible to bury the body without anyone seeing, at least it wouldn't look like a murder. Or perhaps

Imperiale was afraid he wouldn't be capable of killing Patrizia with his bare hands. The car gave him the courage he lacked, it was a more sanitised method, a method that didn't force him to look his victim in the eyes, to hear her breathing and feel her skin on his.

But the roles of the other two men were still inexplicable, or else were explicable in very different ways. Pasquale could have been Imperiale's hired killer: the car was Imperiale's, but the dirty work was his. Although someone who pays for a murder to be carried out usually tries to keep as far as possible from the scene of the crime and certainly doesn't lend the hitman his car. Alternatively, Pasquale could have been the real father of Patrizia's baby, or it could have been Maestri, or it could have been the Holy Ghost… Damn it, I was once again in a state of utter confusion.

My reflections were interrupted by the telephone, as usual. It seemed like my one remaining link to the outside world.

'Hi, it's Marco. I can't talk. I just wanted to tell you that I started my search. He'd left his wallet on the table in the doctors' room. The usual stuff inside: seventy Euros, driving licence, identity card. The only unusual thing was two train tickets, from Milan to Grenoble.'

'He could have gone to France for a conference.'

'I don't think so. He would have said something: conferences are the only thing he ever talks about. And the tickets were used on two different dates: the first at the end of December, which was a Saturday, I checked, the second three weeks ago, again on a Saturday.'

'To Grenoble, you said?'

'Yes, Grenoble. I really must go now. Bye.'

'Bye.'

He could have been a bit more expansive, but I didn't really care. To tell the truth, the first thing I did when I'd put down the receiver was rush back to the envelope with Patrizia's documents and pull out the identity card. Now at last it told me something.

nom: Vitali
prénom: Patrizia
née le: 13 janvier 1982
à: Grenoble (Isère)

Grenoble. Dr Maestri, supposed boyfriend of the late Patrizia Vitali, makes repeated journeys to Grenoble, the city where she was born. Coincidence?

After the identity card I looked again at the photographs, particularly the one of the house where Patrizia had been happy: without doubt, a house somewhere near Grenoble.

Grenoble! The birthplace, the motherland, where we go to find refuge, where we feel at home even when the world around us has it in for us, where it's easier not to be afraid. I'd found an explanation for Dr Paolo Maestri's trips to Grenoble, a psychologist's explanation, which meant it was a conjecture, a therapeutic hypothesis, still to be tested. But at least, for the first time, even the obtrusive figure of Maestri fitted the jigsaw, and, strange to say, even the missing Pasquale Avvisato was carving out a little place for himself, an uncomfortable place, but a place all the same.

I stared at the photograph of that concrete house on stilts. Even though Patrizia had written on the back that she'd been happy there, I still found it a grim, sad place. It seemed to rise out of the mists, like something in a horror movie. Could I have actually seen it in a horror movie? But

I never watch horror movies. A thriller, then? Possibly. I concentrated, going over a whole series of films in my mind. I had the annoying feeling that I was one step away from identifying that memory exactly: one step, but still too far. I tried to recall more details. The image of the house was associated with an interior full of blood. Nothing specific, just blood. Then I connected the blood with the presence of two people, two actors obviously. Two French actors? The inference was a likely one: if the location was in France, it was reasonable to think it was a French film. Two French actors, one older, one younger. Gérard Depardieu, no. Alain Delon, no. Daniel Auteuil, no. Jean Réno… Jean Réno. I saw his face in my mind: the large nose, the slightly bovine eyes, the offbeat charm. Yes, it was Jean Réno, and the other one, the younger man, was Vincent Cassel. Jean Réno and Vincent Cassel, together, in a thriller. At last, I had it: *The Crimson Rivers*. A weird, dark, atmospheric thriller. I couldn't remember much about it, just those few impressions and a sense of disappointment at the end.

Now I could start to verify my psychologist's hypothesis, to see if I was going in the right direction. First objective: to locate the house, because it was almost certainly there that Dr Maestri went, a house in the region of Isère, though surely not in Grenoble itself. It occurred to me that, for once, Benedetta's double-barrelled name and jet-set connections might come in useful. I picked up the telephone, and regained my voice.

'Hello, Benedetta, it's Anna.'

'Hello, is there any news?' There was anxiety in her voice, anxiety and insecurity: strange, I thought.

'Do you remember the photograph of that strange house

223

among your sister's things?'

'Yes.'

'I need to know where the house is.'

'I haven't the faintest idea.'

'Let me give you a clue. It was used as a location for a French film called *The Crimson Rivers*. I assume that among your friends there must be some film producers, directors, something like that. Am I right?'

'As it happens, I do know a few people in the film business.'

'Then use your contacts and see if you can find out, as soon as possible, where exactly that house is.'

Incredibly, I was giving her orders. My faith in my new insight was putting me in an uncommon position of strength.

'Do you think my half-sister's body is there?'

She couldn't say 'sister', not even by mistake.

'I think Dr Maestri has some connection with the house, which may explain some aspects of the case.'

In fact, what I suspected was more complex than that, but I didn't want to tell her anything until I was sure, or rather, until the evidence spoke for itself.

'All right, I'll see what I can do. Can I get back to you at the beginning of next week?'

'You're joking. I need to know by this afternoon. In fact, keep tomorrow free, we'll almost certainly have to make a journey.'

'All right,' she replied, much too submissively.

Following in detail the plan I had in mind, I dressed in dark colours, even exhuming from the back of a wardrobe a dark grey down jacket that must have been twenty years old. On my feet, black Dr. Martens, another souvenir from my protracted adolescence.

As it was nearly midday, I had a quick bite to eat. Then I gave my cat a little kiss on the head and went out. On the floor below, I asked the usual favours of Signora Ghislandi and she, as usual, said she was very happy to do them for me. What a saint!

It was sunny today, and there was a sharpness in the air: the kind you get when snow is on its way but you know it's going to take its time. Although it was still early, there were a few cars with skis on their roofs on the autostrada: the weekend was starting. I thought of Marco and his family weekends. Would he send me a message? There were no tailbacks, and I drove easily, until I reached the usual point, the Strada alle Cascine, like a commuter going through the motions, as if the car were leading the way. I told myself that this would be the last time I commuted between Bergamo and here, and I was right. Whatever happens, I'll never come back here.

From a distance, I saw the place where Patrizia had been knocked down. I stopped exactly where, according to Alina, Imperiale's BMW had done. I looked both ways to see if anyone was coming. The road was deserted. Then I accelerated. When I reached the exact spot where the car had hit Patrizia, I took my foot off the pedal and looked at the speedometer. Eighty-five kilometres per hour. A few more metres at that speed and I would have overturned. But Imperiale's car, which was now Marco's, the car where we had made love, was built especially for dirt roads. God knows what speed he'd been going at when he knocked Patrizia down.

I drove on, passed the Bonos' farmhouse and, when I reached the junction, took the other side road until I came to the little wood. I pulled up, trying to guess the exact place where Abdel had seen the 4x4 parked. Then I got out and opened the boot. I took out that mass of tied plastic bags which had been there since time immemorial and set off. I wondered if there was any risk of getting lost, but it struck me that if I could lose my way in a small cluster of trees no more than two hundred metres in diameter I ought to be admitted to a psychiatric ward. The second question I asked myself concerned the spot where Imperiale might have dug the hole. In the middle, I told myself. And I went straight to the densest part of the wood – which wasn't really all that dense, even though, as forests went, it was the best you'd find within a radius of fifty kilometres. Between the tall branches, the sky was perfectly visible, blue and serene. Looking around, I realised the view was clear, apart from a few threadbare bushes, a few skeletal trees. Even from what ought to have been the most hidden part of the wood, you could see the refuse heaped up at the side of the road: a mattress, a fridge, a wash basin broken into many fragments. On the ground, on the other hand, there was nothing to be seen, no sign of digging, no trace of holes, pits, graves, anything like that. Only scrub and earth, and not loose earth, but compact, solid earth. But would earth thrown down about three months earlier to cover a body still appear loose anyway? If I didn't find the burial place, did that mean there wasn't one or simply that it was no longer possible to distinguish? Or simply that I hadn't been able to find it? I started to search more carefully, feeling a bit like a boy scout looking for tracks to obtain his explorer's certificate. Dried leaves, fallen branches, brambles, waste paper carried on the wind, a few rocks, but no holes. I widened the radius of my search, but there were still no holes. I concentrated, pretending to be afraid. Right now I wouldn't need to pretend, but this afternoon I did. I pretended I was Imperiale, I was there at dawn and needed to dig. Yes, I told myself, I'm Giovanni Imperiale, I've just taken my shovel and gone into the wood. I look around. There's no one. Everything is still dark, no fires, no lights. I'm about to start digging, but suddenly hear a noise and see the lights of a tractor. Yes, there they are, on the road leading to the Malpensata farm. And if I can see the tractor, the person on the tractor can see me. I'm in the middle of the wood, but I'm still too close to the road. I have only one solution: go further, towards the other road, the one where, in a couple of hours, I'll kill Patrizia, the road where the prostitutes hang out, but they aren't there now, this isn't their hour, the prostitutes I mean, because I often go with them. Of course, if I move over to that side I'll have fewer trees to shelter me, but there'll be a hundred metres of cornfields between me and the road. I reasoned like Imperiale, focussing on the fear of being discovered. And I found the grave. A rectangle of brown, regular, quite smooth earth, one metre seventy by fifty centimetres, on which nothing had yet grown. If spring had already come, or even if snow had fallen on it, there would probably have been nothing to distinguish that macabre handkerchief-sized patch of dirt from the rest, it would have been swallowed, absorbed, by the wood. But this afternoon it was quite visible. As visible as I was. That was why I had dressed in dark colours. I would wait for night, come back when it was quite dark, and do the most terrible job I'd ever done. A job for gravediggers, or the Carabinieri. But going to the Carabinieri meant telling the world the story of Patrizia, the story of the missing body, and it wasn't yet time for that.

That was how I was thinking up until a few hours ago. Foolish, reckless, conceited. I thought that the discretion I'd guaranteed Benedetta was more important than my own safety. Above all, I didn't think I would be afraid. What an idiot I was!

I tied three plastic bags to the branch closest to the grave, so that I could find the place again, then, like Tom Thumb, tied one every fifteen or twenty metres along the route as I walked back to my car.

'A hot Vov, please.'

'I'll bring it to you straight away, signorina. Take a seat.'

I still like it when they call me 'signorina'.

I sat down at a little table near the window, with a view of the deserted Piazza della Liberazione. I wondered if Magenta was always so empty at this hour. Two or three groups of young men, heedless of the cold, were the only splash of colour on the grey of the pavement. Separate splashes of colour, in fact, depending on their origin: the North Africans over by the portico, the Lombards from Rho or Pozzuoli on the stone benches, and the Eastern Europeans standing in a group towards the Via Garibaldi.

I waited for the warmth of the Vov to enter my bloodstream and stop my continued shivering, then looked at my watch. It was four-thirty and I hadn't yet heard from Benedetta. Best to give her a push.

I dialled her number.

'Hello, Anna, I was just about to call you.'

Of course. When you're fed up with waiting for a phone call, the other person was always just about to call you.

'Did you get what I wanted?'

'I had to call half a dozen people, but in the end I found out the location of the house in Patrizia's photograph. It's in a village called Livet, in the municipality of Livet-Gavet, about thirty kilometres from Grenoble.'

'Let's go there tomorrow.'

'But I can't tomorrow, I have a work appointment.'

'On a Saturday?'

'Yes, Saturday is a day like any other.'

'Cancel your appointment, because I think we're going to find all the answers we're still missing in that house in Livet.'

'Can't you tell me what it's about?'

'For the moment it's only a hypothesis, I don't want to say anything until I have some more evidence. Then the truth will speak for itself.'

'Why are you making such a mystery of it?'

'I'm not. It's just that I've already accused a man of murder without having any evidence, and I don't want to make the same mistake again. I don't want to say a word until I've had confirmation.'

'And when will you have it?'

'Part of it tonight, as soon as it's dark. The rest tomorrow, when we go into that house.'

'Then I'll call you later to make arrangements for the journey.'

'All right, but I'll have my mobile switched off about ten. Try me later.'

We said goodbye. Narrowly avoiding spilling it over me, I finished my Vov, which was now cold. I still had five hours to kill. I did what girls today do when they feel something coming that's too much like silence and solitude: I grabbed my mobile and called Stefano.

'Hi, are you in the office?'

'Yes, and in a mess as usual.'

'I'll let you go, then.'

'No, don't do that. I just meant that this business of the layoffs hasn't been sorted yet. How are you? Did my tip about *Have you seen them?* prove useful?'

'It may have been useful, but it's a bit early to say. Anyway, things are fine. Actually, I wanted to know what's up with you.'

I didn't want to tell him I'd called him because I had nothing to do. Besides, it wouldn't even have been true. I'd phoned him because, once again, I needed him, because the 'reasonable' part of my unconscious foresaw the danger and I wanted to hear his voice – it might be the last time.

'Nothing new at work, but there is something about the five-a-side. Do you remember what the guys and I used to say to each other as a joke if the game was ever cancelled at the last minute?'

'Of course, you used to say, "Before going home an hour early, best to call first so you don't find your wife in bed with someone." But you never phoned me, so obviously you trusted me. Either that or you wanted to catch me in the act.'

'Of course we never did call, it was only a joke. We said it again only the other evening, when we were due to play against Giorgio's colleagues and they didn't show up. We were due to have a game and then go for a pizza together. Instead of which it was cancelled and at seven-twenty we went home.'

'And one of you found his wife cheating on him?'

'Sebastiano.'

'The one who always played in an Argentina shirt with

the word "champion" on it?'

'That's right, the fair-haired guy.'

'And what exactly happened?'

'I don't know. All I know is that within twenty minutes he phoned all of us to tell us about it, to tell us that the joke had a basis of truth. He even sounded amused, but I think it was some kind of hysterical reaction.'

I didn't know whether to laugh or be angry. Not because of Sebastiano, about whom I didn't give a damn, but because Stefano seemed to find the story surprising – a man who'd cheated on me so many times, who'd sunk our marriage with his affairs.

I wondered once again if there really were couples who didn't cheat on each other. Is it possible to be in love all your life without having the desire to feel a different thrill, 'try a different bowl of milk,' as a friend of Stefano's rather crudely put it? Is it possible that cheating really can help a marriage, or is that just another alibi?

'The worst of it,' Stefano went on, 'is that now we've blown that line. No one will dare make it again.'

'You still have all that joking in the showers.'

'Oh, yes. There's always Luca throwing cold water on someone while he has his eyes closed and his head full of shampoo.'

His good mood had returned and I wanted to say good-bye there and then, while he was still chuckling and I felt close to him.

I left the bar and took a walk around Magenta. I stopped at a hardware shop and bought a pair of work gloves. I'd have liked to buy a shovel, too, but I was afraid that, under questioning by the Carabinieri, someone might remember me and I preferred to rely on the folding shovel I had in the car. Would the Carabinieri ask questions about that grave in the wood one day? Would they find my body? Yes, because this is where my memories end and the present begins, the nightmare I'm living through right now.

To be precise, the nightmare began three quarters of an hour ago, at twelve minutes past ten, when I pulled up at the side of the road near the little wood. The immediately preceding hours had passed without a trace, I'd wandered the streets, had a bite to eat, and the time somehow faded away. As soon as I got out of the car I took the folding shovel and the torch from the boot and put on the gloves. I followed the trail of plastic bags, removing them from the branches and counting them to make sure I hadn't forgotten a single one, and hadn't left a single fingerprint. As for footprints, they don't matter: tomorrow I'll throw my old Dr. Martens in a bin, and as I wear size thirty-nine it's quite likely they'll think the prints are a man's, especially as digging up corpses isn't usually women's work. When I got to the thirteenth bag, I knew I was nearly there. I removed the three hanging just over the grave and the work started, and with the work the fear.

Here's where the neck of the sweater starts. A high roll-neck. With my glove, I brush away the last layer of earth. I'm tempted to go further, to touch the jaw bone, but I resist. Not with my hands, I tell myself. I grab the shovel again and give a few delicate little knocks. I shine the torch and the whole castle of theories, hypotheses, conjectures I've built since this morning, since I started thinking like a psychologist again, finds its foundation: a black beard, Pasquale Avvisato's long black beard, emerges between the grains of earth.

I feel a grim satisfaction, as a counterweight to the fear: everything I was thinking has turned out to be true. Perhaps not everything, but as far as the first half is concerned I was right: Imperiale's first victim was poor Pasquale, the young man from the South, the chemist who told his parents he had found work in a small factory in the area. I try to imagine what's behind this young man's death, what motive drove Imperiale to kill him. I try to make an effort of the imagination, I've been trying since this morning, but all I can see are the usual stupid reasons for violence: filthy lucre, angry quarrels, the sordid desire to impose your will on someone else. No aesthetics of crime, no complex plan, no cold reasoning. There'll have to be an autopsy to establish if he was stabbed, or struck with an iron bar, or, like Patrizia, knocked down by a car. There'll be an autopsy, but I don't have any doubts. Behind everything is a simple, everyday story, the kind you read in the papers. Inside me, something starts to hope that at least Pasquale Avvisato's death hides a love that ended badly, a passion beyond the limits of the human, but it's a futile hope: I know, I believe, I sense that Patrizia's fate is linked to Pasquale's by a thread less noble than love. In any case I'll have the answer tomorrow, when I follow in Maestri's footsteps.

On the road, a car has passed, the kind that scares me, the kind that are solid at the back. I stop, hide a little, and take a better look. It's one of the many SUVs, but it seems light in colour.

Run, get away from here, now. I pick up the shovel, in order not to leave any traces. At the first phone booth I'll call 113 and report the presence of the body, perhaps I'll even accuse Imperiale, but without giving my name: what would be the point? I don't have any evidence against Imperiale. But it's not up to me to produce evidence: the police will see to that, or the Carabinieri, or the magistrates. Not me. As for saying that it was Imperiale who knocked Patrizia down, Benedetta will have to decide – and we need evidence for that, too.

Yes, I'm going now, and even the fear passes.

As I'm collecting the shovel, my eye falls on the groove I've dug in the earth, a groove with Pasquale's body at the bottom of it. I look down and feel pity for the body. It occurs to me that if I don't cover it up again the animals in the wood will make a complete mess of it.

Hold on: it already is a complete mess...

And yet, almost against my will, I start to throw loose earth back into the hole. I cover up the beard, the chest.

I stop for a moment to rest, to give my back a break.

Another SUV stops by the prostitutes. How many of these vehicles are there? How many people have thirty or forty or eighty thousand Euros to throw away on a car?

The SUV I see now is dark: it might be black.

I ought to hide, but it's as if the finding of the body has deactivated my alarm circuits: the tension has fallen, I feel like an empty sack. I watch motionless as the girl gets in the car and closes the door, by the light of the fire. Still motionless, I stand there waiting for the car to drive off. Instead of which, it reverses, preparing to make a U-turn. 'It's someone who knows where to go to get it over with quickly,' I think. What I don't think of is the most important thing, which is that when the car is halfway through its turn, its headlights are pointing straight at me. I realise immediately, but immediately isn't soon enough. I see the tilted oval headlights, like almond-shaped eyes. I see the Porsche Cayenne and I only have a second's doubt. Then the driver sees me. He switches the headlights on full beam. Standing with the shovel in my hand, I project a long, spectral shadow amid those of the trunks and branches.

Any last doubts have gone. The right-hand door opens, the girl gets out, or rather, she rolls out, pushed from inside. The Cayenne starts moving. Its headlights disappear for a moment, as the front of the car dips in passing from the road to the field. Then the beams start to sway: Imperiale is coming straight towards me.

Adrenal glands, thalamus, hypothalamus, hippocampus, amygdala, corticotropin, adrenaline, everything starts doing its duty: fear is active again. I run, forgetting all about my backache, forgetting about everything except the SUV that's coming straight at me. I know it'll only take fifteen seconds to reach the undergrowth, then it'll be a direct clash between me and the killer. I run some more. I turn. The SUV is further away than I thought. I run, straight on, hitting my face on the low, thin branches. I turn. The SUV is still at the same point: motionless, stuck. I don't know what's stopped it, perhaps its very bulk, perhaps the fact that it's more for show than anything else. I stand there long enough to see the plump outline of Imperiale get out and start to run. But now the advantage is mine: I'm about fifty metres ahead of him, perhaps more. I run, and run, and run. I stumble over a root. I fall and get up again. Seventy metres. I run, I keep running. Eighty metres, and only fifty to reach my car. I run. Ninety metres, twenty to the car. I run. I'm there.

I'm glad I left the door open. I throw myself inside and only now, feeling a pain in my shin, do I realise I'm still holding the shovel. I throw it on the back seat, take off my gloves, and turn the key. He materialises in the rear-view mirror, red in the glow from my rear lights.

I mustn't make a mistake, I mustn't make a mistake, I haven't made a mistake since I was studying to get my licence.

And in fact I don't make any mistake. The clutch slips a little and the car starts. I see him for the last time, then the darkness swallows him.

I try to imagine his next move. He'll turn back, get his car out of the field and come after me. But in a minute I'll be on the main road and he'll still have to go as far as the Bono farm, reach the fork, take a right turn... Or else he'll choose to dig up Pasquale's body and take it away, to avoid discovery: but will he have the courage to take those bones clothed in flabby, decomposed flesh in his arms?

I feel reassured, but then I think of a third possibility: he has my address and I'm sure he recognised me. What if he goes directly to my home and waits for me there?

As soon as my wheels touch the asphalt on the main road I turn left, towards Magenta, to avoid the junction with the Strada alle Cascine. I keep looking in the rear-view mirror, obsessively. At a traffic light I almost crash into the car in front, but there's nothing worrying behind me. I avoid the centre of Magenta. I take the bypass and aim for Abbiategrasso. The traffic is flowing well. There are cars, but the sight of them comforts me: not too few to leave me alone with the killer's Cayenne, not too many to slow me down.

At Abbiategrasso, I take Route 494 and drive into Milan along the Naviglio Grande. It seems the easiest way to enter the city, perhaps because I know it well.

My glances in the rear-view mirror become less compulsive. I've won and now I'm starting to believe it. However partial, however temporary my success, I've won, I've grabbed hold of part of the truth and I'm close to doing what Benedetta is willing to pay me for, I'm ready to wipe out the shame of a missing corpse.

But I can't continue to keep this piece of truth to myself.

I'd prefer to put it in an anonymous letter, but I don't want to give Imperiale the time to move the body. I think of the dangers I run with a phone call. Will they locate me? In TV series, the rule is: if the call is a short one, they can't trace it.

So I prepare what I'm going to say, take out any inessential words, train myself to say it fast, then faster, then as fast as possible.

In the meantime, I've reached the centre of Milan. Going back to Bergamo is out of the question. One more reason to nail Imperiale as soon as possible: I can't stay on the run for a long time, my finances won't let me. I recall a couple of decent-looking small hotels near the Central Station. In about ten minutes I get to them and start to look for somewhere to park. At my third circuit of the block, a place becomes free, in the Via Vitruvio. I pull up, but before opening the door and getting out I take a good look round. I see a small group of immigrants arguing in loud voices, which I find quite reassuring.

The hotel I've chosen is in the Via Benedetto Marcello. There's a phone booth opposite. Perhaps it's a bit too close, but I tell myself that even if they traced the call they couldn't drag everyone in the neighbourhood out of their beds. Before going in, I go over the little speech I've learnt by heart, then repeat it a second and a third time, faster each time.

I go in. I grab the receiver, but it slips out of my hand: the fault of my woollen gloves. I try again. I dial 113.

'Police, go ahead.'

'I've found a dead body in Vittuone, in a small wood between the Strada alle Cascine and another side road that doesn't have a name. It's the body of Pasquale Avvisato, who's been missing for three months. He was killed by Giovanni Imperiale, the owner of Vittuone Heat Treatments.'

I hang up and leave the booth quickly, but without running. I cross the street and slip into the hotel. Luckily there's a room available. I pay with my credit card, hoping I still have some money in my account, and go up to the room. I have no desire to talk to Benedetta, or to answer her questions. I send her a blunt text: *Tomorrow morning 9 Via Vitruvio corner Via Marcello.*

A minute late the answer arrives:
OK.

We've just passed Aosta, and Benedetta's coupé is going quite a bit faster than the hundred kilometres an hour which is allowed on this stretch of the autostrada. We don't talk. Since we left Milan we may have exchanged ten sentences, more or less. The main reason we don't talk is because we're waiting expectantly for the final answer, which I think I know but don't want to anticipate for fear of being contradicted by events. And because it's a tough answer, the kind that could hurt.

So we don't talk. I read the newspaper. In Milan I bought the *Corriere* and looked for news of a body found at Vittuone. There wasn't any. Obviously. If everything has gone well, the police found the body after the paper came out. If it's gone badly, badly for me, then they haven't found it. They may even have ignored the phone call from that madwoman who fed them an unlikely story, not even pausing for breath. To make up for it, there are other cases similar to this in the local pages. There's a worker killed in a quarrel over a parking space, a labourer who fell from some scaffolding, a Tunisian beaten to death by a group of his compatriots because he didn't pay for some drugs. In short, there's all the banality of violent death, which doesn't even need reasons, which is sufficient to itself, which explains itself precisely because there is no explanation.

The tunnels are starting. I close the newspapers and also my eyes. I'm sleepy. Last night I slept really badly. It was only to be expected. I alternated between half-sleep and agitated dreams. Dreams, not nightmares. There were no dead people or bloodstained hands, not even the threatening outline of Imperiale: I suppose my subconscious has already put him behind bars, already classified him as harmless. No, there was none of all that. I dreamt that Morgana was ill and

239

Signora Ghislandi was trying to phone me but my mobile was off. And all the while Morgana was getting worse, she could hardly breathe. She was lying on her side, searching for me with her eyes, and I wasn't there. Then I think I had a recurring dream, the one where I'm in a large, crowded lift, dressed only from the waist up, and everyone looks at me as I explain that I left my trousers at home. But I'm not sure I really had that dream: sometimes when I sleep badly I even remember dreams from other nights, other sleeps. And finally, just before waking up for good, I dreamt about Stefano. That hadn't happened to me for at least three weeks, but that, too, is a recurring dream. He and I are making love, nothing more. Gently, intensely, not like a week ago. I dream that he and I are making love in our bed, in the morning, with the light filtering through lowered shutters. I'd prefer it to be something more perverse, steamier, like for instance while we're making love he stops, gets up, opens the door and lets another girl in, politely and calmly introduces her to me, she undresses and tries to get into bed with us and I run off shouting all kinds of insults. I'd like it to be like that, it would mean that I'm processing the break-up, that even the non-rational part of me is reacting to his betrayal. Instead of which it's a tender dream, a teenager's dream.

I close my eyes and the last thing I manage to feel before sleep overcomes me is a great anger towards myself, anger at not having detached myself emotionally from Stefano: when my emotions become too strong, something in me turns back to him.

I'm woken by the sun as we come out of the last tunnel. We're in Courmayeur. On the street there are people trudging along with skis over their shoulders and boots on their feet, on their way to the cable car. And I'm hit again by a hail of memories. Of when Stefano and I went skiing together, and we spent Valentine's Day in a snowbound little hotel, up on the Little St Bernard Pass. There's no memory more indelible than the memory of a place you visited with someone you love. When you go back, you feel as if you're in a time warp: you look at the houses, the mountains, the restaurants, then you turn, expecting to see the other person at your side. For me, Courmayeur is Stefano, there's no other possibility, perhaps there never will be.

'Let's have a coffee,' Benedetta says.

'OK.'

'Let's go to the Posta.'

Obviously she's at home in Courmayeur.

'I think Berthod's, on the square, would be quicker.'

She's surprised that I, too, know the place, that I, too, have gained access here, alongside all the people with double-barrelled names. I have no desire to tell her that skiing trips at the foot of Mont Blanc were among the few luxuries Stefano and I allowed ourselves. I have no desire to tell her, and she wouldn't understand anyway.

'Do as you wish,' she replies, slightly irritated. 'I'm going to Posta, I have an appointment.'

'Here? Today?'

'As I said, Saturday is a day like any other and it's even better to talk in a bar than an office. As it was obvious I couldn't avoid this journey, I thought I'd take the opportunity to make an appointment with this customer, who I can never get hold of in Milan.'

I look at her, without saying a word.

'Wait for me at Berthod,' she goes on. 'Half an hour at the most, and I'll be there.'

I drink my coffee and watch the chair lifts which, as they turn, send off blinding little shafts of light, like needles.

After exactly thirty minutes Benedetta is back. It occurs to me that her story about an appointment was only a pretext to show me that she doesn't change her plans for anyone, let alone me.

We resume our journey. I'm in a hurry to get to Livet, the

village where the strange concrete house on stilts is located. I'd like to get there before Maestri, although it doesn't really make any difference. Probably, I only want things to end quickly: I want the rest of the truth, the part concerning Patrizia's body, I want my cheque, I want to go home.

We enter the Mont Blanc tunnel. Here, too, Benedetta tries to press down hard on the accelerator, but the flashing lights make her change her mind. We proceed at the prescribed speed, for almost half an hour. Then we're back out in the sun, with snow all around. Benedetta switches on the car stereo. There's an Astor Piazzolla CD in it. The music fills the car, isolating it from the outside world. With a milonga in my ears, I have the impression that the landscape is moving in slow motion. Everything – the glaciers, the trees, the houses, the signs, the other cars, even lorries – passes by, but noiselessly: the music has reduced the chaos outside to silence and everything is in harmony.

I drop off again, this time into a deep sleep.

When I wake up, we're in a place called *Le péage de Vizille*, at least that's what the sign says. A few low houses, two or three shops and a large, newly-painted concrete building, probably a municipal apartment block. The snow has almost completely gone, apart from the heaps at the sides of the road, made dirty by waste paper and exhaust fumes. The sun is hidden now, and as we advance into the valley the layer of cloud grows thicker.

Benedetta continues driving, confidently, without any sign of tiring. From time to time she glances at the SatNav, on which arrows and directions appear and disappear. We pass a monument to the fallen Resistance fighters of the Vercors. The road veers to the right, then continues straight on, sinking further into the valley. On our right there's a bare wood, on the left, beside the river, appear the outlines of old disused factories, their bricks blackened by time and coal fumes.

Then at last the sign: *Gavet – Commune de Livet et Gavet*. At Gavet the valley widens slightly and the houses steal space from the forest. The factories still rule the roost, but here they appear more modern, at least some of them, and still seem to be in business. Beyond the factories is the river, and beyond the river other houses, a village for the workers, it, too, blackened by at least a century of fumes.

The sky now is a solid grey, and the clouds cut the mountains in half.

The same sign as before, but this time with a red bar across it, informs us that we are leaving Gavet. According to the SatNav, we're four kilometres from our destination – four kilometres from the truth. Or at least I hope so.

The forest returns, then another village: *Rioupéroux – Commune de Livet et Gavet.*

Rioupéroux consists of two rows of houses lined up along the road. The pavement is virtually non-existent, the fronts of the houses give directly onto the asphalt. No sign of front gardens, no sign of people. Everything is grey, greyer and smokier than anything we've seen so far. Most of the houses are closed up, with rusty iron shutters. On one of them is a faded sign: *Café du Centre*, but the café is closed and boarded-up too. A village that's been abandoned, left desolate. Then, further on, I see a woman pushing a pushchair. She's alone on the street and looks like a survivor, or a madwoman. As the lorries shoot past her, she keeps walking straight on, and seems to be humming a lullaby. I have the impression she wants to push her pushchair all the way to the end of the world.

We pass her and leave the village. The road makes a little curve to avoid a round block of stone, six or seven metres high, with a huge protuberance that resembles a nose. A brown panel says: *Tête de Louis XVI*. In France any roundish mass becomes the head of the guillotined king.

The wood reappears on the right-hand side of the road. The windscreen is beaded with tiny drops. The horizon is low and dark.

*

At last we reach Livet. The SatNav starts beeping. Livet looks exactly the same as Rioupéroux: the same boarded-up houses, the same rust-eaten shutters, the same desolation. Another village facing the road. The buildings are all alike, all except one that stands out at the far end. It takes me a moment to recognise it, then images of Jean Réno and Vincent Cassel running through the night pass in front of my eyes and I realise this is the house in Patrizia's photograph, except that I'm seeing it from the other side. From here, you can't see the tall concrete pillars supporting the protruding top floor. It just seems like an austere house in the mountains, with exposed stone at the bottom and, at the top, plaster of a vague colour somewhere between brown and grey. Between the third and fourth floor is a painted sign, white on a green background, and faded, but the wooden veranda in front of it makes it practically impossible to read: only the final letters emerge: EUX.

'Stop here,' I say, pointing Benedetta in the direction of an unpaved open space on the right. She looks at me questioningly, then pulls up. I get the feeling she's given up trying to understand.

We get out. She opens her umbrella, I pull up the hood of my anorak.

'Let's go round the other side,' I say. She follows me.

We continue along the street, which turns left just after the building and crosses a bridge. I lean on the rail. Now the house looks the way it does in the photograph, with that top floor stretching out over the river and the void, barely supported on concrete legs as thin as a flamingo's. The broken window panes and pots filled with dried plants accentuate its already ghostly appearance. All doubts have gone, the truth is in there – either that or it's lost forever, at least as far as I'm concerned.

We retrace our steps. I open a rusty little gate and we enter the courtyard. Several doors face onto the yard, one of them leading to the stairs. There's no entryphone. Instead of going upstairs, I decide to try the ground floor apartments.

I knock at a door: no answer.

I try again: silence.

I move a few metres and knock at another door. From inside comes the sound of footsteps.

I wait for someone to appear, but nothing happens.

I knock again.

I wait a few more moments and the door opens, just enough for an old woman to put her head through the opening. Her hair, gathered in a bun, is grey but still relatively dark.

'What do you want?' she asks, slightly irritably.

Summoning up my best French, I answer with a question. 'Does Patrizia Vitali live here, by any chance?'

Benedetta looks at me, disconcerted. That means she hasn't yet understood a thing.

'No, nobody lives here with me, I'm alone.'

I've already exposed myself, and only an affirmative answer will save me from looking stupid. I insist. 'If not actually with you, perhaps in this building. She's twenty-three years old, of Italian descent. The lady with me is her sister.'

The old woman looks annoyed, and is about to close the door, but from inside I hear a voice:

'Let them in, Clémentine. I'll be right there.'

Benedetta hears the voice, too, only she doesn't get the message. But I do. I realise that I was right, right all down the line.

We enter a tiny entrance hall, then a wretched living room. Velvet couches, dolls dressed in tulle, mismatched chairs and various knick-knacks placed on low tables. Leaning out of the window, a fluffy toy of a red cat.

'Please sit down,' the old woman says.

We sit down, but a moment later, by some instinctive reaction we jump to our feet again: Patrizia has come into the room, pressing with her hands on the wheels of her wheelchair.

We're all motionless, turned to stone. Then Clémentine leaves us alone, closing the door behind her.

In front of her, sitting in a wheelchair, Benedetta has the answer I didn't want to give her, even though I knew it. That ticket for Grenoble found by Marco in Dr Maestri's wallet had clarified my ideas: Paolo Maestri really was Patrizia's boyfriend and she must still be alive, in France, near Grenoble.

Patrizia has tears in her eyes. I don't know if they're tears of pain or emotion. Benedetta is like a statue. At last she's found her again, but she doesn't approach her, doesn't embrace her, doesn't even greet her. I don't know if it's because of the surprise, the disappointment at finding her alive, or because she still doesn't understand. I'll have to try and explain, present my conjectures, hoping that Patrizia will confirm them.

I'm about to say 'Let's sit down', but stop myself just in time: the usual embarrassment when you're with a person in a wheelchair. I say nothing and sit down, and Benedetta follows suit.

I turn to Patrizia. 'My name is Anna Pavesi and I'm a psychologist.'

'Yes, I know. Paolo told me.'

'Paolo is Dr Maestri, is that right?'

She nods but can't speak, her lower lip is shaking too much.

'Then you also know,' I continue, 'that we thought you were dead.'

She nods again. I realise that she won't say anything for a while, that it will be up to me to keep the ball rolling, alone, as usual.

'Is it all right if I reconstruct what I think happened?'

Silent consent.

'Let's start with Pasquale Avvisato.'

They both look at me questioningly, Benedetta wondering who on earth this man is, Patrizia wondering how I found out about him.

'Let's go over the facts as briefly as possible, because, basically, it's a simple story, really quite an obvious story. Pasquale is killed by Imperiale, Patrizia's employer. The reasons I can only imagine: a quarrel, perhaps over Patrizia, perhaps something to do with work, or money, I don't know. I also imagine that after a while Imperiale starts to be afraid that Patrizia knows what happened. Or perhaps even witnessed the murder. So he decides to kill her, too. He buries Pasquale's body, then waits for her on the road: he knows she comes by there on her bicycle. As soon as he sees her he knocks her down with his car. He's even ready to turn back and make sure she's really dead, but someone arrives and he's forced to escape. But Patrizia isn't dead. She's taken in a coma to the local hospital in Magenta, where her boyfriend works. Except that Dr Maestri isn't on duty: he arrives early that afternoon, just in time to see Patrizia regain consciousness. That's when she tells him what happened. She probably tells him about Pasquale's murder and the fake accident. She's scared, scared that Imperiale might try again to kill her. And it's here, in my opinion, that Maestri decides to take matters in hand.'

I stop for a moment to see if Patrizia wants to take up the story, but clearly she's not ready yet. I approach and start to address her directly.

'It was Paolo who thought up the idea of the fake death, wasn't it?'

'Yes.'

We've gone from silence to monosyllables. A good sign.

'Dr Maestri puts you in a drug-induced coma and alters your medical records, even simulating your death and making a false report of the facts.'

'Yes. He thought the only way not to take any more risks was to pass me off as dead.'

'But the idea of escaping to France was your suggestion.'

'He asked me where I'd felt safest in my life and I told him it was here, with Clémentine.'

'And Maestri took great care to get things right. With help from his uncle, who's an undertaker, he even faked your funeral. And while Imperiale and Signora Bono were following the burial of an empty coffin, you and your boyfriend left Magenta and came all the way here. Am I wrong?'

'No, you're absolutely right.'

'I still don't understand,' Benedetta says.

'Let's start again from the beginning, but this time, Patrizia, you have to help me.'

She nods again.

'Tell me about Pasquale.'

'I met him at the factory. He'd come in the evenings, when most of the workers had already gone. Imperiale used him to prepare the chemical substances for the various treatments, but wouldn't hire him officially. When we got to know each other better, he told me Imperiale kept telling him he'd hire him in the New Year.'

'Were Pasquale Avvisato and Imperiale on good terms?'

'At first, everything was fine, but then things turned bad. I never saw them argue, but when we were together in the bar, those two or three times it happened, Pasquale would tell me that they often had violent arguments because the poor devils who worked on the chemical treatments were risking their skin and their health. The machinery was old, there wasn't enough ventilation, and even the dumping of the waste was against regulations. He was convinced that Imperiale was bribing the safety inspectors and he would tell him that to his face. He was fearless, Pasquale, an idealist, someone who wanted to change the world.'

'Did you see Imperiale kill him?'

'Yes. It was the evening before the accident. They came into the mechanical workshop through the door from the yard. They were shouting. They didn't know I was still in the office. I heard Pasquale say, "I'll report you." But I didn't know what about, probably about those dangerous processes. After a while, through the windows of the office, I saw Imperiale pick up a big monkey wrench and hit Pasquale in the face. Pasquale collapsed and he carried on hitting him, like a madman. I was scared. I went out without making a noise. The last thing I saw was Imperiale with his ear to Pasquale's chest and that was when I realised he was dead. Once outside, I took my bicycle to go home. That must have been when Imperiale realised that I was still there. He must have heard the noise of the padlock knocking against the grating of the building where the bike was tied. But I didn't realise straight away, it only occurred to me later, when I woke up in hospital.'

'Why didn't you go to the Carabinieri?'

'I was afraid to go alone and Paolo wasn't there, he was in the United States. In fact, at that hour he was on a plane and I couldn't even call him on his mobile.'

'But wasn't it more dangerous to keep quiet?'

'Like I said, I never imagined that Imperiale had seen me. I just wanted to wait for Paolo to get back, then I would go with him to the Carabinieri.'

I pause for breath and look at her. I look at that wheelchair, the kind I, too, almost ended up in. All at once, the resentment I've been feeling towards 'poor Patrizia' in the past few days vanishes. In front of me I no longer see the demure girl, the little plaster Madonna: there's only a young woman whose life has been shattered. I ask her about Maestri, and how she met him, and her eyes light up.

'It was at the end of July. I had to take one of the workers to hospital, a Tunisian boy who'd broken his leg falling from a ladder. Imperiale asked me to go with him because he didn't speak Italian. They admitted him and Paolo took over his case. It was afternoon and I stayed there for a while to keep the boy company. Paolo heard me talking in Arabic and his curiosity was aroused. We chatted a bit and it got late. I asked him if there were any buses to Vittuone and he offered to drive me home. That was it. That was how it started.'

'And is it still going on?'

'Of course. We want to get married. Right now, he's in Grenoble, at the hospital: they may offer him a post. We've decided to stay here.'

'But why didn't anyone know about your relationship?'

'Because it was ours. Paolo doesn't have any friends and doesn't get on especially well with his colleagues. He says sharing his work with them is more than enough, his private life has to stay outside the hospital.'

'But you could at least have talked to Signora Bono.'

She smiled. 'Her less than anyone. Vittuone, Corbetta, Magenta: they're not far from the city, but the atmosphere is very provincial. If I'd told Signora Bono, within a week everyone would have known, and sooner or later the rumour would have spread to the hospital. No, finding each other, Paolo and I, I mean, was a stroke of luck and when luck comes to people like us it's better to keep it close to our chests, without talking too much about it. I'm lucky to have Paolo with me.'

She considers herself lucky. Despite everything. As if, instead of being in a wheelchair, she's sitting on a deckchair of a cruise liner. She's lucky to have Paolo with her, but for how long? How long can we make our happiness depend on the presence of another person?

'They said I'll remain paralysed forever,' she continues.

She adds nothing else to that. As if to say: I'm happy anyway. As if to say: Paolo is all I need. Or else as if to say: Paolo is all I have, and I have to make him be all I need.

It occurs to me I don't have Paolo, or Stefano, or Marco. All I have is Morgana. But then I cross my legs and I feel ashamed, because they can still move. For the moment.

Fear grips me again. What if Imperiale is still at large, what if they didn't arrest him? I suddenly ask, 'Would you be prepared to go back to Italy and testify against Imperiale?'

'No,' she says, categorically. 'I was in a coma for six days, I died and came back to life, I've moved house, I've come to

Livet because Imperiale knew my old address in Domène, Paolo is changing his job. All that, just to help me forget. I won't go back, not for anything.'

I don't know if I should insist.

'They said I'll remain paralysed for the rest of my life,' she repeats. And this time her tone is different; it's a tone that puts paid to any further discussion. Then she adds, 'I was hoping for something better in life.'

And I think of all the women who could put that sentence in their family motto, starting with me.

Benedetta is frozen. She doesn't know what to say, what to do. Perhaps she feels guilty. Perhaps she's simply uncomfortable and can't wait to leave.

'Why did you come to Italy without telling me or my mother?' she asks.

I find it hard to judge her tone of voice, I don't understand if there's reprimand in it, or affection, or simply the neutrality of an obligatory question.

'Because after father and mother died, you were all I had left. I wanted to find you, I wanted to see if we could really be sisters. That was why I couldn't just turn up on your doorstep like a refugee. I couldn't say to you, "I'm here, I don't have anywhere to sleep, I don't have a job, I don't have money." I wanted to meet you and say, "I'm living near you now, I have a job, and a roof over my head, let's see each other from time to time, with no strings attached, just to feel that you're there, that you're my sister".'

I'd like to see Benedetta apologise, throw herself at her feet, say that now she'll give her all the love she denied her before, but nothing happens, or almost nothing. Benedetta goes close to her, strokes her cheek and says, 'You can count on me now.'

Then she opens her purse and takes out her chequebook. I take a glance and see that it's from a French bank. She writes a cheque, folds it and gives it to Patrizia. Perhaps I'm deluding myself, but I had the impression that in making that gesture that was so normal for her, her hand trembled a little. I saw, or at least thought I saw, that the amount was written in shaky handwriting.

I go out, because I want them to talk, they must talk. But I don't know if Benedetta will be capable of it.

I go into the yard and take another look at the building. The old woman joins me.

'This was the house of the man who owned all the factories around here,' she says. 'He had those protruding verandas built so that he could have a bird's eye view of his factories on both sides of the river.'

I thank her for the clarification and go out into the street. It's stopped raining, but the asphalt is still shiny, the only shiny thing in this opaque world of old smoke and exhaust fumes.

I think over the whole affair and of how that combination of fictions, tragedies, broken and mutilated lives, was born out of a simple gesture of anger, out of the invincible banality of evil. I think over the whole affair and a song by Francesco Guccini comes into my mind. I hum the beginning to myself:

What a squalid little story is the one I have to tell you, just a stupid little story like so many...

I keep walking. Looking at the houses, I realise they're not as identical as they appeared at first glance. At the time, they must have wanted to distinguish the dwellings of the manual workers from those of the clerks and those of the bosses. I imagine Livet in the days when her industries were fully functioning, the days when the boss kept an eye on his factories from above. And I imagine the days when they closed everything, when they said, It's over, we don't need you any more. People start to leave. Two or three moving vans every morning. One by one doors are barred, the shutters come down. Until there's nothing more to close, nothing more to move. What became of the people who worked here? Were they 'recycled', the way companies and machinery are?

Soon Benedetta will come out of the house and say, 'Shall we go?' Once in the car she'll make out a decent cheque for me, too, and hand it to me without smiling, without thanking me. I'll look at it and I'll be pleased, at least for a while. And then, as dozens of people disappear every day, in a few weeks or a few months I'll get a call from someone who's spoken to Benedetta, someone who thinks I'm a psychologist who specialises in searching for missing persons. I'll try to persuade them they're talking to the wrong person, that I'm not the one who can help them, but they'll tear off a cheque, I'll think about my bank account, and the last time I had any work, and I'll give in. My 'recycling' has begun.

Acknowledgements

This story, although it may not be apparent, is also a story about friendship.

So thank you to Andrea, Antonio, Edoardo Jr., Edoardo, Federico, Francesco, Giacomo, Gianguido, Gustavo, Leslie, Mauro, Nino, Peo, Pier, Pippo, Roberto and all the others, the Monday friends who for 450 Mondays have been running with me, chasing a ball.

And thank you to Enrico and Sophie, Marco, Paolo and Cinzia, my long-time friends, who have always run with me, even without a ball.